Belinda's Rings

Belinda's Rings

a novel

CORINNA CHONG

NeWest Press

Copyright © Corinna Chong 2013

LIBRARY AND ARCHIVES CANADA CATALOGUING IN PUBLICATION

Chong, Corinna, 1984–
Belinda's rings / Corinna Chong.

Also issued in electronic format. ISBN 978-1-927063-27-9

I. Title.

PS8605.H654B44 2013   C813'.6   C2012-906583-8

Editor for the Board: Douglas Barbour
Cover and interior design: Natalie Olsen, Kisscut Design
Cover images: azalea © Morphart Creation / Shutterstock.com,
squid © KUCO / Shutterstock.com
Author photo: Emily Zhang

NeWest Press acknowledges the financial support of the Alberta Multimedia Development Fund and the Edmonton Arts Council for our publishing program. We further acknowledge the financial support of the Government of Canada through the Canada Book Fund (CBF) for our publishing activities. We acknowledge the support of the Canada Council for the Arts which last year invested $24.3 million in writing and publishing throughout Canada.

#201, 8540–109 Street
Edmonton, Alberta T6G 1E6
780.432.9427
www.newestpress.com

NeWest Press

No bison were harmed in the making of this book.
printed and bound in Canada   1 2 3 4 5   14 13

For my brother and sister,
in whom I see what I hope to be.

⚭

Hybridize or disappear; family *in* place.
— FRED WAH, *Diamond Grill*

1 Bathyspheres

SQUID'S GOT THREE MOTHERS who can't spank him.
That's what my stepdad Wiley used to say when Squid
got into the goo. Back when he was a baby, you had anything
gooey and Squid'd find it. Peanut butter, craft glue, ketchup,
little bits of melted tar on the street — smeared all over his
cheeks faster than you could say 'fudge.' That was code in our
family for 'Squid is covered in something gooey,' except you
had to yell it out, *FUUUUUDGE*, like a swear word. Mum
doesn't know that people say 'fudge' to mean another f-word,
so sometimes I'd yell it right in her face to make Jess laugh.
Jess never did it herself, squeezed her eyes shut like she was
jumping off a building whenever she yelled fudge. She didn't
yell nearly half as loud as me, either.

The problem with spanking was that it didn't work. Mum
only tried it once, in the supermarket. I was there and remember it perfectly. She'd let him out of the shopping cart
to toddle around. He was just little. Only a couple months
before he'd still had that mini-drunk-person sort of walk that
made me want to follow right behind him, holding out my

arms, thinking he could topple over any second. By this time he'd gotten to the stage where we had to actually run after him 'cause he'd take off when you weren't looking. But we were in the cereal aisle and we didn't think he could do any damage, so we let him scamper around. He liked to punch the cereal boxes, the ones on the bottom shelves that no one wanted anyway. So he was punching, punching away, and every box he could reach was getting a punch, Squid made sure of that. Mum was looking at the generic brand of Frosted Flakes, the one that came in a big milky-coloured bag with no box, so most of the flakes were crumbled into powder.

That's sick, I told her. Can we please just get the Kellogg's?

It's all the same, Mum said. You're just paying for the name.

It looks disgusting, I said, holding the bag up to the fluorescent lights. I will not eat that. It's like sawdust.

That was when I was in grade six, and my friend Marnie would come over after school to watch TV. She was obsessed with Frosted Flakes, the Kellogg's kind. We always had a bowl each. I couldn't give her the generic brand. She'd notice. But while I was arguing with Mum, neither of us noticed that Squid had stopped punching. He was standing in front of us with a giant grin across his face. You could see all his pointy little baby teeth.

He'd stuck a fist into his diaper and got it all covered in — goo. Shit. This mustardy-brown, pasty kind of shit. The Squid special. And now he was waving the gooey hand above his head, his feet hammering the linoleum. Mum and I stood there for a second, staring at him, and then we both lunged at the diaper bag sitting in the shopping cart. Fudgefudgefudge, I said, Mum and me both pulling at the Velcro flaps and our hands just getting in each other's way. That gave Squid enough time to walk up to a lady who was bending down for a box of Grape Nuts. He swung his mucky hand like a club — SPLAT —right on her back. Squid's four fingers, imprinted in yellow slashes on her black suede coat.

The lady dropped the Grape Nuts, cranked her head around to look. She couldn't see the damage, but her eye caught Squid's pasty hand waving as he ran down the aisle squealing. Mum chased after him with tissues, her handbag slapping her ribs.

The lady stood up slowly. I thought she might puke, but she just stood there, her tongue jutting between her teeth. She was watching Mum chase Squid. So was everyone else. There were a couple of snickering high-school boys with a basket full of Doritos and Mountain Dew. A mom with her baby perched in the cart, quietly nibbling a soggy Arrowroot biscuit in two hands. They waited for what they expected. Punishment. I waited too.

Mum caught Squid by the collar and reeled him in. She grabbed both wrists and held his hands out in front. When she whipped her head to flick the hair out of her face, I could see her eyes darting around, noticing all the people watching her. It might have been the way the lights reflected off her eyeballs, but she looked like she was about to cry.

That was when Mum spanked him. Let go of one of his wrists and *thwack*. Squid's eyes bulged, his hips pulled forward, his little bum caving in on itself. He spun around and looked at Mum. At first, his face started to crumple up, and here we go, I thought. But then he just stopped. Blinked. His face smoothed out again, and his mouth did this funny thing where it turned into an oval. It was hilarious. A perfect oval, aimed right at Mum's snarling face. And then he laughed, gleefully, like one of those evil Chucky dolls from the horror movies. Ran down the aisle, feet going so fast that his wobbling body could barely keep up. He disappeared around the corner, Mum trudging behind him.

I watched Grape Nuts lady peel off her coat. She rooted around in her purse for tissues. It was hurting my stomach not to laugh.

I'm really sorry, I told her. I offered some fast food napkins I had stuffed in my pocket.

Can you believe that child? Grape Nuts lady said. She had this really embarrassed smile, and she was trying not to look anyone in the eye.

That mother needs to learn a thing or two about discipline, she said.

Oh I know, I said. I shook my head, and so did she. I was surprised how easy it was to play the part. At that moment, I was just some random girl shopping by herself. Another stranger, eyeing that bad mother's abandoned shopping cart with the gummy bears and Chef Boyardee and cheap bologna.

It boggles the mind, she said. I held her coat by the shoulder-pads as Grape Nuts lady swiped at it with balled-up napkins. I wondered what 'it' was exactly that boggled the mind — Squid or Mum.

What did you feed him, Grace? Mum asked me when we got to the van. She smeared a baby wipe between Squid's fingers, bunching and folding.

I don't know, I said. Cheerios. One of those cans of creamed corn?

The Heinz ones? Mum asked, huffing out one of her it's-all-your-fault sighs. You know the Heinz ones give him diarrhea.

I thought it was just the beans ones that made him do that, I said. Besides, it's not my fault. He's a baby, last time I checked.

Mum plonked Squid into his car seat and buckled him in, didn't bother to readjust his scrunched-up hood behind his neck. I climbed in next to him, pulled his hood out from under the seatbelt. Mum heaved the door shut so hard the whole van shuddered, like she always told me never to do.

It was the first time I knew — really knew — I was alone. Me, separate from Squid and Mum. Mum drove home like a zombie, arms limp and back hunched. Even from the back seat of the van I could tell she was making movements she'd memorized from driving this route again and again, week after week. The sound of the brakes at the stop sign, the rhythm of the engine, the timing of the turn signal, left here, then right there, familiar as a song that gets overplayed on the radio. I watched a few raindrops river down the window and imagined us underwater, all separate, in our own little bathyspheres, roving around the deep ocean. We were trapped inside, looking for the same route to the surface.

◯◯◯

Back then, Squid was going through a vegetarian phase. If we tried to hide a little morsel of sliced ham in his mashed-up squash, he'd just suck off all the squash and eject the cleaned ham chunk neatly like a tiny VHS tape.

The funny thing is that squid — the giant kind, with eyes the size of dinner plates — are carnivorous. When I first read that in one of Wiley's *National Geographics* — *giant squid have eyes the size of dinner plates* — I imagined being eaten by a squid. I don't know why. Maybe it was the mention of 'dinner.' But I imagined the tentacles shooting out, all of them at once, and cinching around me, wrapping around and around. And for some reason I wasn't wearing any clothes, so I could feel the slimy tentacles slithering all over my body. I felt the suction cups sucking great big purple rings into the skin of my arms and legs, my naked back. My cheek squishing into an enormous black eye, my mouth filling with jelly flesh. I imagined it like a great big squiddy hug, except the squid squeezed so tight that my ribs broke and my lungs burst like balloons.

I found out later, when I really got into marine biology, that it wouldn't happen that way. Squid actually only use two of their tentacles — the two longest ones, shaped like spears at the ends — to grab their prey. The other eight tentacles are really just for show. It's only because they look so different from us — foreign, like they belong to another world — that we find them so threatening. It's like that old saying goes: we fear what we don't understand.

I

THE MAN SITTING NEXT to her on the plane was dressed in a suit. Idiot, Belinda thought. Only an idiot would wear a suit on a nine-hour flight. Belinda had worn her pajama pants and an old t-shirt, but she still felt restless after the first hour. She'd taken her shoes off and wrapped her feet in a blanket. She'd tried curling up in a ball and taking a nap, but her feet kept slipping off the seat. Every few minutes she'd feel her back slumping, her bum creeping to the edge of her seat, and would promptly shimmy herself upright. It had been so long since she'd flown; Belinda wondered if this discomfort was an indication of her aging body. But the man next to her hadn't moved. He had his headphones on, and he'd been staring blankly at the headrest in front of him.

Belinda wondered if perhaps the man was crazy. She'd recently learned that there were a lot of crazy people in the world, and many of them could mask it very well. Belinda herself had even married one. Several of the mental disorders she'd been reading up on sounded just like people she knew. She was convinced that one of her coworkers, Sabrina, had

Histrionic Personality Disorder. In fact, Sabrina's ploys to get attention were almost sociopathic. She'd once stolen a cupcake from the supermarket at the mall, and when the security guards caught her she told the manager some sob story about being so poor she was starving. Later that week, Belinda had seen Sabrina sitting on a restaurant patio downtown, drinking martinis with a strange man. She had met Sabrina's husband before and it definitely wasn't him. Sabrina saw her walking by, but she didn't smile or wave or pretend not to notice. Her eyes followed Belinda down the street as if to say, I'm glad you saw me, I hope you tell. That kind of behaviour wasn't normal.

She thought that the man next to her might have Obsessive Compulsive Disorder. That would explain the suit and the rigid posture. It seemed to her that OCD had been running rampant in the last couple of years. The effect of a reactionary society on impressionable minds.

He glanced over when Belinda took out her magazine. It was the latest issue of *The Circular Review*. Belinda got a subscription for the eyewitness accounts. The first issue she received in the mail included one from an English woman named Velta Parr, who claimed to have witnessed a crop circle in the making. The account was written with such elegance that Belinda felt she could hear Velta's voice through the pages, the story thrumming like a melody. She still remembered the details: Velta had been walking around Bryony Hill with her husband on a humid and still day. It was early in the season and the corn was stiff and light green. The air felt so thick they were having trouble breathing as they walked up the hill, which she noted was highly unusual. All of a sudden the stillness broke with several huge gusts of wind rolling over the fields, turning the corn into a sea of turbulent waves. A pillar of light pierced through the grey sky and shone directly on the cornfield. It was so bright that the field became a mirror of undulating white light. The trees at the edge of the field were leaning, bowing to the ground under the force of the wind, and then a band of mist came charging between them, eddying into a shimmering whirlwind. The wind began to whistle above her head; she could feel its pressure pushing down upon her. Her body was covered in pins and needles and when she turned to her husband his hair was standing on end like the bristles of a broom. The grain stalks around them were bending into smooth arcs as the wind raked over them. Under their feet, a spiral began to grow out of the field, beginning in the centre and whorling outwards. It took only a matter of seconds to form, and then the gust swept off into the distance, leaving miniature whirlwinds in its wake. Velta and her husband watched the small whirlwinds comb the grains into pristine concentric circles for several minutes. By the time the winds had dissipated and died off, the sun had almost set. At dusk they returned home, silent and enraptured by their strange encounter.

The words flowed through Belinda like scripture. But it wasn't only the words she remembered. Velta had included four illustrations drawn with hundreds of thin, delicate ink lines layered on top of each other. It amazed Belinda that the drawings looked realistic and three-dimensional, and yet when she examined them closely, all she could see were haphazard lines like stray horsehairs. Up close the drawings appeared wild and spontaneous, but the picture in its entirety was most definitely exact and intentional. The vigourous precision infused in each scratchy line told Belinda that this account was the real thing. No person could put herself into a drawing with that level of intensity if she didn't truly believe in it.

Belinda decided to take a painting class after admiring Velta's drawings. Painting seemed easier than drawing; painters could get away with splashing colour all over a canvas and calling it a masterpiece. But she wanted to represent her own encounter with the same careful passion as Velta, and she always felt that her words were insufficient. For the first time in her life, she felt that she had something profound to express.

In the first few classes they had to learn about colour theory. They did a paint-by-number colour wheel with acrylics, and the students, all Belinda's age or older, struggled to keep their brushes from crossing the laser-jet-printer lines. Belinda managed to mix a perfect orange, which her teacher told her was fit for a pumpkin. But when it came to painting actual pictures, Belinda might as well have been a three-year-old with finger paint. Every form she tried to render — a house, a tree, a sky — ended up looking disproportioned and flat, cartoonish. And she didn't want to bother taking the time to mix her own tints, so she laid down blobs of bright red, blue, and yellow and swished them around the canvas. She painted a few scattered circles and squares to practice controlling her shaky lines. Abstract, she called it.

Her teacher stood at her easel and cocked his head to the side as if there were actually a recognizable form embedded somewhere in her painting.

Kandinsky, he announced. Your style is reminiscent of Kandinsky. You should look him up.

Belinda had never heard of Kandinsky but was flattered anyway. After class she went to the library and asked the librarian if she'd heard of Kandinsky, the painter.

Ah yes, the librarian said. Kandinsky, first name Va-silly. He's very famous — you've probably seen his paintings. *Concentric Circles?*

Excuse me? Belinda sputtered. She'd never encountered this librarian before. This librarian could not have known that she had seven books on crop circles and other unexplained phenomena checked out from the library.

Here, the librarian said, I'll find the call number for you.

WASSILY KANDINSKY, the cover said. Beneath the text was a picture of a painting: a grid of twelve circles made up of rings in rainbow colours. The inside jacket named the painting *Squares with Concentric Circles*.

Wiley had said, Huh, how 'bout that, when Belinda told him about the coincidence. He said the painting looked like a kid had done it.

That's beside the point, Belinda said.

Oh, he said. So what's the point? Wiley was never quite on the same level. But then most men weren't.

2 Mirrors

WHEN SQUID STARTED SCHOOL, Mum said it wasn't a proper name to be calling him anymore. But I don't care, I still call him it, even though Jess nags me, *all the kids are gonna make fun of him.* All the kids make fun of him anyway, and besides, Mum cheated when she named him, just stole the name Sebastian from her sister. I have a cousin back in England named Sebastian, who's older than me. Older than Jess, even.

It doesn't *matter,* Mum said when I reminded her, rolling her eyes.

But what if Auntie Prim comes to visit, I asked.

Oh for Chrissakes, Grace, she won't, was all Mum said. I could tell by the way she tried to shut me up so quick that Wiley didn't know about the cousin. But Wiley didn't seem to care about names, anyway. All he cared about was that his firstborn child inherited his long piano-player fingers.

Unlike Mum and Wiley, I think names are pretty important. When I get married and change my last name, I figure I might as well change my first name too, while I'm doing all that paperwork. Grace is such a boring, geriatric-sounding name.

Mum even admits she wouldn't have called me that if it weren't for Da. He wanted to name me the Chinese word for Grace, and Mum told him she absolutely refused to name me anything that people couldn't pronounce. Lo and behold, I got stuck with Grace. I thought about changing it to something cool and unique like Phoenix, but then I figured it'd be hard to get used to being called something so different. So I decided to make just a little change. Gray. Yep. Scratch the 'c-e' and add a 'y.' I think it fits 'cause it could be for a boy or a girl, and I used to be kind of a tomboy. Also, the sea looks gray when you swim in it. The gray sea — sounds like something from a poem.

That's a colour, not a name, Mum said, but then I said, Gray isn't a colour, actually. It's a shade. That shut her up.

So I figure Squid should get his own name too, like a person deserves. A unique name. People might say it's weird, but what is weird anyway? It's a relative measure. My best friend in Social, Rose — she said to me one time, it's weird how you call your Mom 'Mum,' like with a British accent.

I don't have a British accent, I said.

Yeah, but you say it like 'Mum,' like that.

Well, how the heck do you say it?

'Mawm'.she said, like a yawn.

I laughed. That sounds weird to me. Sounds American. Y'all sound Amurrrrican, I said with a Yankee cowboy accent.

She shrugged, started doodling in her notebook.

Jess still calls Mum 'Mummy,' which is probably weirder by Rose's standards. It's a really kiddish thing to do, but Jess is like that. She just started shaving her legs last year, and she was in grade eleven by that time. I was in the bathroom brushing my teeth one night, and she showed me the Gillette satin-smooth triple-blade razor Mum bought her like she was all proud of it. She tore off the packaging while I spat in the sink, wiped my mouth with the back of my hand and rinsed it, watching the froth swirl down the drain. From the corner of my eye, I could see her reading the little instruction pamphlet.

You're doing it wrong, I told her when she scraped the blades down her dry shin. Jesus, you're gonna cut yourself. You're supposed to do it in the shower. And you do it this way, against the grain. I took the razor from her and glided it up her calf. A few stiff black hairs sprayed out the sides of the razor and fell onto the toilet seat.

How do you know, she said, her face turning red.

I shrugged. I just do. I wondered if she'd seen the disposable razor I kept under the sink. One of Mum's. But she probably wouldn't have figured out it was mine, even if she had, since I was two years younger, and she was supposed to be the first one to do things like that.

If I had been in a mean mood that day, I would have said, I've been shaving my legs for like, a really long time. And then I would've laughed and felt good watching her stand there holding the razor and looking like a little kid, a really sad little kid. Wearing those shorts she's had since grade eight, the ones with the pleats in the front and the spaghetti sauce stain on the crotch. I used to have a pair that matched, minus the stain. I guess it was easier for Mum to buy us the same clothes back then. If you don't like it, then buy your own, Mum said. So I did.

But Jess clings to everything she's ever owned, like a treasure. Like some piece of her will die if she doesn't keep every single little thing with a memory attached. She even keeps her old training bras with the yellow sweat stains in the pits. I've seen them in her dresser. I don't know if she still wears them. They're so stretched-out they'd probably still fit.

And this is who Mum leaves in charge. Mum even said it when she was leaving for the airport. Jessica, you're in charge, she said, even though Wiley was standing right there. Maybe she said it to make Jess feel important. Don't get me wrong,

Jess is miles better than Wiley or me at looking after Squid. Mostly because she can act just like Mum when she wants to.

Here's a secret about Jess: she desperately wants to be exactly like Mum. Just before Mum left, she was copying everything Mum did, which meant that for each thing I did wrong, I got nagged twice. But Wiley got it the worst. They were like a tag-team the way they were ganging up on him. Wiley had been sulking on the couch the whole time Mum was bringing her suitcases out, and when she went over and bent down to kiss him goodbye, he turned his head to the side so she caught his five o'clock shadow instead of his lips.

Mum clucked her tongue, put her hands on her hips. You're a grown man, she said.

I don't know why you need this crop circles trip, he muttered. His eyes were dark and droopy, like a bloodhound's.

Because people need to do something for themselves once in a while, Mum said. You of all people should know that. Jess was standing right next to Mum like her trusty sidekick, glaring at Wiley even though their conversation had nothing to do with her. And after we'd watched Mum's taxi pull away, Jess marched in and told him she would appreciate it if he could get over himself and participate in this family. It's like she records Mum's phrases, word for word, and tosses them out there whenever she feels like it. But Wiley didn't say anything back, just closed his eyes and lay down on the couch, on his side. He put one hand over his ear.

Seriously? Jess said. You're a grown man!

Jess has wanted to be like Mum ever since we were kids. She even wrote it in her diary when she was eight. *Mummy is so pretty. I want to be just like Mummy.* Pretty lame, eh? It was like she *wanted* someone to find it and read it and then think to themselves, My, what a nice little girl Jessica is. It's like she wrote it for her teacher. Too bad the only one who ever read it was me. We had the same diary, except with different pictures on the covers. Mine was white with a rainbow and hers was pink with butterflies, but the locks were identical. We discovered that almost all diaries have the same locks and keys anyway, so what's the point? I remember thinking I was so smart when I figured that out. I thought I was the only one who knew, until Jess told me she knew too. I had three or four other diaries, ones I got as presents and stuff, but I still only used the one. I kept all the keys, though. I kept them tucked under the velvet lining of my jewelry box, as if they were so precious they needed a special hiding place. As if the keys were the secrets themselves, everyone else's deep secrets that they thought no one would ever find out about.

Okay, maybe Jess's diary wasn't quite that lame. I actually felt kind of sad for her when I read it. I still remember what it said because after I read it, I would hear the words in my head whenever I saw Jess looking at herself in the mirror. *Mummy has green eyes and blonde hair and I don't know why I didn't get green eyes and blonde hair. It's not fair. Mummy is so pretty and everyone says so. I told her I wished I looked like her and she said I still had a lot of growing to do, so maybe one day I would. But I don't think I will ever grow green eyes and blonde hair.*

Jess was always — is always — looking at herself in the mirror. But she doesn't do it the way most people do it. I've watched her when she thought she was alone. That might sound creepy, but it's not like I have a little peephole in the wall between our bedrooms or anything. The way our house is set up, there's this mirror in the hall with a little table underneath. Jess always leaves her brush and hair elastics there, even though Mum nags her to put them away almost every day. The hall ends at an open doorway that leads off into the living room, so there's a wall mostly separating the two rooms. When you're in the hall you feel like you're hidden, like no one can see you. But when someone is sitting on the living room couch, the brown one, if they sit at the far end of the couch, it's just the right angle to see the hallway and the mirror through the doorway, but it's far enough away that the person at the mirror doesn't know you can see their reflection. I think I'm probably the only one who knows this. No one else ever sits on that couch because it's at a weird angle to the TV. Also, it's lumpy and the springs stick out like elbows 'cause we used to jump on it when we were little. Anyway.

Jess does this thing where she makes funny faces at herself in the mirror. Except they're not funny to her. I think maybe she's imagining she's a supermodel. She'll dab some lip gloss on and then pout, turn her chin and check out her pout from that side. Then she'll act like she's listening to someone talk, like chatting, nodding along, and then that imaginary person says something really shocking and she gasps and makes her eyes all wide. Then she'll pretend to laugh with her mouth open and her teeth glinting. She'll toss and tilt her head at different angles to see what the glinting looks like, freezing her smile in place. Sometimes Jess lip-synchs some words, but I can't figure them out. Every time she makes slightly different faces, has different conversations, probably with different imaginary people. Maybe she sees some guy she likes. She never tells me which guys she likes, not even celebrity ones. In any case, it's hilarious to watch. But as much as I laugh I also feel sorry for her because I know she's just copying Mum, imagining she has Mum's long eyelashes and green eyes instead of boring dark brown ones.

I try not to look in the mirror too much, because I feel like I never see what I actually look like. I see what my brain thinks I look like, but it's different than what I actually look like. You know when you see yourself on video or in a picture and you think, Ew, is that really what I look like? I sometimes use Mum's bathroom mirror because it has two panels on the sides that are medicine cabinets, and if you open the panels so that they sort of face each other, you can see yourself from a whole bunch of different angles. And if you face the panels in just the right way, you can reflect your reflection, so that what you're seeing isn't backwards anymore, but the way that people looking at you see you. It comes in handy when I'm not sure if my hair looks funny. It might look great from straight on, but then when I see it from the reflection of the reflection, I realize it's totally lopsided. Or there could be a lumpy patch at the back. The first time I figured out how I could look at my hair from the back, I noticed that I seriously needed to dye my hair again, because the bun at the back looked like an orange flower stuck onto the dark brown parts smoothed against my scalp. I couldn't believe I'd been walking around like that.

Sometimes I open the mirror panels and as I'm opening them and looking at myself I catch this angle of my face that I've never seen before, and I think, Whoa, who is *that* in the mirror? I once used Wiley's video camera to make a video of myself, where I pointed the camera at myself and slowly rotated it all the way around my head, 360 degrees. I tried to do it so you couldn't tell my hand was holding the camera and then passing it to my other hand behind my head. But it turned out looking all shaky. After I filmed it I couldn't even watch the whole thing, it was so stupid. At the start you could hear me breathing through my mouth all wheezy, like an old man, 'cause the microphone had been pointed at my mouth.

II

WHEN THE CABIN DIMMED for the movie, Belinda flicked on her overhead light. The man sitting next to her had been taking more unsubtle peeks at her magazine, clearly hoping Belinda would notice. He removed his headphones, and she readied herself for him to inquire about the article she was perusing. The picture was certainly dazzling — an aerial view of the Bythorn Star crop circle in Cambridgeshire. Its outer circle framed a kaleidoscope of iconography: four rings unfurling into a star, contained in a pentagram, and encircled by flower petals. The article discussed how five elongated hearts could also be traced within the form. The cosmological language of symmetry made manifest.

But the man said nothing. His hands curled into fists in his lap. Belinda could tell he was simply brimming with curiosity. She couldn't pay attention to her reading, knowing he was on the verge of speaking to her.

Hel-lo, she said in a friendly voice, a voice she usually reserved for small children and cute animals.

The man looked startled. Hullo, he mumbled, and gave a little nod.

Are you from England? she asked.

Em, no. He cleared his throat and sat up straight in his seat. Just visiting, he said.

Yes, me too, she said. Well — sort of. I mean — I was born there, but haven't been back. For a while. She smiled, and silently thanked herself for having brushed her teeth and powdered her nose after the meal.

He responded with what Belinda guessed was a smile back: a barely perceptible tightening at the corners of his lips.

I'm Belinda, she continued. She held out her hand.

Bartleby, he said, giving her hand a curt squeeze.

Bartleby! she cried, too loud. That sounds very British.

Yes, well, he said, smoothing the front of his shirt. My parents are British.

Oh, mine too! she said.

Really, he humoured her. Ahem.

It's not the purpose of my visit, though, Belinda said, slowly turning the pages of her magazine like cars on a Ferris wheel, so that Bartleby could plainly see each one passing. When he didn't respond, Belinda tilted the magazine in his direction.

See? she said. Did you know that more crop circles are reported in Southern England alone than in the rest of the world combined?

No, Bartleby said, I didn't. Interesting. He cleared his throat once again. Belinda wondered if it was a nervous tic. She'd read that people with OCD were usually quite socially awkward.

There's *vital* research going on right now, she said, slapping the magazine shut. Biological tests and such. We're going to be collecting the samples.

I see, Bartleby nodded. It occurred to Belinda that perhaps she was being intimidating. Oftentimes when she got into the particulars of her research interests, she came off sounding overly erudite until it was too late and the person had shied

away. She felt sorry for Bartleby and his outdated navy pin-
stripe suit, which was already suffering horrible creases at
the waist.

So what do you do, Bartleby? she asked, not altogether
interested. Perhaps if she engaged him in his own interests,
she thought, he might feel less intimidated.

Oh, well I — he began, then paused for a guttural throat-
clearing. Actually, he continued, I'm a biologist.

Ah! Belinda said. A thickness rose up in her chest. She
hoped that Bartelby couldn't see her cheeks reddening in the
dim lights. So you do. . . research also? she asked.

Yes, he said. I study marine life.

A Marine Biologist! Belinda replied, and gave her hands
an approving clap. My daughter wants to be one of those, she
said. She quickly realized that it was an insipid thing to say.
Practically every child, at one point or another, dreamed about
being a Marine Biologist. It was a typical phase.

But she's very dedicated, Belinda added. Her face burned
with heat. I mean, she knows more about the ocean than most
adults, she said. All those strange creatures — she knows all
the names.

Uh huh, said Bartleby. Well, my research is in phycology.

Psychology? Belinda asked.

No. No. *Phy*cology, he enunciated. It's the study of algae.

You study algae? How interesting, she said, and meant
it. After all, who knew one could base an entire career on
studying green slime? He was probably paid quite well. Now
that she'd been conversing with Bartleby, she could see how
he was rather handsome. He had thick dark hair and a defined
jaw-line. Even in his seated position she could tell he was tall;
his feet were pushed under the seat in front of him and yet his
thighs still appeared to float at a cramped angle. She imagined
him standing on his long legs, wearing a white lab coat and

glasses, and pouring solutions from test tubes into beakers.
He could be quite dashing.

Bartleby smiled weakly. He'd probably been teased by countless incredulous strangers about his research on algae. Actually,
he said, there's a lot to know. Marine vegetation is very diverse.

Of course, Belinda said, nodding her head seriously. I'd
believe it. I'm working with a biologist who specializes in
plants. Land plants, mind you. I think he's very highly regarded.
Marshall V. Longfellow?

I'm afraid I don't really deal with those — types of scientists,
Bartleby said.

Oh, yes of course. Belinda swatted the air dismissively. You
wouldn't, would you. It's all very specialized, isn't it? Her voice
had begun to flutter.

I suppose you could say that, Bartleby said.

Yes, well, what do you reckon about this film? Belinda
pointed to the screen at the front of the cabin. I've heard good
things, she said. On the screen, Kurt Russell was pacing deter-
minedly through a grand hall instead of sprinting shirtless and
brandishing a handgun as she expected. Belinda hadn't heard
anything about this film.

Bartleby shrugged. Sorry, I don't really follow the movies,
he said.

Well I think I'm going to watch it, Belinda said, smiling
as though she were about to indulge in a butterscotch sundae.
She couldn't unravel her headphones fast enough; it felt as
though an eternity of speechlessness hung between them
while Bartleby stared at her and she fiddled with the audio
jack.

3 The Rings

MUM LEFT HER WEDDING ring behind. She said she didn't want
to lose it on her trip.

We're going to be in the fields, she said, and we'll probably
have to collect samples. I'm not supposed to wear any jewelry.

Yeah okay, I said, rolling my eyes. Maybe they're afraid that
if you wear metal you'll get sucked into the circle's vortex by
the magnetic force field.

Oh stop it, Grace, Mum said.

Gray, I said.

Crop circles don't suck people in, Squid said. It's not like
a black hole.

How do you know? I said. Have you ever seen one? What if
the aliens are actually making booby traps, like in *The Goonies*?
And all these people get curious and start doing experiments
on the crop circles and doing tours like Mum, and then one
day — *sssschwwuuuuuup* — sucked into oblivion.

Squid curled his finger around his nose. He always does that
when he's worried. When he was really little he used to curl his

finger around his nose while he sucked his thumb, but now he just squishes his fist against his lips when he does it.

You remember *The Goonies*, Squid? I asked. He lowered his eyes, looked at the floor.

Those guys had skulls for those traps, he said softly into his fist. And big rocks. They didn't get sucked into anything.

Squid's been funny about skulls ever since we saw the *homo erectus* skull at the Tyrrell museum and I told him the brain was still in it. It wasn't even a real skull, but he believed it. Once he believes something, he can't un-believe it, not matter how hard you try to convince him.

But I saw it, he'd said, I saw the brain! I asked him what it looked like and he said tofu covered in blood. Mum calls it a vivid imagination.

The day before Mum's flight, Squid wanted to help her pack for the trip. Mum let him help for about five minutes before she told him that's enough, he was driving her insane, 'cause he kept taking things out of her suitcase.

But Mummy, these pants have a zipper, he kept saying, and that shirt has a metal button on the pocket.

Mum called me into her room, told me I had to play Hungry Hungry Hippos with him to keep him occupied. Squid perked right up, Yesssssss, ran to his room to get the game. I followed him out, glaring at Mum as I went. Playing Hungry Hungry Hippos with Squid meant sitting there for practically ten hours, letting Squid hammer madly at three hippos against my one hippo (always the yellow one, 'cause Squid hates yellow), and *still* just pretending I was actually trying to win. Squid got the game from his closet, was grinning at it like it was a triple-layer chocolate cake as he carried it with both hands, out of his room and down the stairs.

We had to pass by Mum's room to go down the stairs, and she'd left the door wide open and had turned on some music to listen to while she was packing. Tina Turner. Makes me wanna dance, she always says. As I was passing by Mum's room, I noticed something out of the corner of my eye. The wooden jewelry box that Jess and I got Mum for her birthday years ago. It was one of the best presents we ever got her 'cause it had little compartments especially made for earrings so that they wouldn't get all tangled together. It had cost us forty bucks, which was a lot for two little kids. Mum had said it was brilliant, almost cried 'cause she knew how much it had cost us. That was a long time ago, so ordinarily I wouldn't really think twice about it. But the reason I noticed the jewelry box that day as I was walking past Mum's room was because it wasn't where it usually was. Usually, Mum kept it in her bathroom on the counter with the lid open. Since she never moved it, it would get stuck to the counter because of all the toothpaste and soap scum and hairspray that would build up around it. Instead of seeing the box stuck to the counter, I had seen it in Mum's hand. I had seen her tucking the earring box between two piles of clothes in her suitcase, letting it hide beneath loose folds of fabric. So much for not bringing any jewelry.

Her wedding ring really did stay behind. She'd stuck the ring inside one of those blue velvet boxes you always see people in movies holding out when they're proposing. She put it under her sink, beside the mouthwash she never used because it was unflavoured and tasted like whiskey. The reason I know is because the morning after she left, I wanted to use her curling iron and saw it there. She'd taken the curling iron. When I opened the box it made that little cracking noise just like in the movies. I think they probably test them in the factories to make sure they crack when you open them so people feel all glamourous when they get one, even if the thing inside is cheap.

I was surprised when I saw three rings inside instead of just one. Her first engagement ring, the one from Da that was yellow gold with one round diamond in the middle, the engagement ring from Wiley with the emeralds that matched Mum's eyes, and the silver band that matched the one Wiley had. All three were stuffed into the slot in the middle of the box. And since it was only really big enough for one ring, they were crammed in on top of each other, and the slot had been stretched out so that there was an ugly gap when you took out the rings. They only fit on my pointer fingers, so I put the two from Wiley on one finger and the one from Da on the other. I wondered if Mum had thrown away the wedding band from Da, tossed it into a well or off a bridge or into the river when they got divorced. Or maybe Da kept it.

It's funny to think that humans are some of the only animals that prefer to stick with one mate for their whole lives. There are actually some species of deep-sea fish that keep the same mate for life. Bony fish of the order *lophiiformes*. Commonly known as anglerfish. I prefer *lophiiformes*, mostly 'cause if you say it with an Italian accent you can fool people into believing you can actually speak Italian. I once told this kid who lives down the street, Dustin, that I knew Italian and he said, Okay, say something in Italian. Lah-FEE-a-FOR-mees! I said, pressing my fingers to my thumb and shaking my fist like they do in *The Godfather*. I told him it meant *your goat is hairy*. He totally believed me. He's only seven — same as Squid — but still.

Besides having a cool name, *lophiiformes* fish look like Pac-Men from hell. And on steroids. Most species are about the size of a grapefruit. The first thing you notice about them is their teeth, 'cause they've got these huge jaws with massive underbites, so their mouths are hanging open all the time. And the teeth attached to the jaws are spiny and see-through, like shards of glass. You can't help but imagine those jaws snapping shut like the evil-looking bear traps you always see in cartoons. The reason it's called an anglerfish is because of this funny arm sticking out the top of its head. The arm has a flag of skin on the end called an esca that flutters in the water, and the fish uses this as a lure, like on a fishing rod, to attract unsuspecting prey. It reminds me of when you play with a cat and all you have to do is dangle a piece of string with a pom-pom on the end and the cat'll go nuts, batting away at the thing for no particular reason. The cat's not dumb enough to think the pom-pom is actually a mouse or something, it's just that he can't help it. He sees a pom-pom on a string and he wants to check it out, get his paws on it. You can probably guess what happens when the little fish come to check out the curious flag that the anglerfish is waving back and forth, *comeandgetit comeandgetit*. Snap. Fish fillets.

Anyway, like I said, *lophiiformes* fish have the same mates their entire lives.

So you mean they're monogamous, Wiley said when I told him and Mum. Depends, I said, on whether you can call them monogamous when they don't have a choice. I don't think Wiley knew the answer to that. But it's true, once an anglerfish chooses her mate, she's stuck with him for life. Literally. When scientists first started studying *lophiiformes* fish, they couldn't figure out why all their specimens were females. And wasn't it funny, they thought, how almost all the specimens they'd found seemed to have parasites attached to them? Turns out that the parasites were actually the males. They'd permanently suctioned themselves to their girlfriends' bellies so that they could survive off whatever she ate. It's kinda like how a baby can eat its mother's food through the umbilical cord, except these are full-grown males who make their own umbilical cords. Typical, Mum said.

It all sounds like a pretty sweet deal. The males just get dragged along and can suck up all the food, as long as they fertilize their girlfriends every once in a while. But don't worry, I told Mum, the female gets her revenge, 'cause as she gets fatter and fatter, her blubbery belly starts to grow around the male fish. Eventually, the male gets totally swallowed up inside her flesh. I imagine it like the Wicked Witch of the West, melting, melting, until there's just a pile of goo leftover. You can call that monogamy if you want.

When you think about it that way, and when you remember that humans are animals too, it all seems kinda silly. But when I was sitting on the floor of Mum's bathroom and admiring how her rings made my fingers look skinnier, I suddenly got this funny feeling in my stomach. Almost like the big drop on a roller coaster. It was the same kind of feeling I got the time I'd stolen a spritz of Rose's mum's perfume when Rose was in the bathroom, and I accidentally dropped the bottle on the floor. I'd stood there with bits of glass around my feet, the spilled perfume soaking into my socks. And that feeling. Roller-coaster gut.

Suddenly I wished I had told Mum I believed her instead of laughing at the UFO picture she drew. It's a spacecraft, she kept correcting me. UFO has too many bad connotations.

Now I know all this kinda makes Mum sound like a whack-job, but it's really not that nutty. It's not like she wears a tinfoil hat and tells stories about being abducted or probed or anything dumb like that. See, Mum thinks she saw a UFO. A spacecraft. When Mum tells the story she insists it was the witching hour, when everyone was asleep but her. Cheesy, I know. Anyhow, the way it goes is she can't sleep, so she goes outside for some reason — Mum would say she felt *compelled* — and stands on the driveway. It's a cloudy night and barely any stars are out. She just happens to be looking up at this particular part of the sky when these lights zoom across it, in a sort of zigzag. Three lights, in the shape of a triangle.

You're sure it wasn't an airplane? I asked when she told us the next morning.

Have you ever seen a triangular airplane? she said, pointing her finger at me. And besides, no airplanes I've ever heard of can move like that, whush, whush. Mum made her finger do a zigzag motion in the air.

Later that evening Mum set herself up at the kitchen table with an old notepad and a pencil. The rest of us were just sitting in front of the TV, except Squid who'd been put to bed. It was weird 'cause we were watching *Star Search*, Mum's favourite show of all time. Since our kitchen is attached to the living room she could have seen the TV from where she was sitting, but she just sat there at the kitchen table with her back turned. Writing away. I could see her elbow jostling up and down.

At the commercial break I came up behind her and said, You know your most beloved Ed McMahon is on?

Mum put her arm over her notepad. Her arm had little goosebumps all over it. Yes, she said, I'm busy.

Whatcha doin,' I said, drawing something?

I'm just thinking, trying to remember, Mum said. She shrugged and sighed at the same time, took her arm off the notebook so I could see.

She'd drawn a triangle with big dots on each corner and light rays coming off the dots like spokes. It was obvious that she'd scribbled little circles over and over again with her pencil to make the dots, because they were all shiny and nearly black, and they'd made indents in the paper. She'd also pressed really hard on the lines connecting the dots, and those lines weren't even straight, wiggled in the middle. You could tell that her picture was probably going to show up as far as five pages down, an etching in the paper that would come out white if you coloured over it.

I laughed at that picture. Didn't say anything, just laughed. It looked like a kid had drawn it. I couldn't help it. And anyway, Mum laughed too. Then we were laughing together and it was like our little joke, 'cause Jess and Wiley hadn't been paying attention. It felt okay then. Mum put her pencil down and turned off the light and we sat down on the couch together for the rest of the show. Now that I think about it, she'd been really quiet after that. I don't think she even made any predictions about who was going to win, how many stars this guy or that girl was going to get.

∞

Jess actually cried when Mum's taxi pulled out of the driveway. It was weird to see Mum in a taxi, especially since the van was parked right next to it and Wiley could've driven her to the airport. But he was inside by then, hadn't bothered to come out onto the driveway in bare feet like me and Jess and Squid. He could've been crying too, who knows.

But Jess cries all the time. It drives me nuts. She cried in *The Little Mermaid* when King Triton hugs Ariel and Ariel says, I love you Daddy. Seriously. So when she started to cry while we watched Mum's taxi drive down the street and turn the corner, I just tried to ignore it.

Lookit your feet, Squid, I told him, and when he did I tickled the back of his neck with a bird feather I'd found in the grass. He giggled, swatted the feather away and it floated out of my hand. I caught it and stuck it in his hair.

Robin Hood, I said, Prince of Squids.

Squid laughed again, his hands trying to find the feather.

Jess glared at me, wiping her hand across her runny nose. Don't you even care? she said. Aren't you sad that Mummy just left us here?

I shrugged. Why? I said. It's not like we're gonna starve or something. We've got enough food in the house for a nuclear winter.

You think *food* is the problem? Jess snatched the feather out of Squid's hair, tried to throw it on the ground. But it just floated away, skimmed down the driveway in the wind.

We're only kids, she said, Mummy can't leave us with this kind of responsibility. That's another thing about Jess. She likes to feel sorry for herself. I think it makes her life less boring.

You're seventeen, I told her. Remember?

God, Grace. Don't you get it? Jess leaned in close to me so Squid couldn't hear. Mummy left to get away, she said. From us.

Squid squished his way between us, What did Mummy say?

Mum-my leeeft to get the ay-lee-ens! I sang really loud, to the tune of "Michael, Row Your Boat Ashore." Hal-le-loooooooo-ya! I took Squid's hands and started ring-around-the-rosie-ing.

Jess didn't tell me I was being a total jerk, like I expected. Maybe she was just glad that Squid forgot what he was asking.

III

BELINDA TRUSTED CROP CIRCLES for their shape. A circle
seemed natural, an instinct. She had a hard time believing
that the wheel took thousands of years to imagine. After the
in-flight movie, with Bartleby dozing next to her, Belinda was
flipping through the complimentary travel magazine from
her seat pocket and found an article on ancient Mesopotamia.
It explained that the very first wheels were used to make
pottery. Travelling long distances simply didn't occur to early
humans; for the sake of survival, they needed to stay close to
their families. They shared food, huddled together for warmth,
invented language and art. A clay pot was more valuable than
a chariot.

Belinda had spent over two years researching crop circles
and related phenomena, from their earliest recorded history
to the present day. The early crop circles were simple. Single
shapes, unadorned, drawn with immaculate symmetry. Each
circle seemed to mark the landscape like a map, as if to signal
a treasure buried in the ground beneath. But some of the more
recent crop formations had begun resembling objects — a key,

a flower, a strand of DNA — and these, Belinda knew, were the circlemakers' attempts to appeal to human aesthetic sensibilities. Only humans would be naïve enough to insist that a key could carry universal symbolic significance. The fanatics called them 'pictograms,' dissected their angles to reveal the Golden Triangle or a set of cosmological coordinates that could be read like a treasure map. Geometry was Belinda's most hated subject in grade school. She could never, would never believe in reducing relationships to mathematical patterns. A circle was a circle, no beginning and no end. She needed to believe that life was unmappable.

Belinda had left her mother's home when she was seventeen, and she'd never looked back. Her first attempt to cook for herself involved pouring frozen peas directly into a saucepan, no water. She could remember standing there, watching little pools forming around each individual pea, dismissing her feeling that the slight hissing sound of ice against heat wasn't quite right. She watched until the peas had deflated and turned a sickly green because she hadn't known what else to do. Since then, she'd learned everything she knew about caring for herself the hard way, and yet she never felt any desire to return to her mother's. She'd long ago lost any desire to even think about her mother.

Now her own eldest daughter was seventeen and a baking aficionado. Self-taught. Jessica could bake a moist and fluffy pineapple upside-down cake and a perfectly formed crème brûlée, but would only shuffle her feet at the mention of culinary lessons or a part-time job at a restaurant. Having a good, responsible mother had its drawbacks, too. Belinda knew she was a good mother, despite what her conscience told her.

When the girls were small, passing strangers would assume they were adopted from Vietnam. They gave the girls candy, twinkled their eyes at Belinda's benevolence. Once, a one-eyed man gave Jessica and Grace five dollars each. They had been walking to the food court in the mall to get Orange Juliuses, which Grace always expected as a reward for behaving. The man was limping in their direction. He was limping with such strain that Belinda wondered what he could be doing out of bed and walking around the mall by himself. As he came toward them she saw that he had a glass eye, and considered that perhaps he couldn't see. She steered the girls around him but he lifted his hand, and Belinda understood this as a plea to stop.

The man said nothing, but carefully sifted through each of his coat pockets as if he were looking for a grain of sand. She noticed the veteran ribbon patched to his breast pocket and immediately felt that anything she could think to say would be disrespectful. He smiled when he'd found what he wanted. Then he pressed a small roll of paper into Jessica's hand and another into Grace's. He bowed his head to Belinda and hobbled away.

If she'd known at first that what he'd given them was money, she might have protested, insisted the girls were hers and didn't need the charity. She couldn't decide why he had even thought it necessary to give them money at all — to buy treats? To send to their Vietnamese relatives? To ease the burden on Belinda? Whatever his intent, the girls were dazzled and couldn't care less. And Belinda had felt good about the way the man had bowed to her, tilting his glass eye down to her feet.

Years later she got a job in that mall. She started out at Talbots selling blouses and pantsuits to old ladies. She was employee of the month for four months straight. She had no idea what she'd done to deserve this title; she'd shown up for work on time and stayed awake through her shift, which she supposed was all they expected from her. Getting the job at Merle Norman was a milestone. Wiley had taken her to a French restaurant for dinner on the day she received the job offer. She found it mildly irritating when the waiter whisked the napkin from her wine glass and laid it like a dead snake across her lap, but the food was quite good. She boasted to Wiley that employees at Merle Norman got benefits and free sample kits of the latest skin creams and newest eyeshadow colours. Wiley had never had a job with benefits. She did most of the talking and ate her meager dish slowly while he nodded and stole glances at his empty plate. He found a mint in his wallet and tore the wrapper into tiny little pieces that he collected in his unused spoon.

The managers, she explained, Betty and Abby, told her during the interview that they always had to remind the younger girls to come to work looking fresh and clean. Mist-kissed, they called it. That was their way of telling the girls not to wear too much makeup.

Those girls are so young, she'd told him. They leave the house looking like circus clowns.

Wiley said he was sure she'd be able to teach them a thing or two. No one was more naturally beautiful than her, he insisted.

Belinda disagreed and overlooked his compliment. She hated compliments like that — tawdry lines that could be fed to anyone. She didn't think she could teach them anything, she said, because they didn't know how to see themselves yet. And that would just take time.

Belinda's first day on the job, Abby pulled her aside just before her lunch break. Abby said she wasn't sure if they'd gone over this in the orientation, but at Merle Norman they liked to portray a certain image. As she spoke she examined Belinda's face as though it were covered in blemishes. It's a look we call *mist-kissed*, Abby said, spreading her fingers like fireworks. She asked Belinda to sit in the salon chair at the back of the store so she could demonstrate exactly what she meant. Abby gave her a little cotton ball soaked with blue-green chemical and Belinda had to remove the makeup she'd applied over her crow's feet and her pale lips and her stubby eyelashes that morning. Her colour fell away in beige smears. She'd had to ask for five more cotton balls to uncover her skin, and Abby stood at her side the whole time, watching Belinda saturate each ball, her lips pursed in a reproachful moue.

When Abby had finished dusting her face with powder and blush, sweeping her eyelids bronze, daubing her lips a pale rose, and brushing on mascara, Belinda looked in the mirror and couldn't see any makeup. Her cheeks were ghost-white, her eyes feathered and dim. Her wrinkles stood out like scratches on a plate. Abby insisted Belinda keep the makeup so she could try it out at home. Belinda smiled, but said nothing. She wanted to be grateful, but it felt like an imposition. She'd been using makeup on her face for years, and only she understood the broad curve of her jaw, knew the grey vein that swam beneath the skin under her right eye and the way her lips looked stretched and thin without dark lipstick. Only she could have her every imperfection committed to memory.

For the next two weeks, Abby kept asking Belinda how the new makeup was working out for her.

Fine thanks, Belinda would reply, and then retouch her lipstick from a cranberry tube. The light pink lipstick that Abby had given her, along with the other muted makeup, sat on Belinda's vanity collecting dust from the day of the makeover. Eventually Abby stopped asking, but her face showed that she knew.

◌◌◌

Belinda called home from a payphone as soon as she landed at Heathrow. It was midnight London time, 5:00 PM Calgary time. Grace was reticent, as usual. When Belinda asked her what she was doing, she said she didn't know.

You don't know, Belinda repeated. And what does that look like, exactly?

I dunno, Grace said. Doing nothing, I guess.

Belinda wasn't in the mood to act put-out. That's great, honey, she said. Sounds like you're getting some good relaxation time. She could hear the murmur of Wiley's voice in the background.

Have to run, catch my shuttle, she said before slamming the receiver back on its base. For a few moments, the phone box chimed like a faraway bell tower, dampened by immeasurable distance.

4 Piano Lessons

JUST THE OTHER NIGHT at the dinner table, Jess brought up
that it had been exactly a year since Mum went to Wiltshire.

None of us said anything. We just nodded our heads and
stared at our plates as if we'd done something horribly wrong,
but of course none of us had. I think Squid even smiled a bit,
more because of the weird silence than what Jess had said.

But the way Jess had brought it up like that, out of nowhere,
it felt like an anniversary of sorts. Like some kind of milestone. It got me thinking about everything that had led up
to that point, and whether it meant something more than
what it seemed at the time. A year seems like a long time
and a short time all at once. And when I started to imagine
I was back there, a year ago, things seemed to look different.
Remembering that time makes me picture myself like Dorothy
from *The Wizard of Oz,* stepping from the black-and-white
world where things are simple and into a world of a zillion
different colours. And it seems like I'd be missing something
if I didn't try to remember it all, every little detail.

Funny enough, I started skipping back even further, years, way back to the days when I was young enough to pretend to make pemmican out of woodchips and dance to Whitney Houston around the living room wearing a pink tutu. It seems somehow like all of it matters now that I'm older, even some of the stupid things me and Jess would do when we were little kids.

For a long time Jess and I thought it was funny to say Oooo, piano lessons, whenever people on TV were about to kiss. You know how they always have that fake audience track that laughs when something's supposed to be funny and whistles and hoots when something juicy's about to happen? Well, instead of hooting and whistling we'd say Oooo, piano lessons, and that made it like a joke so that we could pretend we weren't being all girly and getting excited over the gushy parts. We'd rub our pointer fingers together like shame-shame while we said it. If Mum were in the room she would just smile, pretend she didn't know what the hell was so funny.

Do you even get it? I once asked her.

Oh, you girls are so silly, was all she said. Mum always pretends not to get our inside jokes.

She started her piano lessons way back when she and Da were still married. Usually she did her lessons out of the house, and she never said anything about them. I never even thought about her going anywhere while we were at school and Da was at work, 'cause when we got home she was always there, cleaning up the house or making canned ham sandwiches like she'd never left. A lot of times I'd forget that she even did piano lessons until I'd hear her slowly plinking away at something like "Mary Had a Little Lamb" after dinner when Jess and I were out on the deck or the swing-set. She'd always stop playing as soon as we came in.

I don't think Mum ever learned to play a hard song. Or if she did, we never heard her play it. She never said anything about her teacher, either. We didn't even know his name was Wiley until that day he came to our house.

Like the coyote, I said when Mum introduced him. Mum laughed, her embarrassed laugh.

Precisely, Wiley said, and I smiled even though I didn't want to. Then he played 'Eye of the Tiger' on our piano. I remember thinking it was majorly cool, but I was pretty little then. The dust from the outer keys got all over his fingers and he wiped them on the legs of his black jeans, leaving five faint grey streaks on the back of each thigh.

Did you see Mummy? Jess whispered to me as we ran up the stairs to her bedroom. She shut her door behind us and then leaned her back against it. She was grinning, had her fingers bunched up to her mouth and was nibbling at the nails.

Didn't you notice? she said. She pulled a strand of hair from the end of her ponytail and wound it around her pointer finger. Mummy was twirling her hair, like this, she said. Jess made circles with her finger, twisting the hair around it. The loose ends flapped at her ear.

Yeah, I said, she was also laughing funny. Like hee!hee!hee! all squeaky like that. Wiley had been playing all these '80s rock songs, and Mum had stood next to the piano watching him, laughing even though nothing was funny.

And did you see her playing with her necklace? Jess said. The one Daddy gave her for Christmas?

And tapping her foot! I jumped up and down.

That was just to keep time to the music, dummy, Jess said. She rummaged around in her dresser drawer, messing up all the piles of panties that she'd folded. She tried to hide what she was doing, but I saw her slide her diary out from inside the drawer.

Now close your eyes, Jess said, and I did. I knew she would be getting the key from underneath the pencil container on her desk.

Okay, Jess said, and when I opened my eyes Jess was sitting at her desk with the diary open, and she was drawing a line down the centre of a fresh page. I watched her print neatly in purple ink with her Minnie Mouse pen.

SPY NOTES. SATURDAY, JUNE 14, 1991. 1:32 PM.

Mummy	Wiley
twirling hair	joking around
laughing funny	showing off on piano
playing with necklace (present from Daddy)	smiling a lot

sitting close together on piano bench (legs touching)

Was that it? she asked. She started counting on her fingers, chewing Minnie's ear on the end of her pen.

What about tapping her foot?

Jess rolled her eyes. I told you, she said, they're practicing piano. You have to tap your foot when you're learning to play piano.

But Mummy doesn't normally tap her foot, I said. Not when she listens to the radio or Michael Jackson tapes on the stereo in the kitchen.

Even though I was too young to explain it then, I knew that it was really the *way* Mum was tapping, how she moved her body. Like she was dancing. The way she was rocking her hips ever so slightly you could tell that she wanted Wiley to notice. And when she sat down next to him on the piano bench and they started their lesson, she'd been *concentrating*. She'd let us stand at the side of the piano and watch their lesson for a while, and I'd never seen her eyes like that before. So focused. Wiley was playing something slowly, just with one hand, so Mum could see how he did it. She had watched Wiley's long, bony fingers crawl across the keys, staring at them like she was watching him do a magic trick instead of just play a few simple notes.

Mum told us to go entertain ourselves 'cause she kept screwing up with us watching. That's when we got Jess's diary. Then we hid under the dining room table, listening to Mum and Wiley talk in the next room. We took more notes. Jess even tried to record their conversation, but it got boring, and she couldn't write fast enough anyway.

No, no, Wiley said. That's a B-flat. You keep playing B.

Hee!hee!hee! Mum giggled.

No, he said, it's laaaa, not laaa.

Jess wrote *getting frustrated — little bit mean* under Wiley's name on the list.

That was the only time they had their weekly lesson at our house. The funny thing is, from what I remember, neither of us even thought about Da. He was away at a conference that weekend. We didn't wonder whether he knew about Wiley coming over or not, or whether Mum even wanted him to. But he must have found out somehow because a little while later, Mum and Da were arguing in the basement. That was their favourite place to fight, I think 'cause they thought we couldn't hear them when they were down there. Jess and I were watching TV right above them, and we could hear them yelling, but it was true we couldn't hear *what* they were saying. After a while we got used to it, let the sound of the TV drown it out. But we both jumped when the door flew open and Da stomped through. He sat down on the couch next to Jess, put his feet up on the coffee table.

YOU CAN'T SELL *MY* PIANO! Mum screamed from downstairs. Then she was quiet.

We looked at Da, but he didn't seem to notice. His eyes were on the TV. His face hadn't changed.

Mum stayed in the basement for a long time. Da had left the door wide open, but we didn't hear anything. She stayed down there, silent, while Da watched two episodes of *Full House* with us. He was laughing at all the jokes, even the lame ones that Kimmy made. During one of the commercials, he got out this old bag of shrimp chips and started eating them right out of the bag instead of putting them in a bowl like Mum always told us to do. The shrimp chips were the kind that made your breath stink, and they'd been sitting in the cupboard for months.

Those are stale, Jess told him, looking at him with her lips all curled, as if he was eating toad legs or live worms.

They're good, Da said with a full mouth. Try some. Da can never tell if things are stale. And he never remembers that we think shrimp chips are sick and smell like crotch. They don't even sell them at the regular grocery stores, just the Chinese ones, 'cause no one else would buy them. Da finished the whole bag, and afterwards he kept sucking his teeth, ssssstch, ssssstch, and Jess would glare at him every time he did it.

By the end of the second show I couldn't remember anything that had happened in the episodes. I had been wondering the whole time what Mum was doing down in the basement with the cement floors and all those pipes and the furnace and the deep freeze and boxes stacked on shelves and nothing else. I tried to imagine her thinking about something, and what she would think about. But all I could imagine was her sitting on the floor, her knees pulled up to her chest, staring at the wall.

I wish Da still lived in that house, because now when I think about that basement it was actually a pretty neat place. All cool and dark with only one naked light bulb dangling from a wire,

the feeling of the damp cement on your bare feet, weaving
between the pipes that came up from the floor and disappeared
into the ceiling, making shadows move across the walls. When
I was little I thought there was a ghost living in the furnace.
Kind of like Slimer from *Ghostbusters*. I thought that the ghost
traveled in and out of his furnace home through the vents, and
that the fluffy dust on the ventholes was actually ghost slime
that rubbed off every time the ghost passed through.

But then one summer we got a whole lot of rain. At one point
it rained practically every day for a week, and Mum said she
felt like she was back in Wiltshire the way it was coming down.
The news reports started talking about all the houses that were
getting flooded in their basements, and this girl Courtney came
to school one day with big bags under her eyes, saying that
she spent the whole night helping her dad move furniture and
scoop water with a popcorn bucket. She said her dad had to get
a big pump like the ones they use for swimming pools to suck
all the water out. I'd never heard of floods in people's basements
before. I pictured waterfalls pouring through the windows,
Courtney and her dad clinging to a floating washing machine.

Ever since then, whenever I thought about our basement
I imagined it underwater. And as soon as I saw it underwater,
it became a sunken shipwreck, hundreds of years at the
bottom of the sea. Deep enough that no one could find it,
so all the treasures were still locked up in the freezer, which
I imagined was actually a huge treasure chest. The reddish-
brown pipe with the knob on the side was a periscope, the
rack of Da's old suits was a pile of skeletons, their clothes
half-decomposed. The other floor-to-ceiling pipes were pillars
of coral, and the plastic sheeting hanging off the walls was
flowing veils of seaweed.

Of course there would be creatures living down there. Not
ghosts. People often think that life only exists in nice places

with lots of food and plants and sunlight. For a long time people thought that nothing could even live in the deep ocean, until some scientists decided to drag nets and found nearly five hundred new species in only a few days. You'd think it would be common sense to check before you say that life can't exist somewhere. People just don't like to believe in things they can't see. Creatures that live in dark places. Monsters.

But some of those creatures, some of the ones living in the deepest darkest parts of the sea, are pretty much the most efficiently evolved animals ever. Take, for instance, the spookfish of the genus *chimaera*. When you hear that name you imagine some kind of jellyfish with a skirt of long white tentacles, a floating sea-ghost. But actually, it gets its name because its skin is nearly transparent, like the thin layer of skim milk that stays in the bottom of your glass. It's got these huge balloon eyes that stick right out of its head like gum bubbles ready to pop, with no pupils or anything. The eyes face upward to catch the minuscule amounts of light that filter down into the deep waters. And get this: it uses mirrors inside those eyeballs to reflect the light onto a second set of retinas that face down. Basically, spookfish can see in opposite directions at the same time. Hard to believe, which may be another reason that people call it the spookfish. They'd rather think of it as a ghost, something not real.

It looks like an alien, Mum said when I showed her a picture. Like those aliens with the big eyes. I groaned and Mum said What? even though I've told her a million times I'm sick of hearing about aliens. Mum is the opposite of those people who don't believe in things until they see them. Mum only believes in things she doesn't see.

IV

IT WAS LATE IN London. Belinda had pre-booked a room for
the night at the Renaissance Hotel, a five-minute shuttle-ride
from the airport. It had been years since she'd stayed in a hotel.
She followed behind the bellboy, who wasn't actually a boy but
an older, white-haired man, as he lugged her two suitcases and
duffel bag down the hall to the elevator.

Visiting England for an extended period, Ma'am? he asked,
wheezing.

Yes, well — sort of, she said. I haven't decided yet. Are you
sure I can't take one of those bags from you?

Quite sure, he said, setting the bags in front of the elevator
doors with a thump. Belinda pressed the 'up' button. They waited.

Are you meeting a group in the morning? he asked.

I'm catching a train, Belinda said. To Salisbury.

Salisbury? he said. I'm from there. My mum lives there still.

Belinda smiled. What a coincidence, she said. I mean —
that I'm going there. I'll be meeting some people. Not family.

The elevator doors opened and Belinda stepped inside.
The interior was covered in mirrored panels, walls and ceiling.

Belinda looked around her, examining the various angles of her reflection. The bellboy dragged her bags inside, watching her.

A tad unnerving, isn't it? he asked. It's as if you can't escape yourself.

No, no, Belinda said. It's interesting. I like it. It's like being inside a telescope.

He chuckled. A rather large telescope, that is, he said.

Well, she said, the bigger the better. The bigger they are, the further you can see.

Hm, he said, scratching his neck. I suppose that's true. But you'd see very little from here. Bloody cloudy this time of year, he said, giving her a wink.

That evening, she couldn't sleep. It was the jetlag, she told herself. She could always tell she was tired when memories began to invade her thoughts. Old memories, some of them even false, fabricated by her wandering mind. Almost all of them were staged in her mother's garden at the home in Wiltshire where Belinda grew up. There were several about Prim, although Belinda knew she couldn't possibly have accurately remembered her. But that night, she saw a scene in her head that she had seen before; it returned to her from time to time, like a recurring dream. As a child, she had a curious fear of the sour cherry bush that grew in a shaded spot along the side of her mother's house. The bush was spindly from lack of sun, and the scant peppering of cherries that would appear on its branches each year looked to Belinda like beads of blood. For the longest time, a sheet of newspaper had been lodged at the base of the bush, and whenever Belinda saw it there, she thought of a person — Prim — squatting there, using the newspaper as a mat, like a homeless person. Prim was skeletal, her skin gray with dirt. Her mouth gaped, a dark, empty hole.

Of course, Prim had never been homeless and starving, at least to Belinda's knowledge. She decided that the spot under the cherry tree was where Prim would go to hide from their mother. Belinda couldn't remember if she'd made this decision when she was a child, or as an adult looking back. But each time the image returned, Belinda reminded herself that it wasn't real. It came from some recess of her mind that had been shut away long ago.

Belinda called Calgary again, hoping to get Jessica. It was three in the morning her time, but only eight PM their time. Sebastian picked up.

Mummy? he said. Guess what, I remembered all the words. I sang today and I remembered all the words!

You sang? Belinda asked, smiling to herself. That's right, she said, it was your concert today. That's great, honey. Just great. She felt her eyes burning, but she quickly wiped them. It wasn't the end of the world, she told herself. She couldn't possibly be there all the time.

Is Jessica there? she asked, sniffing.

Yeah, he said. But Daddy's right here. He wants to talk to you. She could hear Sebastian passing the phone over before she had a chance to protest.

Bell? Wiley said. He sounded like he'd just woken up.

Have you been sleeping on the couch again? Belinda asked him.

Yeah, he said mid-stretch. Can't sleep in the bed without you.

Oh for Chrissakes, she said, you're going to ruin your back.

Doesn't matter, he said like a sulking child.

You're acting ridiculous, she said. It's a bad example for the kids.

I can't help it, he said. I'm. . . depressed, okay? I've been having these terrible thoughts. . . Wiley had been brandishing that word — *depressed* — for months. His depression was like mould on bread: you could cut off the visible patches, but the infection was still there, infused into each atom of every cell.

Please come home, he whined.

I just got here, she said. I can't. This is something I have to do. A long silence followed.

I have to go, Belinda said. I've got to go to sleep. She hung up, and reminded herself that it was not constructive to call home so often. They would be fine without her.

For hours after, Belinda couldn't stop her mind from whirring. She'd pushed her thoughts away from the phone call and back to her conversation with the bellboy. It had lasted only five minutes, but in that time it had struck a chord. Telescopes. She believed that the telescope was the truest scientific instrument ever invented. An arrangement of mirrors, angled to face one another, with the power to collect, reflect, and magnify light. The telescope brought near what was far, revealed new worlds. But its lenses could not capture anything that didn't actually exist in the visible universe. For Belinda, it disproved the existence of God.

The photographs of the Eagle Nebula were Belinda's proof. The Hubble took them just the previous year, although scientists had known of the nebula since the eighteenth century. It was named after its shape: the cosmic gases and stardust spread to form wings and a hooked beak. Belinda could remember seeing the photos for the first time and feeling the sudden urge to cry, then thinking herself a nitwit for getting emotional over a cluster of stars. One of the photos showed three arms of billowing auburn clouds reaching up into a starry expanse of blue-green mist. If it weren't for the stars, Belinda might have mistaken it for an aerial photo of a sandy delta pouring furiously into the sea. It was a scene that undoubtedly occurred all the time in outer space, and yet to Belinda it appeared to be a monumental event: either the miraculous beginning or the glorious end of something beyond human understanding. Scientists hypothesized that the dark areas in the clouds were the birthplaces of protostars, which sounded to Belinda like an easy guess. The photo had been appropriately named "Pillars of Creation," as if it were taken directly out of an ancient Greek myth.

Looking back, Belinda realized that what she'd really been emotional about was her own naïveté. The Eagle Nebula was 6,500 light years away from earth, and its wings spanned twenty million light years. It had become clear by looking at those photos that the human race knew nothing beyond the petty workings of the earth, and that God was just a way to fill the void left by ignorance. The telescope could only offer evidence that the universe was so vast it might as well be endless.

That was when she began her research. She went to the public library and found an article that explained how the Hubble worked on the same basic principles as all reflective telescopes. She discovered that in their simplest form, telescopes were made up of concentric shafts that slid in and out of one another. If you looked straight-on at the lens of a collapsed telescope, you would see a series of circles radiating from the same centre, like the ripples made by a raindrop in a puddle.

Concentricity. She'd been as moved by the images of the Hubble as she'd been by the first images she'd seen of crop circles. Then there was the UFO sighting. And the coincidences kept multiplying and circling back to each other the more Belinda thought about them. They were all signs, radiating from the same centre. She wore her coincidences like rings, all on one finger. They travelled with her wherever she went, and each was just as important as the rest.

5 Old vs. New

I SKIPPED SCHOOL THE day after Mum left. Just fifth and sixth period. But I'd never skipped before. I always worried the school might call Mum's work number, but it turns out they just have this automated calling system where a recorded voice says *Your child missed one or more classes blah blah blah,* and usually it gets left as a message on people's home answering machines. So the trick is, if you get home before your parents, you can just erase the message and they'll never know. Of course, I only found this out when Mum was gone anyway, so it didn't matter.

After fourth period, I just kind of walked out, down the hallway, got my coat from my locker, and walked casually out the front doors. The whole time I felt like a criminal, like I was swiping a pearl necklace or a video game. A kid in my grade had been caught stealing a Nintendo expansion pack at the mall a few days before. Simon Fulton, nerd extraordinaire. One of those frizzy-haired kids with braces you never would've thought had it in him. I had to keep telling myself to walk slowly, look casual, look casual, and I kept looking behind me, side to side, in case any teachers were around. When I got close to the doors, I started running. I couldn't help it. I was even holding my jacket together, pulling it over my ribs, like I was clutching that new Smashing Pumpkins CD I'd been wanting underneath.

My mission was to get to Squid's school. The week before, he'd told Mum he'd be singing in the assembly and he was all excited until Mum reminded him she'd be gone by then. She didn't even say sorry. He made a face like he'd just dropped his ice cream cone in the gutter. I'd decided then and there that I was going to show up at the assembly and surprise him.

I knew the number 77 bus would stop in front of Squid's school. The number 77 is the bus I take every morning, except Squid's school is somewhere further along the route. Earl Grey Elementary. It's a cinch to remember 'cause my name's in it, except spelled 'Grey' instead of 'Gray.' I like to imagine myself as the school's mascot, Call me Earl Gray, dressed up in shiny purple pantaloons and a wide-brimmed hat with a green feather.

When Mum told me Squid would be switching to Earl Grey Elementary School, I asked her if he was going to learn how to make tea all day. Mum just looked at me.

Like the tea, I said, Earl Grey. Get it?

Don't discourage him, Mum said, making her lips into thin wrinkled lines. I hadn't known it was a special school, a 'developmental learning' school. I just thought it was a funny name.

Maybe your school is shaped like a giant teacup, I said to Squid on the morning of his first day.

No, he said with a big silly smile on his face.

Are you sure? I asked him. I put on my best confused expression. I heard it was shaped like a teacup, I said, and the handle is a slide that takes you from the third floor to the second floor.

Really? he said. Squid loved that, even though he knew I was faking it. I saw him eyeing the handle of Mum's teacup the whole time he was eating his cereal.

Mum says they won't make me do the mad minute, Squid said.

Oh yeah, I said. I remember the mad minute. I narrowed my eyes and stroked my chin like an old man remembering some ancient tale. I hated the mad minute. Way to make kids feel bad about themselves. So I can't do a whole bunch of useless math equations in sixty seconds flat — who cares? I suggested to Squid that we get Wiley to fire up the barbecue so we could burn all his mad minutes, but Mum said Are you crazy? For . Chrissakes, Grace, don't put crazy ideas in his head.

Crazy ideas, crazy ideas! Squid cheered. He bounced up and down in his chair like it was made of rubber.

Old Wiley would have been all for the idea too. He'd get that big toothy grin on his face, like a little kid. And then he'd say something really cheeseball. Something like Let's rock! And then the singing would start.

Wheel-a-Fortune Sally Ride! Heavy meddle suicide! Complete with air guitar. Anytime anybody mentioned something about fire, Wiley used to break out in "We Didn't Start the Fire." Old Wiley practically lived for '80s rock. But when I asked New Wiley about burning Squid's mad minutes, he looked at me as if I'd just clubbed a baby seal to death.

Why would you want to do that? he asked. When did you become so . . . destructive? He took a slow sip of his beer. He was sitting on the patio, watching Mum weed the back garden. He didn't say anything else after that, just shook his head, watched Mum shuffle around on her knees, digging in the dirt.

New Wiley hadn't left the couch since Mum dragged her suitcase out the front door. In the morning I'd found him asleep sitting up, head back and mouth lolling open. There was a bag of

Cheezies lying on his belly and he had orange powder smeared all over his face and down the front of his shirt. It looked like he'd been snacking in his sleep.

I knew Wiley wouldn't notice if I skipped school. Probably wouldn't care, even if he did. But neither would Old Wiley, for different reasons. My Social teacher in grade seven, Mrs. Clarke, once gave me 78% on a news article I wrote about Jim Morrison's suicide, said that it wasn't a 'current event.' Wiley called her a prune-crotched ol' battle-axe. Excuuuse me? Mum said, her nostrils flaring. That made it even funnier. Basically, that sums up what Wiley really thinks about school.

Anyway, once I'd gotten off school property and was waiting at the bus stop, I didn't feel so bad anymore. There was an advertisement on the bus bench for Len T. Wong: putting a personal touch on home-buying. Somebody had drawn on the ad with permanent marker so that it said PLen T. Wong: putting a personal touch on homo-buying. There was a picture of Len T. Wong too, with a pointy Fu Manchu drawn like an icicle on the end of his chin and a black comb-over scribbled across his shiny bald head. I sat on the bench, thought about the time in grade seven when Julie Sanders pointed at the little black hairs sprouting out of my chin and declared to the whole cafeteria that I was turning into Genghis Khan. I looked up and down the sidewalks. Nobody.

Then I heard the sound of the school doors slamming behind me. Footsteps. Gavin Mills appeared on the sidewalk, started walking towards me. His long hair was hanging over his eyes in greasy ropes, so he didn't notice me sitting at the bus stop at first. I stood up. Sat back down again. For some reason, my heart started beating really fast. It wasn't 'cause I was afraid that Gavin would tell on me. I knew he wouldn't. It wasn't 'cause I liked Gavin either. It was just this weird feeling where I felt like running away. Away from the bus stop and

away from PLen T. Wong and his ugly prosthetic Fu Manchu.
I stood up again.

Gavin looked surprised when he saw me. He smiled. I realized
I'd never seen Gavin Mills smile before, except that one time he
told Sabrina Chowdhury that her tits were showing. We'd been
outside for field hockey, and she wasn't wearing a bra under her
Bow Valley High gym strip. You could see her nipples, and one
of them just happened to be sticking out like a pushpin right
in the hole of the 'o' in 'Bow.' Gavin had smiled that sly, tight-
lipped kind of smile that guys never use on other guys. But the
smile he cracked when he saw me was a real smile, complete with
teeth. I smiled back, couldn't stop myself, even though I knew
it made me look like a horse 'cause my upper gums show too
much. I stood right in front of the bench. My arms felt like limp
noodles hanging at my sides so I put my hands on my hips.

Hey, Gavin said, combing his hair back with his fingers.
It fell right back over his eyes and he flicked his head, held it
kind of up and to the side so the hair would stay tossed across
his forehead. You skipping? he asked.

Yeah, I said, I didn't feel like listening to Mr. Pearce ramble
on about the House of Commons.

We finished that unit like three months ago, he said.

Oh really, I said, I guess I don't pay much attention. I laughed.
It came out sounding really high and chirpy. I could tell by
Gavin's face that he thought I sounded like a total ditz.

But you always get good marks, he said, scrunching his eyebrows. Didn't you win the Social award and the LA award last
year?

Oh yeah, I said, that was a long time ago. That was Junior
High. It was just a dumb award thing, it didn't really mean
anything.

You got those plaques, Gavin said, with your name carved
in them.

Yeah, I forgot about those. I don't even know where they are anymore.

Gavin gave me this *are you kidding me* kind of look. He could tell I hadn't forgotten about the plaques. Actually, they were hanging on the wall in Da's home office.

Anyway, I said. I started putting my backpack on for no particular reason. I gotta go.

Aren't you waiting for the bus? Gavin said.

Yeah, that's my bus, I said, pointing to a bus waiting at the traffic lights on the other side of the road. I forgot which one I was supposed to take, I told Gavin as I started jaywalking across the road. Gavin just stood there, watching me. I hadn't noticed that a car was coming and it screeched to a stop in front of me. A little Aah! sound came out of my mouth and I ran to the other side, staring at my feet.

Gavin waved when I got to the stop. I watched the bus coming up the road, pretended not to notice him. I could feel cold sweat soaking through the pits of my t-shirt.

The bus was a number 37. I had no idea where it would go. I got on and chose a seat at the back. When I looked out the window I saw Gavin standing up on the bus bench. I don't know why. He wasn't doing anything, just standing and staring straight ahead like a statue, his greasy hair flapping around his ears in the breeze. Everyone on the bus was looking at him. As we drove away, I could see Len T. Wong's eyes between his spread legs, following the bus down the street.

I didn't think about what I was going to do until we turned the corner. I was about to ring the bell for the next stop so I could get off and run across the street to wait for the 77, but then I didn't know if Gavin was going to be getting on the next 77. So I just sat in my seat and started biting my hair, which is what I always do when I'm nervous about something. One day you'll cough up a hairball, Jess always says when she sees me doing it. Not likely, Mum had once corrected her, she'll need surgery if she's got a hairball. Hair gets lodged in the small intestine, Mum said, I saw it on TV. Ever since then I've pictured this ball of brown hair with food bits all stuck in it, sloshing around in my gut, but it still doesn't stop me from biting my hair.

The bus was one of the old-style ones with the long sideways benches at the back, so that when the bus was really full you'd keep sliding into people's hips every time the bus stopped and started. The public transit booty-bumper. But luckily since it was the middle of the day there was just me and this other guy sitting on the bench across from me, chewing purple gum and smacking his lips really loud.

The bus must be going to the LRT station, I told myself. I was sure that all the buses going in this direction went to the LRT station after the high school. I could get off there and figure out if there were other buses going past Squid's school. I looked at my watch. It was 1:17 PM. I had time.

Where're ya goin,' girlie? said the gum guy. He lifted the brim of his ball cap so that it stuck up in the air. The sun coming through the windows made his forehead shine.

Nowhere, I said. I mean home. In my head I said, None of your business. Girlie yourself. He nodded, started chewing his gum vigorously, making his chin wobble up and down. He took off his cap and there was a bald patch on his buzzed head, right smack in the middle.

What's yer sign? he asked.

Ssorry? I said. I almost laughed out loud.

You look like a Capricorn, he said. He yawned, tilted his head back. His tongue was stained purple. Then he looked at me again with his eyebrows perked up, and his eyes looked wet from yawning so wide.

Ooookay, I said. I turned to the window and watched K-Mart

fly by. Let the traffic light be green, I told myself. Let the next three traffic lights before the station be green.

You a Buddhist? he said, and then quickly — I ask because I don't wish to offend her majesty the Bali-Bali Queen of the Forbidden City. He pushed his thumb into the side of his nose, sniffed. Cackled to himself.

I almost piped up about how I was actually born in Canada and I'd never been to China, but I stopped myself when I recognized the slur in his voice, the way his head rolled back on his neck. Wiley once told me you could see under people's skin when they're drunk, right down to the bones. I knew it was just a figure of speech, but it made me think of the alcohol like some kind of acid, so when the person swallows it all their skin comes sizzling off, like burning from the inside out, until the charred flesh is just lying in scraps on the ground and only a skeleton is left. My school owns this life-size skeleton that they keep in the storage room next to the Science lab, and a few years ago these grade twelves got ahold of it somehow and hung it from Mrs. Desoto's ceiling. They'd strung it up by its neck with fishing line so that the feet were touching the ground as if it was standing on its own. And they strung up the hands too, so it looked like the skeleton was flapping its arms like bat wings. People said they heard her scream from the basketball courts outside. It's funny how a useless dead skeleton can give people the willies but a live person with skin covering a skeleton isn't considered scary at all. If you think about it, the skin is kinda like a costume, a cover-up for how people really look, which makes its pretty ironic that people dress up like skeletons for Halloween.

Anyway, by this point the bus had reached the last traffic light before the station. I was literally just about to breathe out an audible sigh of relief, let my neck uncrimp itself so I could stand up and wait by the door. And then — we turned left.

Instead of going straight through the lights to the LRT station, the bus turned left and merged onto the highway faster than I could think to yell out STOP. I just sat there letting my cheeks get hot and watching the trees along the side of the road go whooshing by. I put a strand of hair fatter than a cigar in my mouth, and my teeth were practically chattering. I thought about talking to the bus driver, but I didn't want gum guy to hear.

Sometimes I wonder how I get myself into these ridiculous situations. Then I remember it's my bad karma. Mum says there's no such thing as bad luck, so I say karma instead, 'cause it's basically the same thing. I've got another five years to live down because I broke the giant mirror that Jess used to have mounted on her bedroom door. We were fighting about something dumb, probably who was going to look after Squid, and I stormed out of her room and slammed the door. It was weird 'cause I've slammed her door dozens of times and nothing ever happened. But that time, the whole thing just fell right off. Did a belly flop on the carpet. It didn't shatter either, like you would expect. Only cracked into a whole bunch of pieces, so it sounded like a stack of newspapers being dumped on a concrete floor. I didn't even know I had done it until I heard Jess moaning like a humpback whale. When I opened the door the mirror was lying flat on the carpet with all the pieces in place, like a jigsaw puzzle just waiting to be stuck together. And that was that. Seven years bad karma. It was an ugly mirror anyway.

When I finally got off the bus I was close to tears and it was 1:44. I was on some random street that I'd never seen before and I felt like my throat was packed with stones. I didn't know what else to do but cross the street and take the next bus going back in the other direction.

I was going to be late. No way was I making it to Squid's school by two o'clock. I started whispering to myself, you stupid, you stupid, stupid idiot, how could you be so stupid, you fuck, you fucking stupid. I almost thought about killing myself right there, it was that bad. I imagined, just for a second, that it was me hanging from Mrs. Desoto's ceiling, the fishing line pressing a thin bluish streak into my neck. And I hated the gum guy, really really hated his guts, loathed the very thought of that freak-nut and his revolting purple tongue.

Eventually I found a bus stop, and when the bus came the driver told me it would take me back to the LRT station. I must have looked really relieved then, 'cause the bus driver said he would tell me when we got there, and then he pointed out where I could catch the 77 as I was getting off at the station. That made me feel a bit better.

I made it to the school by 2:28, and the assembly was still going. When I got into the gym the kids were in the middle of singing a song about chicken soup. Squid was up there on the risers, first row, singing away. *In February it will bee-ee. My snowman's anniver-sa-ree-ee.* Since he was at the front you could see his arms were stick straight and his hands were in little fists, pressing at his sides. Somebody, probably his teacher, must've told him you have to stand up straight when you're singing, because he was all stiff like a toy soldier.

I had to climb over someone to get a seat on the fold-down chairs they'd set up under the basketball nets. Squid must've noticed me then. When I looked up he was grinning like crazy. He was smiling so big he could hardly sing, couldn't form the words properly 'cause the corners of his mouth were way up at his ears. His back was even straighter than before, and his fists were practically vibrating he was so happy. He couldn't stop smiling, you could tell he was trying to 'cause he'd lost where he was in the lyrics and he was looking all confused. The kid beside him belting it out, *Happy once! Happy twice!*

Happy chicken soup with rice! I was pretty well cringing in my seat, saying in my head Jesus Christ, Squid, quit grinning, you look like a doofus. He managed to chime back in at the end of the next verse, *Blowing once! Blowing twice! Blowing chicken soup with rice!*

And then a weird thing happened. All of a sudden, I started to cry. I started thinking about how ridiculous it was that Squid was so happy to see me, that he didn't care that I was late, and then I was crying. It just happened, like that. One minute I was thinking Squid looked like a dork and the next minute I had tears brimming at my eyes. All these images were flashing through my head: making gingerbread houses with Squid, having water-balloon fights with Squid, letting Squid tear off the tinfoil for the pan of McCain Superfries we were making and Squid getting all excited about the spiky tear-off thingy. It was like a movie montage reeling through my brain. I had to bend down and pretend I was getting something out of my backpack, but then the tears started dripping on the floor and I had to wipe my hand across my face. I could feel the lady sitting next to me glance at me. I unzipped my backpack, shuffled my binder and lunch bag around. I didn't know what else to do so I kept shuffling and just hoping the crying would stop.

V

THE GRAIN WAS WOVEN with riddles. Canola, wheat, maize, barley, linseed, and rye. Their brittle stalks would snap if you tried to bend them by hand. Before Belinda knew anything about crop circles, she assumed that the shapes were mown out of the fields, the stalks razored off. She'd seen the front-page stories in the tabloids speculating that UFOs had been landing in the fields, stamping the ground beneath with their spinning discs. The increasingly intricate designs quickly debunked that theory, but another convincing explanation had yet to take its place. Unorthodox wind vortices couldn't explain how the grains of one stem bed had been bent at different heights to create defined layers like trifle, or how these layers could be swept in opposite directions. But crop circle theories fell by the wayside as soon as those two opportunists from Southampton insisted they had masterminded the phenomenon. They claimed to have dragged a plank attached to a rope to flatten the grains. Belinda was certain this was just a ploy to gain attention and notoriety. The manmade crop circles could be picked out on first glance by even the least discerning eye;

they were crooked and lopsided, the lines wavered, and the flattened grains were smattered about the ground like road kill. They were a joke compared to the true circles, in which the stalks were bent at near ninety-degree angles and brushed like hair into perfectly symmetrical forms. The stalks were not flattened, but hovered inches above the ground. Their seeded heads had been swept into neat parcels of cresting waves. No evidence of footpaths leading into or out of the field. And besides, there were simply too many occurrences — more than one hundred each year in England alone, and dozens more across the globe — to be attributed solely to the work of two silly pranksters.

For Belinda, the most fascinating evidence came from Marshall V. Longfellow's article on the anatomical anomalies found in grains taken from crop circles. She was finally sitting on the train, nearly on her way to meet the man himself. She had a copy of Dr. Longfellow's seminal article with her, which she'd already decorated with highlights and penciled notes. She'd practically memorized it, but she took it out of her purse and looked over her notes again, as a distraction. She'd been chewing her nails incessantly as she waited for the train to start on its way. For a moment, she wondered what Wiley and her children might be doing, if they were sitting at the breakfast table, eating the toaster strudels she'd bought on Sebastian's request. But then she realized it was two in the morning where they were. Everyone would be in bed. She quickly turned her eyes back to her article, back to Dr. Longfellow's inspiring words.

He was an American biophysicist, and a legend in crop-circle research. He had been the first researcher to take samples and analyze their molecular structure, and he found that the plant cells had in fact been altered at the site of bending. The results of his tests suggested that the grains had been manipulated by microwaves, heated at the nodes and flexed into shape in the same way a piece of glass can be rendered malleable under flame. Some of the stalks even showed evidence of singeing. When the bent nodes were dissected and examined under microscope, they appeared to have burst from the inside out. A series of concentric circles radiated from the centre of each ruptured node, branded into the plant cells like minuscule tree rings.

Belinda couldn't fathom why the skeptics had largely dismissed Longfellow's findings. She guessed fear. It was evident, at any rate, that the grains had suffered some sort of trauma, and yet Belinda preferred not to think of it this way. She'd seen photos of one crop circle in a field of flowering canola, where each delicate yellow petal remained intact and untouched. The formation looked like a giant Easter wreath dotted with thousands of flowers, all nesting gently among the combed stems as if tucked into place by an invisible hand. If the incident had been traumatic, surely the canola flowers would have died. Surely the grains wouldn't have continued to grow in their horizontal positions without making any attempt to regain their vertical posture. But they accepted their alteration willingly, continued to live, and even to ripen. Belinda saw it as a testament to the beauty of adaptation.

When Belinda was a child and still living in her mother's house, they had a lopsided houseplant. Her mother kept it banished to a dark corner of the living room and it grew sideways, sprouting long, gangly arms that reached out in search of scant sunbeams. Her mother insisted it stay there because she bought it specifically to decorate that corner. To move it would defeat its purpose. The plant grew teardrops for leaves, and they gathered on the ends of the pale, limp stems. Every week when the time came for Belinda to water it, she thought of her sister.

Prim had left when she was fifteen years old and never returned. Belinda was only a baby at the time. In her mother's embittered way, she made the subject of Prim taboo. She isn't anything special, her mother insisted. Only a bad girl.

Of course, this only made Belinda more enamoured with her. She knew that Prim looked like her, with the same green eyes and dense blondish-brown hair. Their neighbour, Mrs. Fields, had given that away when she patted her on the head and remarked that Belinda was a spitting image of her sister, but that she hoped she was better behaved. Belinda had also deduced that Prim had the same wide ankles and square, boyish feet. Her mother had once told her, when none of the boots in the local store would fit her feet, that stocky ankles and feet were the Harris family inheritance, and not one of the ladies on the Harris side had escaped them.

But as a teenager, when Belinda thought of her sister, her stockiness was not a burden but a symbol of strength. Prim's green eyes were luminous, not mossy, and her hair thick and luxuriant rather than unruly. She smoked cigarettes, the long curl of smoke wisping from her lips like a question mark. She dated boys, which, Belinda had intuited, was part of the reason for her fallout with their mother. Belinda had imagined Prim as a more confident, more beautiful, and seductively mysterious version of herself. Perhaps even a future self. Prim was the Snow White that Belinda aspired to be, banished from the house by her evil mother and noble in her bold independence. In Belinda's mind, wherever Prim had gone she had undoubtedly married the man of her dreams, and this was all she needed to be sublimely happy. Belinda was content to believe this, and didn't want any evidence that proved otherwise. It was naïve, but it allowed her to believe that you didn't need a good mother to turn out all right.

The lopsided plant had been Belinda's bridge. It had been there all along, since before Belinda's birth, a living witness to Prim's existence. Years later, when she moved out of her mother's house, Belinda took the plant with her. She placed it on the kitchen windowsill in her apartment and watched the stems rise up from the soil after only a few days. She kept the soil moist and rotated the pot every so often, allowing the sun to pour over each leaf with equal attention. Within two months, a tiny flower bud had pushed its way out of the soil. And eventually, the bud unfurled into a lush, fuchsia-pink bloom. An azalea. Her mother had never known, had always assumed it was just a plain green plant. She had never given it the chance to be an azalea.

Belinda liked to believe that the plant had disguised itself for all that time. It became what it needed to be according to the circumstance. When she married Dazhong and moved to Canada, she'd had to leave the azalea with her neighbours. She had often wondered what forms it had taken since then, how many transformations it had undergone. In the twenty-one years that had passed, she had never once allowed herself to believe that perhaps the azalea had died.

6 The Other Grace

THERE'S THIS OTHER GIRL named Grace who was in my math
class last year. She's gone to the same school as me since
elementary. Everyone mixes us up, even teachers. My math
teacher would sometimes accidentally hand her homework
back to me, so I got to see her marks. She always got 90s,
which was how I knew right away it wasn't mine. She's on
the debate team too, and just before Mum left she won some
big competition. The next week they put up posters all over
the school about it, and everyone thought it was me. On the
morning of the day I skipped fifth and sixth period, this dumb
kid in my homeroom, Ricky, said, Hey Grace, what'd you win?

It wasn't me, I said. I'm not on the debate team.

I thought you won something, he said. Some contest.

It's not me, I said. It's the other Grace. The Chinese one.

Aren't you Chinese? he said. This kid, he just keeps going.
I think maybe he has ADD.

No, I said. I crossed my arms and looked the other way,
pretended there was something interesting happening over
there. But it was first thing in the morning and everyone was

just sitting at their desks, zoning out. I thought about the other Grace. I knew I would be seeing her in second period. She usually dressed in pink corduroys, worn white at the knees. No matter what colour she was wearing on top — purple, neon green, yellow — she still wore those pink corduroys. She pulled the waist up way too high. She always tied her mussed black hair back in a low ponytail with a red velvet scrunchie, and you could see the flecks of dandruff at the roots from miles away. She spoke with a Chinese accent, and when she talked, I couldn't help but notice the little daubs of frothy spit that had collected at the corners of her mouth and turned all white and crusty. Her breath smelled like sausages.

Even though I was pretending to ignore him, I could tell Ricky was thinking about something. He was all quiet, and he was still looking at me, at the back of my head. I could just *feel* his eyes looking at me. Ricky's one of those kids who's just — well, like a kid. Which is funny 'cause I think he probably failed a grade or two, which would make him older than the rest of us. But it takes him a long time to think about things, and you can see his lips moving when he's thinking, like he has to talk to himself. And when he doesn't get something, he just says it, *I don't get it,* waves his hand around, doesn't care if everyone's laughing at him. Once, during attendance, I saw him poking his mechanical pencil in his ear. He had the pointy end stuck right in there, and his thumb was click-click-clicking the other end to make the lead come out. When he pulled the pencil out of his ear, slowly and carefully, the lead was sticking way out, with a little hunk of orange wax pierced on the end. I almost puked.

But you have a Chinese last name, Ricky said. See, he just doesn't let up. It's like he's too dumb to get how annoying he is. I could feel my cheeks getting hot. Other people were starting to look.

That's only 'cause my dad was born in Malaysia. I don't even live with my dad, okay? Christ, what's with the twenty questions? Whoa, tou-chy, he said. Held his hands up like he was surrendering. As if I was some kinda bank robber just 'cause I didn't want to answer a bunch of questions first thing in the morning. As if it made no difference, what's the big deal, what does it matter that I wouldn't be caught dead wearing corduroys OR the colour pink, I don't speak a word of Chinese, my hair is always clean and it's brown not black, not to mention I think hair scrunchies are butt ugly.

Fine, I said. It came out really loud, and everyone looked. I stood up. Slammed my textbook down on the desk for effect.

You wanna know what I won? I yelled. I won fifty thousand bucks! I threw my hands up in the air like I was tossing confetti.

Ricky's eyes went all wide. He started kind of half-smiling, like he wasn't sure whether to laugh or not.

I won — a platypus! I won a lifetime supply of candy! There — are you happy? I put this big fake smile on.

My homeroom teacher — Mr. Steeves — called it an 'outburst.'

Would you like to tell me what brought on that little outburst? he asked me in the hall. I told him I was stressed out, that Ricky was bugging me.

He kept calling me by the wrong name, I said. It's Gray, not Grace. I prefer Gray. I asked Mr. Steeves if he could change the attendance sheet, change my name to Gray so he wouldn't forget when he called my name. I just hate it when I get called the wrong name, I said. I just do.

But that wasn't really the reason. Even if I tried to explain it, Mr. Steeves wouldn't understand. Really, I was only trying to be funny. Some people had laughed. But it was like this quiet kind of laughter, like the same kind of laughter you'd hear the times when Ricky said he didn't get it. And after a couple of seconds I sat back down at my desk and didn't feel much like fake smiling anymore. At that point I got this sudden feeling that I just wanted to go home, really bad. I'd been wearing the same green hoodie with torn cuffs for the last two days because Mum hadn't been there to harass me about laundry. I hadn't really realized until then that the hoodie fit me like a potato sack, and the fabric on the sides was starting to pill so that it looked like a cat had been scratching at me. I thought about standing up and walking out, but I'd never done anything like that before, and besides, I hate it when people get all dramatic.

That evening I went rummaging through Mum's old clothes from the '70s and found this tube shirt with little frilly sleeves that hung off the shoulders. The thing was so stretchy that when you held it up it looked like only a five-year-old would fit into it, but when I put it on it hugged me really well. It had orange and yellow stripes going across it. I thought it looked cool and retro, and it was tight enough that the stripes curved around my boobs and made them look perky.

The next morning was Friday, and I was up really early, before my alarm went off. The sun was just coming up by the time I'd gotten dressed and washed. I'd even put some mascara and blush on. I learned how to apply blush years ago when I watched Mum practicing on Wiley. It was when she first got her job with Merle Norman and she had to pass a bunch of tests to be a *Certified Makeup Artist,* Mum's terminology. See, they have this hierarchy at Merle Norman where the older married ladies get to do all the fun stuff like applying makeup and piercing ears and building towers of eyeshadow boxes. They make the younger girls, the ones who only work after school and during the summer, sit at the cash register and Windex the vanities. So Mum had to prove to the biddies who'd worked there for twenty-odd years that she was worthy of powdering faces and curling eyelashes. The funny thing was she was really nervous.

She practiced every night for more than a week before she was ready to do the makeup tests at work. Toner all over, two dabs of concealer under the eyes and blend, curl the lashes and give two coats of mascara (brown for the blondes, black for the brunettes), ask for a smile and swirl blush on the apples, swipe to the cheekbones and ta-da. I'd get all those stupid phrases stuck in my head listening to Mum chant to herself while she carefully grazed Wiley's eyelashes with the mascara wand as if it was covered in hydrochloric acid.

Swuuuurl the blush, she'd say to herself, making little circles on Wiley's cheeks. And swipe. Jess once asked her if she'd ever thought of practicing on us, because wouldn't that make a lot more sense?

Wiley's got the cheekbones for it, Mum said. And besides, you girls are too young to be wearing makeup.

Wiley was a good sport about it 'cause he was still Old Wiley back then. He just sat there trying to watch TV out of the corner of his eye while Mum had her face right in his, peering at each and every lash to make sure the mascara was even. He came out looking like a drag queen every time 'cause Mum kept putting on way too much of everything, *just lemme even it out*. One time, when Jess and I had been out somewhere, we came home to the sound of Mum squealing with laughter. We found them in the kitchen, Mum keeled over laughing with tears in her eyes, and Wiley, his face all made up, standing in a pair of Mum's pink high heels with a purple feather boa wrapped around his neck. He was wearing these old denim cutoffs and one of Mum's silk blouses patterned with flowers.

Hey, Jess said, pointing at Wiley's boa. That's from my old Halloween costume! We both burst out laughing, and Wiley strutted around talking in a high-pitched voice while we laughed with Mum until our stomachs ached, and finally Mum said, Oh dear, oh dear, I'm just no good at all.

She ended up passing the tests anyway, but only 'cause they weren't really actual tests, just something the Merle Norman ladies did to keep themselves busy. Good thing too, 'cause I don't think New Wiley would've been much fun to practice on.

Mum had never shown me how to apply makeup but I thought I did a way better job. Granted, it was pretty easy to look better in makeup than Wiley. I stared at myself in the mirror for quite a while. I thought I looked pretty good wearing the stretchy shirt. With my eyelashes all curled and darkened and my cheeks pink, I looked like one of those go-go dancers from the old New York night clubs. I did a go-go dance for myself and wished I had a pair of leather knee-boots. I was pretty sure that people at school were going to notice I looked different, say things like Wow, did you get a makeover?

On my way down the stairs, I ran into Wiley. I think I jumped a little bit because it was the first time I'd seen him off the couch in three days. That and he was smiling up at me like he'd just found the Land of Narnia. His eyes were practically twinkling.

Jesus, I said, what are you doing up so early? I had stopped on one of the middle steps, and Wiley was standing three steps below me.

Early? he said. It's six-thirty, and it's a beeeeeautiful day. You look nice.

Thaaanks, I said, eyeing him like Sherlock Holmes. He looked wired, as if he had an electric current flowing through his veins. All of a sudden I wanted to cover my bare arms and shoulders. I tugged the shirt down to cover the sliver of stomach skin that was peeking out.

What the heck is up with you? I said.

Wiley chuckled in that *if only you knew* kind of way. What's up with me? he asked. Life! he said, sweeping his open palms around the stairwell. Life is what's up with me!

Oookay, I said, pushing past him down the stairs. I need breakfast, I told him.

Wiley followed me into the kitchen. I wanted to tell him not to follow me, but it just seemed weird. I couldn't think of a good reason why he shouldn't follow me in his own house. I just had this funny feeling in my stomach, like something bad was going to happen, which didn't make much sense 'cause I'd lived in the same house as Wiley for seven years and never felt that way before.

Don't you want to hear my resolution? he asked.

Umm, I dunno, I said. Do I? I opened the pantry and started looking at the cereal boxes. I knew I wanted Cap'n Crunch but I didn't want to have to look at Wiley so I just kept tapping my finger on box after box, pulling them out a little bit and then sliding them back in.

Well, Wiley said, taking a seat at the kitchen table. I thought you'd be happy to hear that the self-pity ends here. I've resolved to stop being ruled by your mother's whims and just start living for *me*. He plonked his finger down on the table.

Good for you, I said. I hoped that keeping my back to him would make the sarcasm even more obvious.

No, no! he said. I swear! Enough feeling sorry for myself. I shouldn't have done that to you and Jess. His voice was all wistful and even though I wasn't looking at him I could tell he was hanging his head like a bad dog.

What about Squid? I said.

Yeah, he said dreamily, Squid too. You know what? His voice brightened up again.

I shut the pantry doors, turned around and looked at him like *Jesus Christ, what now?*

I'm gonna do something nice for him, he said. I'm gonna do something really nice for my son. He deserves that.

Yeah, I said. Well.

Wiley nodded, as if I'd said something worth agreeing to. Then his eye caught the frilly sleeve of my shirt.

What are you wearing? he said.

It's just one of Mum's retro shirts, I said.

Wow, he said, looking me up and down. A lady already.

I giggled and immediately wished I hadn't. It was a reflex. When I was younger Wiley used to call me such a lady whenever I made gross burps or spilled food all over the front of my shirt. I could tell he secretly loved it so it always made me giggle. But it wasn't funny when it wasn't a joke. It made me feel like crawling into myself and hiding.

I ran out of clean clothes, I said, looking down at my crossed arms.

You look so — *happy*, Wiley said. Healthy. His whole face broke into a cartoon grin. I'm happy for you, he said. I'm happy that you're happy.

Whatever, I said. I have to go to school.

But you haven't had breakfast, he called after me. I was already halfway up the stairs. I didn't hear him following behind me so I went to Squid's room first. Squid was still in bed, and he'd thrown the covers off onto the floor and was spread like a starfish. His pajama shirt had ridden way up to his armpits so his bare tummy was sticking out. The rays of sun coming through his curtains landed right on his belly, making it look white and smooth as a freshly baked sugar cookie.

I didn't really know what I was doing in there. I didn't want to wake Squid up. Instead I sat on the end of his bed and watched his night-light slowly fade out with the rising sun. And I thought about how Squid used to visit the furnace in the basement whenever Mum turned the heat up, wasn't afraid of the fire and noise like most little kids. The first time I showed him the furnace I made him kneel in front of it and watch while I ran upstairs and cranked the heat. I expected to hear a scream and the patter of little feet, but he was totally silent. I found him still kneeling, peering in through the furnace slats at the pilot flame.

Isn't it spooky, I said.

The fire is blue, he said, as if nothing that's blue could ever be scary.

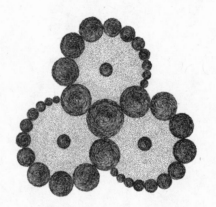

VI

THE TRAIN RIDE FROM the hemline of London to Salisbury was three hours of rolling fields dotted with grey cities like lingering fog. Though she'd traveled this very route twenty years earlier, the landscape seemed entirely different to Belinda. Quaint thatched-roof cottages stood like dusty museum artefacts, remote and inhuman. When she was a child, the cottages were everyday fixtures as much as petrol stations. She never questioned the significance of the roofs or the little straw animals perched atop their peaks like beacons. An owl lived on one street, a squirrel and a pheasant on another, an ominous blackbird with one brown eye on the house up the hill. Only after she moved to Canada did she learn that each animal represented the thatcher's signature — a symbol of his ability to master his medium. Belinda allowed this idea to resonate in her mind with images of swathed crop circle grasses, wondering to whose mastery they bowed.

Belinda had never wanted to be a mother. It was the men who had wanted children. With Dazhong she had agreed because it felt like the next step. She was twenty-one and couldn't envision an alternative to motherhood. Wiley had wanted one of his own; a mini-Wiley to play with, like a doll. But Sebastian looked everything like Belinda. Even his eyes, although Wiley's blue in colour, were the exact same walnut shape, and fringed with the same long, dark eyelashes, as Belinda's.

Some time after Sebastian's birth, Belinda admitted to herself that the decision to have children was almost always motivated by selfishness. Children were a way to feel useful, and she had admittedly enjoyed feeling useful for some time. It was satisfying to know that someone needed you deeply in order to survive. But the satisfaction had long since worn off, and she had become nothing more than a faceless provider.

Of course, now that she'd had children she had no regrets. Misgivings, perhaps, about how they would turn out. Jessica and Grace were so restrained and unconfident, and Sebastian wasn't nearly restrained enough. What had she done differently? During Sebastian's tantrum phase, Wiley preached about discipline from his high horse of inexperience. Nothing wrong with playing it rough every so often, show them who's boss, he'd say. Belinda had outlawed spanking after the incident with Grace, and it had been a regular point of contention that simmered between herself and Wiley like a thick soup, wafting occasional reminders under their noses.

You know how I feel about spanking, she'd said, for the dozenth time. And anyway, it doesn't work. He thinks it's funny.

That's because you don't *mean* it, Wiley said, pointing a finger between her eyes.

So I'm supposed to batter my child with passion, is that it? Belinda said.

Well, it worked for Grace, he replied, and immediately looked sorry.

Belinda gave him a look that said *watch it.* That was different, she said. I told you we're not talking about that. Ever again.

Yeah, fine, Wiley said. But remember, Jess had the same problem as you.

Belinda did remember. It had happened when Sebastian was two and Jessica was looking after him while Belinda and Wiley were out for an anniversary dinner. Sebastian had thrown one of his signature temper tantrums because Belinda wasn't there to put him to bed. She resented Sebastian's fixation on her as much as she resented Wiley's unsolicited advice; as far as she could tell, she hadn't done anything to provoke either. In those days, even going out for dinner meant dragging a train of guilt along, because conditions had to be perfect for Sebastian to go to sleep at bedtime without a fight. As the routine normally played out, the television would be turned off at eight o'clock and Sebastian would sit at the piano bench with Wiley. He was allowed to listen to Wiley play one song (usually 'Every Rose Has Its Thorn') while he drank his special milk, which had been warmed (not too hot) in the microwave with a dollop of vanilla extract. Then Belinda would lead him up to his room, make him climb the stairs on his own to tire him out. She'd sit on the edge of his bed and read to him from a book while he twisted his tattered blankie around and around his wrist until its tight coils spiraled all the way up his arm. When his eyelids finally drooped shut Belinda would set the book down and rub circles into his back. The circles needed to be smooth and even or Sebastian would moan, flip over, and flick his eyes wide open in defiance. To keep herself from falling asleep she made a silent game out of it, trying to draw the circles perfectly round and smooth, applying the same degree of pressure over Sebastian's back as it rose and fell with increasingly broadened strokes. Sometimes the lower half of her body would go numb under the strain of keeping her movements exact. She counted each complete circle until she reached one hundred; only then was it safe to consider making her exit. If she lifted her hand too quickly he would jolt awake, so Belinda had developed an art of gradually lessening the pressure with each sweeping revolution until her hand just barely brushed the surface of Sebastian's pajama shirt.

The elaborateness of this process often left Belinda feeling mournful. She'd allow her palm to drift off Sebastian's back like a sail catching the wind, and in her drifting hand she imagined herself, untethered, white and floating in no particular direction. Nobody else could ever possibly understand this ritual; it was knitted between Belinda and Sebastian, an unseen umbilical remnant. It was a suffocating obligation.

Naturally, Jessica's efforts to mimic the routine failed miserably. Sebastian had stood in the kitchen and screamed until his knee-locked legs trembled and his special milk was puddled between his feet. Jessica had tried to carry him up the stairs but he wriggled free and scurried back into the kitchen, his socks sopping up the milk and wiping it across the floor. He'd gone straight for the utensil drawer and pulled out a steak knife, and when Jessica came ripping into the kitchen after him he threw the knife at her. The blade only scraped her arm, but Jessica took it personally, as she always did. She told Belinda she hadn't known what else to do; he had an evil look on his face, as if he'd wanted to kill her. So she whapped him on the bum. And Sebastian just stood there. She spanked him again, harder, and he growled. Like a wild dog, Jessica had said. When she started to cry, he laughed.

Belinda and Wiley came home to find Sebastian watching television and Jessica on hands and knees, a teary Cinderella, mopping spilt milk with the kitchen rag. The smell of vanilla had lingered in the kitchen for days. Belinda found its scent in soaps and perfumes quite sickening ever since.

It certainly wasn't normal. Sebastian had an imagination that blinded him to consequences. But although she worried about where this tendency would lead him, Belinda feared even more the possibility that Sebastian, that all three of her children, might someday see through her. That they might eventually come to resent her resentment, feed her the same guilt she fed to her own mother. The scenario had the potential to carry through generations like a disease.

Belinda convinced herself that the trip to England was as much for her children as it was for herself. She was setting an example: decide what you want from life, and don't be afraid to pursue it. Dr. Longfellow had called her commitment *soulful* in his last letter. *That kind of passion will serve you well in our line of work,* he'd written. A passionate mother was better than a wholly disinterested mother. Belinda's mother had never been soulful about anything, not even the cross-stitching projects she insisted on filling her time with. Belinda would try to rest her little chin on her mother's shoulder and tell her how lovely the angel looked, or how expertly she'd stitched the apples on the trees, and her mother would grimace as though she were suddenly looking at a pile of vomit. Rubbish, she'd say, it's only a lark. And yet the aida cloth was conveniently laid across her lap and the embroidery thread tangled in her fingers whenever Belinda wanted to play checkers, bake a cake, or go to the playground. A lark that flew high over Belinda's head.

Belinda hadn't spoken to her in eighteen years. Her mother still sent them parcels at Christmas, too big for Belinda to hide, and a card on her birthday. The card always contained three crisp Canadian $50 bills, which must have required a special trip to the bank. The price of forgiveness. Belinda kept the cash for years, in case of emergency. She slotted the bills into an envelope that she taped under the top drawer in the kitchen, where no one else would find them. It was better to pretend that ties had been severed.

, Double-Take

WHEN I WAS IN grade three I had this best friend named
Michelle. I called her Shelley, even though nobody else did.
It seemed to suit her 'cause she was the colour of those small
white seashells that glow when you hold them up to the sun.
When we hooked our arms we looked like a yin-yang symbol,
we contrasted so much. I wished more than anything that
my skin was as milky and smooth as hers instead of brown
like tea. And instead of stick-straight dark hair like mine,
she had fine curly hair that was so blonde it was practically
white. She spoke with a very soft and high-pitched voice, the
kind of voice a bluebird in a Disney cartoon would have. Her
arms and legs were so bony I actually believed that if I held
her hand too tight, tiny little cracks would appear and travel
all the way through her hand and up her arm and the whole
limb would shatter into a million pieces. But I adored her for
being so white and breakable. When I think of her now with all
that fine curly hair and those bony arms and legs I see her as a
human incarnation of a porcelain doll, which is funny because
I treated her like my baby. I dragged her along everywhere

I went and made sure she got to bounce first when we played King's Court at recess. I gave her seven of my scratch-and-sniff stickers to trade because her mom wouldn't buy her any. She had butter sandwiches for lunch every day, so I always broke off a piece of my chocolate-dipped granola bar to give her for dessert.

For the longest time I didn't know she was poor. And not poor in the way that we were, in the way that Mum said we were, *Don't you know how poor I am,* when I asked if we could go to Chuck E. Cheese's two weekends in a row. Shelley was poor enough to have to wear flip-flops to school up until October when Mrs. Goldsmith gave her a pair of hand-me-down running shoes. They were obviously boys' shoes with their wide soles and their fat blue stripes on the sides, and they looked totally ridiculous on Shelley's little bird feet. When she came to school wearing them for the first time I marched her right into the corner of the coatroom before anyone else could see her, hissed into her face, What the heck kind of shoes are those to be wearing? Those are for *boys,* silly! I made her take them off and I threw them into the garbage along with all the banana peels and snotty tissues and sandwich crusts.

I don't have any other shoes to wear, she said. She stood there in her socks watching me.

Socks are better than those ugly things, I told her. Besides, they clean the floor every day here so what's the point of wearing shoes? I hooked my arm in Shelley's and walked her into the classroom, making sure to veer around the spots where old grey gum had been mashed into the carpet.

You would think, just by looking at her, that Shelley would be the kind of kid who'd cry if someone threw her shoes in the garbage and made her walk around in her socks. But she didn't. She didn't bat an eye, acted like this kind of thing happened to her every day. She didn't seem worried at all about what she would do when everyone went outside into the muddy grass and puddles at recess, or when the end of the day came and she had to walk home. Of course, none of that stuff ended up being a problem because Mrs. Goldsmith noticed right away and made me fish the shoes out of the garbage.

Thinking about it now makes me want to cry. I think about Shelley watching me toss out the shoes she was given like they were trash, and the worst part was that she didn't say or do anything to stop me. The fact that she didn't cry or whine or even look shocked at all is probably the saddest thing I can even think of. I was the kind of kid who would throw a tantrum and tell Mum I hated her when she wouldn't let me have a lava lamp instead of a regular night-light. I can't even imagine what kinds of things Shelley had to put up with when being forced to wear shoes that had just been picked out the garbage and were covered in sticky brown juices and crumbs wasn't the biggest tragedy she'd ever experienced. To her, it wasn't even a tragedy at all.

I try to tell myself that even though I was an insensitive brat, I was still a good friend to her. I like to think that maybe I helped her forget about all the depressing stuff in her life and just have fun being a kid. We had some good times together. We made up an Ewok language and when anyone else was around we'd speak only in Ewok, shake our heads when people said Huh? We were only able to memorize a handful of words so we basically had the same dumb conversation every time, something to the effect of How are you today, I am fine, Do you like rollypolly berries, Yes I do. We thought words like rollypolly definitely sounded like Ewok because they were cute and fun to say. The only word I can clearly remember writing into our Ewok dictionary was 'ooba.' That meant goodbye.

In our schoolyard, there was this long grass that grew all along the chain-link fences. The grass grew really tall because the mowers could never cut that close to the fence. Shelley and I used to collect the grass, pull it up by its roots and weave it together for our Tarzan rope. We imagined that once we'd lashed the braids together, we'd have one rope long enough and strong enough to tie to a tree so we could swing from it. I think every kid has a fantasy of living in the jungle and swinging through trees from ropes. When you're a kid you can imagine how it would feel to jump off the branch of a gigantic tree, tall as a skyscraper, your stomach falling right out, your arms hanging on for dear life and your whole body clenched and ready to get schmucked — but then all of a sudden every-thing becomes slow motion. You see another rope hanging from another tree slowly coming towards you, and then you realize that all you have to do is reach right out and grab it. And you would feel like the whole jungle was built just for you, like there would always be a rope hanging for you wherever you needed it. It would feel like freedom.

Shelley and I never got far enough to figure out how to connect the grass braids because we left them lying in a pile against the fence and someone stole them. I don't know why we didn't find a better place to keep them. Maybe we knew that it wouldn't work anyway, wanted to save ourselves the disappointment.

For a long time I didn't think about Shelley. I'd almost for-gotten all about her until I had the crop circle dream. It had only been two days since Mum left. Remembering the way I felt when I woke up makes me want to call it a nightmare, but there wasn't anything particularly scary about it, really.

In the dream, Mum was sitting in a field. There was tall grass all around her, so tall and dense that you wouldn't be able to find her unless you looked down from the sky. She was sitting on her knees in the middle of a circle where the grass had been cut short, and it looked like the circle had been cut to fit her body perfectly. It seemed like I was sitting right in front of her except I couldn't have been because there was only just enough space in the circle for her. Her knees were brushing against the wall of grass stalks.

Then she reached out and took a handful of grass. The sound of roots pulling up was like ripping stitches out of denim. But the roots weren't thick and gnarly like I expected. They were very long and thin and flowy, like hair. And when she combed her fingers through the roots to separate them into strands, I noticed that Mum's hands were also long and thin and white, with see-through fingernails. Shelley's hands.

I still get goosebumps just thinking about it. It was like I was seeing Mum as a ghost. It felt like it was happening in real life, as if wherever Mum was at that moment, she might be actually, truly, dead.

You know how dreams always make perfect sense for the first few minutes after you wake up? You think, Thank God it was just a dream, as if all the crazy stuff that happened in your head could feasibly happen in real life. Then you try to tell someone about this crazy dream you had, *Isn't that funny? Isn't that messed up?* and they look at you like, So what? Big deal. It always turns out to be one of those 'you had to be there' stories. That's why I didn't bother telling Jess when I went to her room in the morning to see if she was awake yet. That and I didn't really feel like sitting there on her bed like a mental patient while she pulled out her dream dictionary and prattled on about the symbolic meaning of grass.

Besides, it was Saturday morning, and Jess was busy being her usual worry-wart self.

We can't just *leave* him here, Grace, she kept saying. Not with Wiley acting like a total head-case.

We can't tell Da we aren't going for dim sum either, I said.

I know, she said, rubbing circles into her temples with her fingers. It drives me nuts when Jess does things like that. I know the only reason she does them is 'cause adults do. The other thing she does when she wants to act stressed is pinch the bridge of her nose between her thumb and finger and scrunch her eyes up, like she's got a migraine or sinus congestion. When she does those things I just feel like telling her how ridiculous she is, that she's such a melodramatic wannabe-grown-up.

Christ, relax, Jess, I said. It's not like he'd be alone.

Jess paced over to her bedroom door, closed it and locked it even though Wiley was in the garage, all the way at the opposite corner of the house.

Have you *seen* the kitchen? Jess said, her eyes bulging.

Why yes, I have, I said chirpily. It's blue with white cabinets, what's your point? I knew that Jess was referring to the stacks of unwashed dishes, the dried-up splotches of Coke that had been spilled all over the stove elements, the balls of used tissues spilling out of a cough syrup box that was sitting in a red puddle next to the sink, the counters dusted in fine, technicolour-orange Cheezie powder.

Seriously, Grace. There were nine empty Cheezie bags in the garbage. Nine!

Scandalous! I gasped. If he's eating Cheezies, God knows what else he might do!

Jess gave me the look of death, crossed her arms tight over her chest. I could tell she was trying her best to think of something mean to say.

You may not want to hear this, she said, because I know you're like best buds and all, but Wiley is — disturbed. Mentally. Mummy told me.

And whatever Mum says is true, right? I laughed. I made it sound like I was laughing at her, but it was more to cover up the fluttery feeling in my stomach. I thought about what had happened the day before. Wiley's wired look, his 'resolution.'

Jess narrowed her eyes. What is that supposed to mean? she asked. It wasn't sarcasm. I felt sorry for her, being seventeen and still so naïve.

I guess we'll just have to take Squid with us, I said.

Yeah, right, Jess said, 'cause Daddy'll love that.

We'll just tell him that Squid loves Chinese food, and he reeeeally wants to come.

Jess bit her lip. You're not going to tell him about Mummy being gone, are you? she said.

Of course not! He'd probably make us stay at his house.

Probably, Jess agreed.

See, Da suffers from chronic obliviousness. It's not really his fault, since he only sees us every couple of weeks, but he seems to think that time just stops when we're not with him. To him we're still two little girls aged seven and nine. Once, after I let it slip over the phone that I was home alone with Squid, he drove to our house and gave me a cheque made out to Mum for two hundred dollars. Tell her to get a babysitter, he said.

Da was waiting in the car outside our house like usual when he came to pick us up for lunch. I went up to his window to ask about taking Squid along while Jess and Squid waited inside. He said okay but I could tell he was annoyed about having to pay for an extra person. I just pretended not to notice his grouchy tone, ran back inside and told Jess and Squid to put on their shoes. Then I went to the back door and opened it, peeked into the garage.

We're taking Squid with us for lunch, I told Wiley. He was rummaging through the utility shelves, trying to pull out an old dusty drill tangled up with an extension cord. His hands were pulling at the cords as if it were a matter of life and death. Finally, they came free.

Lunch? he said, holding the tangled cords up like a web. Man, I haven't eaten since yesterday! He tossed the cords on the floor, on top of a pile of other tools.

There's leftover pizza in the fridge, I said. And tons of other stuff. You'll be fine.

Oh sure, sure, he said, waving his hand like a traffic cop, *move it along.* Got too much to do in here anyway. Don't worry about me. Don't worry about me at all, I'm a big boy, I'll take care of myself. He giggled, mechanically. You have fun, he said. Let loose.

I left quickly, put on my shoes without bothering to tie the laces, and went out the front door.

When I joined Jess and Squid in the car, Da was suddenly acting all cheery. He was asking Squid about school, and he had his fake happy face on where he smiles with his teeth parted, the way he does when he's talking to his boss about the high grades Jess and I always get in school, *she got a 98% on her exam, which subject was it again?* Squid didn't know any better, having only talked to Da maybe twice in his entire life. Since Da has always treated our house like quarantine, I wasn't even sure how long it had been since he and Squid had seen each other. But Squid nattered on about his assembly, how he remembered all the words to the songs and he never used to be able to remember things so good.

As soon as we sat down at the restaurant, Squid announced, I really really really like Chinese food. We'd coached him.

Da smiled, looked genuinely surprised. Really? he said. You should tell that to her. He looked over at Jess as she sat down next to him. He pinched her cheek and Jess scowled, made a whiny noise.

See? Da said. Chinese is the best food.

All the oil gives me cramps, Jess said.

Naw, Da shook his head. Oil is good for you. It helps the digestion.

Hah, no it doesn't! There is absolutely no way oil is good for you.

You should become a doctor, Da said. Do some tests and find out for yourself.

Jess rolled her eyes. Yeah, yeah, she said, you already know I'm going to be a doctor.

Good girl, Da said.

I'm going to be a pet store owner, Squid announced.

Da frowned. When he frowns, he does it mostly by wrinkling his forehead, and the wiry hairs of his eyebrows furl out like caterpillar legs.

Except my pet store will only have amphibians, Squid continued. That means animals that can swim in the water or walk on the land.

Jess cut in before Da's eyebrows could furl any further.

He's got a toad, she said, don't you, Sebastian?

Princess Leticia, Squid said. She's a fire-bellied toad.

Hm, Da said. He started looking around the restaurant, snapped his fingers at one of the waitresses. Jess looked at me like *Oh my God, does he really have to do that?*

Some of the other people sitting in the restaurant looked over at our table, looked first at Da, then at me and Jess, then at Squid, then back at Da. I could just see the wheels turning inside their brains.

What about you, Grace? Da said. Still going to be an eye doctor?

Ophthalmologist, I said. And no. I've wanted to be a Marine Biologist since, like, grade eight.

Good money? Da asked. He took two plates of bao from the waitress' cart and set them on the table.

I dunno, I said. Don't care. That's not why —

Da started clucking his tongue at the plates of food in front of him, his way of saying he didn't want to hear the rest of it. Meanwhile, Squid had grabbed a bao in his fist and was bent over his plate, already shoving the last bites into his mouth. Da did a double-take. A smile spread across his face.

Hey, Jess snapped at Squid, laying her palm flat on the table. Food to the face, not face to the food! We're not barbarians.

It's good, isn't it? Da said, still smiling. It's my favourite too.

Squid nodded, his cheeks stuffed full. Jess made such a show of rolling her eyes that her whole head rolled along with them.

In the car on the way home from the restaurant, I started to feel sick from the Chinese food. I thought about how people always try to talk to me and Jess in Chinese when we're out with Da, but it never happens when we're with Mum. And then I started thinking about Shelley again. I thought about how Mrs. Goldsmith had nicknamed us Ebony and Ivory, and I was always jealous because it was way better to be Ivory. I remembered feeling sort of relieved when we stopped being friends after grade three because her family moved away to the southwest and she had to change schools. But thinking about it made me feel really sad, sadder than I had felt at the time. I had made her a card and given it to her on her last day at school, and the card had a unicorn on the front that I had traced from a picture book. I thought it was a really good drawing, and I even coloured the unicorn's hair purple — Shelley's favourite colour. On the inside, I wrote a poem and drew a border of hearts around it in purple smelly marker. At the bottom, I signed my name, and then a big OOBA, with sad faces in the O's. Shelley had opened it carefully with her little white hands, scanned the words, and slotted the card back into its envelope. Thanks, she said, with a slight smile. And then she was gone.

VII

IT WAS THE ARCHAEOLOGIST that made her want to leave
Merle Norman.

She and Wiley had gone on a weekend trip to the Radium
Hot Springs for their third anniversary. Sebastian was not
even two; she'd still been carrying the weight from the
pregnancy. Her thighs and buttocks felt thick, weighed down
as though ham hocks were lodged beneath the skin. The hot
springs had been Wiley's idea, naturally. Skipping just one
province over to a mediocre small-town tourist attraction
could barely be called a vacation in Belinda's mind. She had
expected the hot springs to be natural; she pictured pools
of bubbling Technicolor water carved into jagged rock,
mountains rising up on all sides. Instead, there was a concrete
pool, painted with a sky blue bottom, seating all around the
perimeter. Like a hot tub, but larger. The real hot springs were
somewhere else, protected from view, while the water was
filtered into the pool. Of course, thought Belinda. They're too
special, too important for us, the regular people.

Only twice did they actually swim — soak — in the pool. The first time, there were six men in the water when she emerged from the change room. Wiley was taking his time. She considered turning around, retreating back into the change room as though she'd forgotten something — a towel. But one of them had already spotted her. He eyed her, one arm propped on the rim of the pool as though wrapped around the shoulders of an imaginary woman. His expression was entirely neutral, but unyielding. Belinda resisted glancing down at her jiggling thighs as she walked across the pool deck.

The men seemed to be together — colleagues. The one man continued to stare, apparently in a sort of daze while the chatter of the others flitted around him.

For me, it's the wrist, one of the men said to the others. Doctor says it's carpal tunnel. Repetitive strain.

You sure he meant your golf swing there, Ed? another chortled, showing his giant square teeth. The five men laughed to themselves. The sixth broke his stare on Belinda, sank deeper into the water as she descended the first step into the pool.

The men then fell quiet, a thin line of tension knotting between them. She could feel her skin flushing, and hoped they would think it was the heat of the water.

Hi, one of them murmured, giving Belinda a small nod.

They were probably oil executives, Belinda thought to herself. Rich people on a weekend retreat, compliments of the company. Bigwigs. Her throat tightened.

Wiley then emerged from the change room, dripping from the shower.

You were fast, he said, zipping across the pool deck.

For Chrissakes don't *run*, Belinda hissed. Wiley looked like a drowned rat with his shorts plastered to his thin thighs, the hair matted and slicked all over his skin. He plunged himself into the pool up to the shoulders.

Ahhhhh, he sighed.

For a moment, Belinda considered pretending she didn't know Wiley. She smiled at him politely. But no, she realized, the men had seen, had heard them talking to one another. Although, to an outsider, she told herself, any one of these men could be her husband. She could have married a rich oil executive; why not? She had chosen for love. Back then, it had been for love. But there hadn't been any other choice. Love or loneliness. Some women could choose loneliness; Belinda seemed to be missing the trait that allowed for it. A certain hardness. But for these moments, when it was still possible to imagine that Wiley was not her husband, she could pretend she had it. She could even convince herself.

As she soaked in the pool, she stretched these thoughts out, made a game of it. Imagine, she thought to herself, you are swimming laps in a pool. A real pool, like the ones they use for swimming tournaments. You are young, nineteen, maybe twenty, your thighs, your body, are slim, svelte, smooth as plastic. You cut through the water, you glide on the surface. It's not a chore to swim — it's invigorating. You sweat, the water cools you. When you come up for air, you see a woman sitting in the hot tub. She is the only woman at the centre of a group of men, most of them balding, overweight. She is alone. She is radiant in her white suit. None of these men can touch her.

Wiley gave her arm a nudge, making her twitch.

Isn't that right, Bell? he said. Lived in Alberta for fifteen-odd years and never been west of Cochrane. The staring man perked his eyebrows.

I suppose, yes, it has been that long, Belinda replied. I haven't had a reason. Until now.

And then, a woman entered from the change room. She seemed familiar with the surroundings; she walked casually across the pool deck, slid into the water like a hand into a glove.

Belinda was conscious of herself staring, in a trance just like the man had been. But she could not help it. This was the woman she had just imagined; the exact woman — blonde, slim, young, sure of herself. She smiled at Belinda and sat just a few feet away.

Belinda forced herself to turn to Wiley and act as though she was involved in his conversation. She tried to picture what she looked like to the young woman, whose eyes she could feel upon her. Her belly began to suck itself in, even though it was concealed under the water.

When she glanced back over, the woman was closing her eyes, her neck resting against the edge of the pool. Her face was delicate, flawless, skin slightly rosy from the heat. Her hair was a natural blonde, glowing under the sun. When her eyes flicked open they fell directly on Belinda's.

In that moment, something strange happened. One of Belinda's false memories flashed in her mind — another image of her sister, Prim, and herself as a toddler. It was summer, and she could see herself and Prim, wedged among the plants that had grown monstrous at the back of her mother's house. The prick of a raspberry cane as Prim yanked her by the wrist to the spot where the garden hose hung, nestled in the weeds, obscured from the view of the kitchen window, behind which her mother was fixing lunch. Prim crouching over her, shooting a jet of water all over Belinda's naked skin, her other hand cinched around Belinda's wrist. Belinda had made a mess, she was sure, but the memory did not reveal what it was on her skin that Prim was washing away. The stony, determined expression on Prim's face told Belinda it was dangerous, perhaps poisonous. But Belinda was screaming, wailing like a torture victim, her tiny limbs stiff and vibrating with the shock of the icy water. She was too young to have learned to speak. And it was too long ago to be an actual, accurate memory.

Hi there, said the woman suddenly. Belinda pulled herself out of her reverie and realized she had been gaping at the woman like a fool. Her face burned.

Sorry, Belinda said, you look like someone I know. Knew.

Oh really? she replied. She scooted towards Belinda, examining her face. Maybe we know each other from work? she asked.

I don't think so, Belinda said. Do you work here? In Radium?

Yeah, she said. I'm from here, actually.

So you work in . . . tourism? Belinda ventured. Or customer service?

The woman laughed. I guess there's not much else in Radium, is there? she said. But no, I'm actually an archaeologist.

Oh, Belinda, said, straightening in her seat. Well, that's very interesting. An archaeologist! And you live *here*?

Yeah, it's great. There's so much awesome hiking and camping around here. I have my own condo, a dog. I live about ten minutes away.

Really, Belinda said. You're so young.

Twenty-one, she said. She smiled, timidly, and it made her look even younger.

Perhaps this is a stupid question, Belinda said, moving closer to the woman, but what does an archaeologist do in Radium?

She laughed again. A lot of people ask that. There's a lot of Native land around here. They need archaeologists to make sure developers aren't digging into gravesites or disturbing artifact repositories, that kind of thing.

I see. Fascinating.

Belinda noticed then that the woman's bathing suit was Nike brand. High quality. The swoop stretched smooth across the curve of her breast. It was the kind of bathing suit one would buy at a specialty swimwear store for an exorbitant price. Jessica had once asked for a Nike swimsuit for her birthday.

Belinda had not been inside the store for more than five minutes before she headed straight back out empty-handed, spooked by the price tags and the saleswoman's lofty talk of specially engineered swimwear fabrics.

Belinda continued to make small-talk with the woman, the two of them forming a unit separate from the men. Still, Belinda felt out of place. Isolated. She and this woman — more accurately, girl — were from different worlds. The girl talked about spending long hours working out in the field, ankle-deep in mud. It was tough work, gritty. It was not anything like the life of Indiana Jones, she insisted with a practiced chuckle, as though she'd made the comparison dozens of times before. Although Belinda could accept that it wasn't like the movies, to her, it was even more glamourous. Every day this girl sacrificed her time, her comfort, probably even her safety, for her work. She was committed to uncovering secrets that had been buried in the earth for hundreds of years. She had wisdom, knowledge that people admired. What would it be like, Belinda wondered, to have your entire life figured out at twenty-one? Belinda hadn't even thought it possible. But this girl had the whole package: a professional job, money, a dog, the freedom to spend a weekday afternoon soaking in the pool. Where would Belinda be now, she wondered, if it had been that way for her? Certainly not here, on a substandard three-day vacation with three children at home to worry about. Perhaps she would be on a business trip, sipping mimosas while working on a shiny portable computer in her penthouse hotel room.

Hey Bell, Wiley said, nudging her again. I'm getting wrinkly. Wanna go?

She wished the woman good luck with her work, and as she stood to leave, she noticed a small tattoo on her upper shoulder, near the base of her neck. A circle made up of tiny black hearts. She thought nothing of it at the time, but it would later become what she saw as one of the vital coincidences that brought her to her research. A circle. A sign.

◯◯◯

She'd given up on trying to read. The train had already made four long stops. At this rate, she wouldn't be arriving in Salisbury until noon. But on the positive side, she'd been enjoying the time alone with her thoughts. As the train wove through the green countryside, Belinda saw herself surveying the scenery the way an archaeologist might — as a theatrical stage set against the curtain of history. The stage was only the magical surface of things; what happened behind the velvet folds of the curtain was unsensationalized reality. How many unknown stories remained embedded in those hills of chalk, infused in the splaying branches of ancient trees, waiting to be uncovered?

Stories of crop circles had been a part of recorded history as far back as 1678. An English woodcut pamphlet from that year, entitled 'The Mowing Devil,' told of a miserly farmer from Hertfordshire who refused to pay a labourer the demanded price to mow his field. The farmer told the labourer he'd rather the devil mow his field than pay the sum, and his imprudent wish evidently came true. That evening, the grain blazed as though it had caught fire, but by the next morning a perfectly mown circle had miraculously appeared in the field. The circle was too perfect, the article pointed out, for a human to have made it. A primitive ink illustration pictured a man with the legs and horns of a goat swinging a scythe to flatten the grains. Two rings encircled him, the mown stalks rendered as sharp diagonal lines leaning against each other like fallen dominoes. Leaf-shaped flames danced recklessly around the rings.

Belinda understood how it would have been easier back

then to attribute the miracle to the devil. It seemed too destructive and self-indulgent to be an act of God, and any notion of supernatural forces beyond good and evil had yet to be imagined. In a way, there was something almost sinister about perfect concentric circles, the centres of which could only be pinpointed from the sky. A mark of doom, a bull's-eye.

In fact, the first time she came across 'The Mowing Devil' while reading library books in bed, the illustration sent chills down the back of her neck. It reminded her of Egyptian hieroglyphic drawings, eerier than realistic drawings because they stripped everything to the bare bones and forced your imagination to conjure the details. The white, unblinking eye of the devil seemed wise and all-knowing in its simplicity. She showed the illustration to Wiley, but he only groaned and rolled over.

But isn't it fascinating? she said.

Everything is fascinating to you, Wiley said into his pillow. He flipped over. When are you gonna finish doing all that research? he asked.

Finish? Belinda said, almost laughing. This isn't some sort of temporary hobby, she said. What if I asked you when you were going to *finish* playing piano?

That's different, Wiley said. That's part of my job.

Well, Belinda said, you can think of this as my job. It's what I'm passionate about, after all.

Too bad you can't make any money off of it, Wiley said.

Right, Belinda said. Because you make piles of money as a piano teacher.

Wiley's lips tightened. Go to sleep, he said, reaching over her and switching off her bedside lamp. Belinda sat still for a moment, her book still open on her lap.

I'm going then, she said, climbing out of bed. I'll read in the living room. She gathered her stack of books and put on her slippers.

You're living in books, he said to the darkness as she left the room. They're like stories. It's not real life.

It was true, in a way. Belinda had never actually seen a crop circle. But by that time she had already decided she was going to make her way to England, where she would finally step foot inside her first crop circle. It would confirm everything she believed in. She promised herself that when the moment was upon her, she would remain acutely aware of every feeling running through her body. Many people who had experienced walking inside a crop circle, even some who had been adamant skeptics, admitted they had felt lightheaded and lethargic upon entering the area. Some even reported hearing high-pitched ringing sounds that seemed to drop out of the sky above. When cereologists took soil samples from underneath these circles, the tests detected high levels of magnetism. Belinda saw these as warning signs. Beneath the beautiful, swirling patterns lay a power beyond human control. It occurred to Belinda that uncovering the answers might even be dangerous. She'd read of animal corpses, porcupines and rabbits, recovered from several recent crop-circle sites. The corpses had been severely burnt, although there was no sign of fire anywhere in the field. One charred porcupine appeared to have been shrunk down to half its size like a cooked mushroom.

She knew it was a silly and hopelessly romantic thought, but Belinda felt sure that her first experience walking into a crop circle was going to be life-altering. And now, with every turn of its wheels, the train brought Belinda closer to fulfilling her connection to the phenomenon. In Salisbury, she would meet Dr. Longfellow and join his team of researchers. She felt like a child on a rollercoaster, knowing the big drop was imminent but still breathless with uncertainty.

8 Perfect Circles

SOMEWHERE INSIDE JESS, THERE is a Supermum trying desperately to break free. Mum never liked to bake chocolate chip cookies or banana bread like other mothers, *It's so messy, As if I have time for that,* so Jess took it upon herself to wash the dust off the rolling pin and put on the floral print apron. The first time she made cookies she got flour all up her sleeves, so when she took a break to go to the bathroom she left a skiff of fine white powder trailing behind her. The cookies turned out okay — they were a little too crunchy — but we pretended they were delicious. Squid was too young to know how to pretend to like them, or even to understand why he should try to pretend. He told her they tasted like dry Ichiban noodles, but at that time everything tasted like Ichiban to him 'cause that's all he was eating. Jess really took it to heart though. You could tell because she got all quiet and then reread the recipe in Mum's *Best of Bridge* book a zillion times over.

The problem is that Squid just doesn't have a sweet tooth like most kids. For some reason Jess didn't figure that out for a long time. She got on this crazy baking kick, and kept trying to make Squid be her Oompa-Loompa. I think she thought that if Squid had a hand in actually making the treats, he'd get all revved up for eating them.

Wanna stir the brownie batter? she'd ask him, and Squid would reply, Um, I'd rather not. Squid figured out early on that he could get away with a lot if he spoke like a grown-up, so he was always saying things like I'd rather not. It made us all laugh and coo, *Isn't that precious,* and nobody would care that he wasn't doing what he was asked. So it went on like that for ages, Jess making cakes and tarts and crème de menthe pie and tiramisu and Squid saying he'd rather not help, and the rest of us feeling like we'd puke if we saw another peanut butter cookie but feeling bad when they sat on the counter for two weeks and went stale. But then one day Jess accidentally dribbled some melted butter across the cookbook page and the drip-spots turned see-through. When Squid saw that he decided he wanted to help, but then it was way more fun to draw with the butter than to stir it into the dough. Invisible drawing, he called it.

It's not hurting anybody, Mum said when Jess scowled at Squid's buttery fingers. Mum got him a pad of printer paper and oh boy, he went nuts. At first he was just dunking his fingers in the bowl of butter and making squiggles and dots on the paper, but eventually he started drawing circles. Circle after circle, and then he was getting careful, drawing separate circles and making sure he didn't overlap them. In the end he was dipping only his pointer finger in the butter and watching the tip touch the paper and slowly draw out each line. It was creepy, like being in the Twilight Zone watching six-year-old Squid concentrate on those circles. He drew one of the circles big enough to take up half the page, and he practically had his face on the paper he was concentrating so hard. Then he drew criss-crossing lines like a snowflake inside the circle.

Nice cookies, Squid, I said.

They're not cookies, he said, keeping his eyes on his paper.
They're crop circles. That's why they've gotta be perfect.

Oh really? I said. But didn't you know that nobody, not even
Picasso himself, can possibly draw a perfect circle?

Squid lifted his finger, looked up at me.

Not freehand, I said. It's impossible.

Mum gave me the not-so-fast eyebrows. That doesn't mean
he can't try, she said.

Squid drew four more crop circles before Mum said he had
to stop now, butter costs more money than crayons. She ended
up putting Squid's drawings on the fridge. He hadn't bothered
to tear the perforations between pages, so there was just one
long trail of paper that Mum folded back up and pinned under
a super-strength magnet. I thought maybe the butter would
dry up and the paper would turn white again, but it stayed
see-through and shiny, so you could see bits of the drawings
underneath the top page, a few ghosted lines. For a while every
time I looked at the fridge I thought of the oil-splotched take-
out baggies filled with greasy samosas that Da likes to buy.

Squid's drawings didn't stop Jess's baking spree, though.
Granted, her baking did get better. In my book, Jess is the
reigning queen of pineapple upside-down cake. But it got to
the point where I was thinking in desserts. One of her greatest
successes was this ginormous triple-layer chocolate Oreo cake,
and we got to eat our slices sitting in front of the TV because
a National Geographic show on space nebulas was on and Mum
didn't want to miss it. All that talk about the vastness of the
universe got me feeling really philosophical. If life on earth
were a chocolate Oreo cake, I thought, then human existence
would be the thin layer of gross vanilla pudding in the middle.
The best parts of the cake — the creamy icing on top and the
Oreo crust on the bottom — are above and below us, and it's

a mystery why we're sandwiched between all that spongy filler 'cause we don't taste like anything anyway. It's no wonder we think we're so great when we're stuck in the middle, so far from the deep oceans on one end and outer space on the other that we can't even fathom the kinds of things that live there. I thought Mum would totally agree with me when I told her this, but she just gave me the weird-eye and said I was very imaginative.

My friend Rose once tried to explain to me what purgatory was. She's supposed to be Catholic, but in grade seven Greg Pearson convinced her that the Virgin Mary was actually a prostitute and now she says it's all a load of hooey. Even if she did believe in it, she always skips Sunday school and tells lies in confession, which I'm pretty sure makes her a sinner in the Pope's eyes.

Purgatory is like this place between heaven and earth, she said, and nothing is really good or bad. It's just kind of — blah.

But earth is pretty blah too, I said. So what's the difference?

Well it's better than earth, she said. It's where you go before you can get into heaven. I think you have to get whipped and burned and stuff.

That sounds worse than earth to me, I said. Sounds like hell.

'Kay, forget it, Rose said. I think she could tell I knew she was just B.S.-ing it.

I asked Wiley about it when we were having dinner that night. This was before we found out about Mum's plan to go to England. Squid was over at the neighbours' house eating hot dogs, which was good 'cause he would have gotten all scared hearing us talking about hell and dying. Wiley's parents are Catholic and whenever we went to their house they had to drape a tea towel over their painting of Jesus on the cross so that Squid wouldn't start crying. The first time Wiley explained to him that Jesus was hanging up there by nails hammered through his hands, Squid put on his mittens and refused to take them off. He told us it hurt to look at his hands, and when Mum made him take the mittens off to eat dinner, he kept holding them in fists and tucking the fists under his armpits.

Anyway, I thought Wiley would know about Catholic stuff from his parents, but he was in one of his hyper moods that day, which meant nobody could get a straight answer out of him about anything. Mum asked him how his lessons went and he blabbed on for fifteen minutes about how he was going to create the next piano prodigy.

I can feel it, he kept saying. This Raymond kid, he blows my mind! I swear to God, under my instruction, he's going to be playing with the Philharmonic by age thirteen. Mark my words!

Mum listened while she prepared dinner, told him she was glad it was going well, but the whole time she had this slight smile, lingering just beneath her plain-faced surface. After Wiley finished his rant he kept pacing around the kitchen like he was juiced up on Pixy Stix, opening the oven every few minutes to check on the potatoes as if they were about to explode. At one point Mum had to take him by the shoulders and say, Relax — you're so intense! His whole face dropped into a scowl in one snap motion.

I told you not to call me that, he said. For FUCK'S sake, can't a guy be hungry?

We all froze, stared at him. The sound of sizzling ham filled the silence.

Sorry, sorry, Wiley said, holding his hands up in the air. Just forget I said that, okay?

Jess gave me a scared look, but I pretended not to see it. I just helped Mum take the dishes of ham and peas and potatoes out to the table. Her face was red, but she wasn't saying anything. She wouldn't even look at me or Jess until we'd all sat down at the table and started eating. Wiley bit into a piece of ham and said it was succulent, and that made everyone breathe a big sigh of relief. I felt like someone needed to start a conversation then, so that's when I brought up the subject of purgatory.

So, I said, Rose and I were talking today about purgatory.

All right, Mum said. Not the topic I would expect from two fifteen-year-old girls. She smiled.

Yeah, well, I said. I was just curious. But Rose didn't explain it very well.

Wiley was busy cutting up his meat, not even looking at me. Wiley, I said.

He looked up.

You know about this kinda stuff, right? I said.

Wiley jumped out of his seat, rushed into the kitchen saying, One sec, just getting the pepper! I rolled my eyes at Mum and she shook her head back, *just let it go*. Wiley sat back down, sprinkled pepper all over his plate like he was playing a maraca.

I've discovered I love pepper, he said, watching his plate fill up with black flecks.

Hello? I said.

He set the pepper down, picked up his fork. Sorry, what? he said.

Purgatory! I said.

Oh right, Wiley said, tapping his baked potato with the back of his fork. Isn't that the place where you get tortured?

Not exactly, Mum said. It's more of a . . . state of *being* than a place.

So like something you make up in your head? I asked.

You might say that, Mum said.

It's those goddamn priests, Wiley said with his mouth full. The ones who diddle with the choirboys. They want to convince themselves they're still gonna get into heaven.

I laughed, and Wiley seemed to like that 'cause he smiled.

What are you talking about? Jess said.

Mum cut in. Well, she said, the way I understand it, it's taking into account that things aren't always so black and white.

Rose said it's a place between heaven and earth, I said.

Yes! Wiley said, slamming his hand on the table. That's what I learned. Sunday school — I took six years of it. He wagged his finger at Mum.

Yes, okay, Mum said, some people see it as a place. But that's a bit — simplistic.

Wiley put down his fork. He propped his elbows on the table, folded his hands and pressed them to his lips.

Mum glanced at him, then continued.

Catholics, she said, believe that some people — the ones who were good but did their share of bad things — have to be purified before they can go to heaven. She cut into her potato carefully and mashed up the inside, watching Wiley out of the corner of her eye. He was chewing slowly, staring at her like she had a target on her forehead.

Sounds creepy to me, Jess said.

So what, I said, their ghosts just kind of float around in their dead bodies waiting to get into heaven?

I guess so, Mum shrugged. I don't really know. I guess they believe you don't need to go to a special place to prove you're a good person.

Wiley snickered at that. What a scam, he said. His knee started jiggling under the table. I guarantee you, he said, the guys who came up with that crap are the jerks who disobeyed all the rules behind everyone's backs. They've gotta convince themselves they're still *good people*. He made air quotes when he said good people.

Well, what's wrong with that? Mum said, laying her knife across her plate even though she still hadn't taken a bite of her food. She looked Wiley right in the eye and his knee stopped jiggling. His smile quickly faded away.

For a few seconds everyone was silent. Jess was holding her fork in midair, balancing three peas on the prongs. Neither of us knew who was going to say something next so we just stared at our food.

People make mistakes, Mum said, but they can change.

Does that mean they're not good people? Mum's face was blank, her hands folded. Jess lowered her fork back to her plate.

Then Wiley started breathing really loud through his nose. His breathing got louder and louder and faster and faster until he was practically wheezing and his face started to go pink as the ham on his plate. He looked at me, then at Mum. And then he gave her this look I'd never seen before. A sneer. It was like something straight out of a Grimm's fairytale. It was the same face that evil witches make when they're stirring poisonous concoctions and plotting their evil schemes. I'd never seen someone try to make that face seriously, so I almost started laughing out loud at the table.

There are no good people, Wiley said.

Mum's cheeks turned bright red. She got up from the table and took her plate with her towards the kitchen.

Cunt, Wiley said. He didn't whisper it or yell it. He said it like it was just a regular everyday thing to say like *tennis* or *orange juice*.

When Mum's head whipped around I expected her to look really angry. But instead she looked like a scared puppy. She looked at me and Jess and not even Wiley, didn't say anything. No *Excuuuse me?* or *Watch your mouth!* or even *What the fuck is wrong with you, you fucking bastard?* Just that ridiculous puppy face that made me want to curl up in a little ball under the table. It only lasted a split second, but that was all we saw before she left the room.

And then Wiley stood up, and I could feel all my muscles hardening and my shoulders shooting up to my ears. He picked up his plate and tossed it clear across the room. Potato and peas and shards of stoneware and ham pieces went spewing everywhere.

See? he said to us, spreading his hands. No good people.

He didn't follow Mum to their bedroom, left the house by the front door.

Of course Jess was crying by this point and I really didn't blame her. We'd never heard our parents swear at each other like that, call each other names, break things. That was something people did in movies — the criminals and the psychopaths. I think I probably would've cried too if I wasn't so shocked that I could hardly wrap my head around how chunks of potato got on the ceiling. The Wiley I knew made jokes whenever people talked about anything serious, and used insults like dingleberry and numbskull. That Wiley, the one who marched right out the front door and left it swinging open on its hinges, was totally different. It was as if someone else had climbed into his skin and taken control of his body. But the scariest part about it was that the whole thing made me believe that what Wiley said might be true.

I guess in the end I never really figured out what purgatory was. But I got to thinking. What if this *is* purgatory, what we're all living, right now as we speak? That might explain why nobody's happy and everyone always wants to be some-place else, and why we always want to be better than everyone else. It would explain why people want to believe in perfect and wonderful things without having any proof. It's like somewhere deep down, they know this can't be all there is.

A lot of people don't realize that the first deep-sea ocean-ographers were considered total kooks. Even the smartest and most famous scientists told them that nothing could live down there, it was just a bunch of ooze and dead matter. There's this great line from "In the Abyss" by H.G. Wells that goes, *You thought I should find nothing but ooze. You laughed at my explorations, and I've discovered a new world!* The neat thing about that story is that it was written in 1896, almost forty years before the first deep-sea submersibles were even invented. In the story, Elstead the explorer journeys to the bottom of the sea in a homemade bathysphere and he finds an underwater city inhabited by these weird reptilian fish that have two legs and faces like humans. My favourite part of the story is when the fish people start worshipping Elstead as some kind of God because they've never seen anything like him, and after all, he did float down out of the dark sky in a shiny metal ball.

I like the idea that in the ocean world, the earth is actually the sky and the sky is the unknown universe beyond. It makes me wonder how many layers there really are to this cake.

VIII

DR. LONGFELLOW COULDN'T BE older than forty-five. In a
magazine interview he had mentioned that he received his
doctorate in Biophysics in his mid-twenties (he was something
of a prodigy), and a biographical note on one of his articles
cited his graduation year from Brown University as 1978.
Belinda couldn't be sure if he was married; his research
partner, Monika Treadstone, had been mentioned in almost
every one of his papers. And at the end of his last letter, Dr.
Longfellow had written, *Monika and I look forward to meeting
you.* It struck Belinda as a kind of affirmation, or perhaps a
warning; a gesture akin to a man by himself in a bar laying
his left hand next to his wine glass, his wedding band glinting
in the dim light like a pylon. Monika may have been one of
those women who chose to keep her maiden name. She was a
scientist, after all, and Belinda had noticed that many highly-
educated women claimed to be feminists. Belinda imagined
Monika as tall and thin and wearing a one-piece beige safari
suit, belted tight at her trim waist. Her long raven-coloured
hair would curtain seamlessly over her shoulders, even after

a day of traipsing through the fields and digging for soil samples. She was probably much smarter and even more dedicated
than her husband, always in the lab doing new experiments.
Belinda herself had gone about marriage in the wrong way.
She was no longer reluctant to admit that. Both of her marriages
had been adventurous rather than practical, defiant more than
genuine. Her swift marriage to Wiley, ten years her junior, had
been as scandalous as her marriage to Dazhong. He's *Chineeese?*
her mother had said, indignantly smearing the word. Belinda
had felt sublimely happy to hear her mother say exactly what
she expected, and she spread her hand to show her the ring with
its small, round diamond, the facets winking white light.

You don't know what you've got yourself into, her mother had
said, peering dubiously at the jewel. You don't know what kinds
of values he has. The Chinese have different values. Her words
had sounded cold and snobbish. A poor excuse for her resolute
disapproval. What did she know about love, anyway?

Belinda's marriage to Wiley had been slightly different.
Her mother hadn't even known about it for almost a year, when
Belinda informed her through a letter. She'd only written it
to quell the 'I told you so' thoughts she knew her mother was
having over Dazhong. The letter made it clear that this time,
she'd chosen the right man — an energetic, fun-loving man.
But Wiley had changed after Sebastian was born, and Belinda
couldn't be blamed for failing to recognize the early signs. He'd
acted as if getting married and having children was going to
change the world.

We're perfect together, he'd say. Can you imagine what our
kids will turn out like? With our combined genes? They'll be
geniuses! Beautiful geniuses!

Belinda mistook it for passion.

The heart of Belinda's problem in marriage was her per-
suasive imagination. She had the ability to imagine feelings

into being; if she wanted romance, she could convince herself that Burger King on a Saturday night was unconventional and sweetly modest. In a way, it was empowering. But eventually reality would catch up with her, stripping all her self-imposed happiness down to threads of stubborn tolerance. It seemed to her that the solution was to resist attaching herself, to darn the holes left by her amputated partners and allow her own body to fill her skin.

Belinda finally disembarked in Salisbury just before noon. When she arrived, coated in nervous sweat, at The Viceregal Arms Hotel — a blocky building, curiously striped black and white like a prison uniform — the desk told her that her party had gone for the day. A note in Dr. Longfellow's handwriting read, *Be back after dark.* The terseness of the note tied a small knot in Belinda's stomach. She ordered a pot of English tea to her room that arrived as a bag of Tetley floating in lukewarm water. Then she fell asleep while watching the news on TV, and when the telephone woke her several hours later she considered, for a brief moment, not answering. She could pretend she wasn't there, that she'd gone out on her own to explore.

Hello? Belinda said into the phone. She sounded groggy and prayed that Dr. Longfellow wouldn't pick up on it.

Hello, Mrs. Spector, the man on the other end said. Mr. Longfellow's asked me to inform you that he's in the lounge.

Oh — all right, thank you, Belinda replied. She set down the receiver and sat still. How strange it seemed to her. Even impolite. Why hadn't Dr. Longfellow called her himself? Or come up to her room?

She had ironed her cream silk blouse and black skirt upon settling into her room, so she quickly slipped them on, retouched her makeup and hair, and tucked her wallet and lipstick into a tiny leather purse. She added the notepad and pen from the nightstand, in case Dr. Longfellow intended to give her an orientation or a run-down of tomorrow's schedule. Maybe they had fallen behind in their sample collection without her there to help. Dr. Longfellow had explained through his letters that much of their work would involve long days digging in the fields, taking pictures, and charting maps of the formations. She was anxious to showcase her thirst for knowledge, prove her dedication. She was a fast learner. As she made her way downstairs to the lounge, she walked lightly so her hair wouldn't fall flat.

Dr. Longfellow was the only person sitting in the lounge. Belinda didn't notice him at first, partly because he was sitting in a dark booth in the far corner, but also because he looked nothing like Belinda expected. He stood abruptly when Belinda approached. His red hair coiled in frizzy ringlets to his shoulders and his suit jacket appeared too long for his torso, giving him the appearance of a child wearing his father's clothes. Belinda shook his hand and he didn't return her smile; his pale blue eyes fell away from hers and then flitted about the room as if tossed by a sudden gust of wind. He was slightly shorter than Belinda, and rather severely hunched.

Good evening, he said, brushing his sleeves. The train was late?

Yes, Belinda said, unfortunately it was. I'm terribly sorry. It's wonderful to meet you, finally.

Yes, trains are always late from London, he said, and flashed a thin smile. He sat down in the booth and Belinda took a seat across from him. A cigarillo reclined in the ashtray between them, curling grey smoke.

I'm so excited to begin, Belinda said. The wait has been agonizing.

Is that so? Dr. Longfellow said. He looked intently towards the bar, head moving this way and that, apparently desperate to catch the attention of a server.

Yes, she said. The train took ages! Beautiful scenery, but I'm eager to get out there, you know? She tried to catch his eyes, but they continued to dart around the restaurant. He seemed nervous and disinterested at once, oblivious to the smoking cigarillo dangling its long, ashen hook. She might as well have been talking to herself.

Will Dr. Treadstone be joining us this evening? Belinda asked, trying to put her face in his view.

Eh? His attention flicked back to Belinda, and then he shook his head vigourously. Nonononono, he said. She's not a doctor. You'll meet her in due course.

A server approached their table before Belinda could reply.

You drink wine, yes? Dr. Longfellow asked.

Uh — sure, okay, Belinda said.

He ordered Belinda a glass of house red, nothing for himself. She hated red wine.

Dr. Longfellow settled back in his seat. Your flight was smooth? he asked, taking a bill out of his wallet.

It was fine, Belinda said. I met a biologist, of all things. He was sitting next to me —

The server set her glass of wine on the table and Dr. Longfellow passed him the money. Belinda thanked him.

A bit of an odd man, she continued, but his work sounded interesting. He said he's a phycologist.

Never heard of such a thing, Dr. Longfellow said. He stubbed out the cigarillo.

Belinda laughed. It does sound rather obscure, doesn't it?

Yes, it does, he said, straight-faced. I'm glad you arrived without too many problems.

Thank you, she said. I'm so glad to finally be here.

Good, he said. He nodded. She nodded back, waiting for him to go on.

I'm afraid I can't stay long, he said. It's been a very long day. I'm a person who needs a certain amount of sleep. Nine hours minimum.

Oh, of course, Belinda said. She could feel her face dropping, and forced a smile to lift it. I don't mind at all, she said. She checked her watch: 8:13 PM. You need your rest for all that brain-work, she said with a polite little laugh.

It was a field day today, he said. Lots of wind. It blows the dirt all over you.

I see, Belinda said. Well, don't feel you need to stay here on account of me.

I thought it would be good to meet you anyway, he said. Face to face.

It was very kind of you, Belinda found herself saying. A hot wave filled her cheeks. She took a small sip of wine.

I suppose I'll be off then, if you're sure you don't mind. He stood and slid his hands into his coat pockets.

No, no, not at all, she said. Her voice was suddenly quiet, muted.

Are you interested in seeing Woodhenge tomorrow? he asked, gazing into the distance as though it were a philosophical question. I can get my assistant to take you, he said. I think Stonehenge will be much too busy on a Saturday.

Oh — um, sure, fine, Belinda said. Thank you, that sounds fine. She almost ventured to ask what *he* would be doing tomorrow, but decided against it. She didn't want to sound ungrateful.

Good, he said, nodding. My assistant will call on you in the morning. Pierre is his name.

Okay, yes, I will remember that, Belinda said.

See you tomorrow, at some point, Dr. Longfellow said, still nodding. His hands seemed quite attached to the insides of his coat pockets, so Belinda folded hers in her lap.

Good night, she said. Have a good rest! She forced another smile.

He walked briskly out of the lounge, and from Belinda's seat she could see him climbing the hotel stairs, staring down at his clomping feet.

Belinda felt stunned. What had happened? Was he angry? Annoyed that her train was late? Or was he merely cranky after a long day? Belinda hadn't even had the chance to do anything to upset him. The server came to check on her and drifted back to the kitchen, leaving the lounge empty, silent. Belinda felt unable to do anything but sit and listen, her thoughts melting into background noise. A far-off clink of dishes hung in the air for an inordinate length of time, and her mind clung to the reverberations. She stared blankly, contemplated the objects on the table in front of her as though they were part of a still-life painting. She had never seen wine so still; she could easily believe it was made of plastic. Next to her glass was a delicate roll of ash, now lying in the tray alongside the smushed cigarillo. Detached, discarded. The scene made her feel afraid to move, as if the slightest shift of her body might cause a leathery squeak that could ripple the liquid surface or crumble the ash. The suspended moment expanded and swelled, pushed the meeting with Dr. Longfellow to the past, to the edges of the day where it didn't matter and could easily be forgotten.

And then it came upon her: this must be part of the training. Of course. Dr. Longfellow was sending her to Woodhenge to give his assistant the opportunity to assess her abilities. She'd been naïve to think she could simply saunter in with no experience and immediately work alongside the seasoned researchers. Her book learning counted for little in the field; Dr. Longfellow was testing her ability to apply her knowledge.

She lifted her wine glass and took a generous mouthful. The wine in England didn't taste so awful after all.

9 Amphibians

MUM WAS BORN IN Wiltshire, the crop circle capital of the world, which I'll admit is a pretty weird coincidence. Or maybe it's not a coincidence at all. She said she was going on a 'spiritual journey,' but who knows what that really means? Wiley once said that spirituality is what you make of it, and now that I understand what he meant I think it was a pretty smart thing to say. I could be spiritual about Swiss cheese and nobody could tell me it was wrong. Cheese is my religion, I could say, and who would have the right to tell me my religion wasn't true or real?

Aside from Mum, none of us have ever met our relatives in Wiltshire. Auntie Prim is fourteen years older than Mum, and she moved out of their house when Mum was only two. Mum's never actually said so, but Jess and I figured out that Auntie Prim was kicked out because she got pregnant. Our cousin Sebastian is only two years younger than Mum, and last I heard he still lives at home with Auntie Prim. Since I don't know anything else about him I imagine him like Norman Bates, dressed in a grey wig and a flower-print dress.

Turns out the guy who wrote *Psycho* actually based the character of Norman Bates on a real serial killer named Ed Gein, who skinned his victims' bodies and made woman-costumes out of them. He even peeled the skin off their faces to make masks for himself. Before he got caught everyone thought he was a pretty regular guy, a little odd and maybe a tad too attached to his mother. Meanwhile he was stealing corpses from graveyards to decorate his house — capping his bedposts with shrunken heads and making trophies out of human bones. Who knew.

I couldn't imagine having a baby right now, at my age. There's a girl a year older than me in grade eleven, Lily something, who had to switch to a special school because she got pregnant, but I don't think her parents kicked her out. Jess told me that in grade seven she once saw Lily in the girls' bathroom with a plastic baggie of oregano and a packet of cigarette paper. When Jess was in the stall Lily was showing another girl how to roll the oregano up into joints.

You can't smoke oregano, I told Jess.

How would you know? she asked, so I let her go on talking about how it smelled like burnt spaghetti and how she was afraid to come out of the stall because she didn't want to get beaten up.

I could've told on them, Jess said, as if this were some juicy scandal. But I never told anyone. You're the first.

Ooo, lucky me, I said, but Jess pretended not to get that I was mocking her. It drives me nuts how she acts so scared of anyone who's not a goody-two-shoes like her. She'd never told me the story about Lily and the oregano before, and the only reason she decided to tell me then was 'cause I'd just told her about Lily being pregnant. I think it must make her feel better to believe that certain people are just plain naughty through and through, and will get into trouble no matter what they do.

As much as I'd be totally freaked out about being pregnant if I were Lily, I also think it might feel kind of nice to have a little person inside you, using you as a blanket. When Mum was pregnant with Squid you could hardly see a bump until she was eight months. Squid was all nestled in there hiding, the way he still likes to be sometimes when he's tired. When he was five he built a fort out of a moving box that the neighbours had put outside with the trash. The box was one made especially for hanging suits and fancy clothes in, so it had a metal bar running across the top. Mum let Squid use one of the fleece blankets to drape across the bar so it made a sort of tent within the box. Squid liked to curl up between the drapes of fleece with his stuffed giraffe, which he named Machu Picchu (he heard it on TV). He'd lie in there for maybe fifteen minutes every night before bed, and all you could hear was Squid talking very softly to Machu Picchu. We didn't ask what he was doing because it was the only time we got a break from keeping watch over him. I once stuck my head in the box to see what it was like, and I didn't blame Squid for liking it so much. The lamplight coming through the handholds at the sides of the box made the fleece blanket glow pink, the way it looks when you close your eyes in bright sunlight. And the smell of warm cardboard, like no other smell in the world. If I'd been small enough I would have snuggled up in there myself and taken a nap.

Mum eventually got sick of the box taking up space in Squid's room, so she tossed it in one of the big metal bins outside Safeway one morning after she'd dropped Squid off at school. Pretty cruel. Squid cried for an hour when he found out, and Mum said he had to learn to let things go. Easy for Mum to say. She doesn't even talk to her own Mum anymore, not even over the phone. Every year we get a Christmas parcel from England wrapped in brown paper and twine, and it's become sort of a tradition for all of us to tear and pull and pick at it together because it's got so much tape on it, pressed over every edge and fold. Mum always ends up having to get a pair of scissors to cut it open. For some reason we never think to get the scissors in the first place. Maybe 'cause it's more fun to act like we're ripping ravenously at the parcel, as if there's something irresistible inside. Mum doesn't let us do that with any other presents, *For Chrissake don't tear it, we can save the paper for next year.* The funny thing is that Grandma's parcels are probably the least exciting of all the gifts we get. She packs them chock full of lame stuff like underwear and wool socks, and the year Squid was born nearly half the thing was crammed with Huggies. For a few years all she sent was packages of dry beans, pasta, gravy mix, sardines, and wheat crackers, as if she'd mixed addresses up and sent us a box for the food bank by accident. Mum would sigh while she pulled out all the packages, would try to pretend she wasn't excited to see the five Double-Decker chocolate bars tucked in among the beans. Double-Deckers were Mum's favourite and you could only get them in Europe, but the rest of us didn't really get what all the fuss was about.

When she told us about her trip to Wiltshire, I asked Mum if she was going to visit her Mum and Auntie Prim and Sebastian. She just laughed and wrinkled her eyebrows like she was all surprised, but I knew she wasn't.

Now why would I do that, Grace? she said, as if I'd just asked her to jump off the edge of a cliff. And then she started talking about everything she needed to pack and all the chores she had to do, which really meant the chores that she wanted *us* to do. Of course, she didn't give me the opportunity to ask why she *wouldn't* visit her family. When I was reading the brochure for the Sacred Britain Crop Circles Tour, I pointed out to Mum that it said the trip only lasted eight days.

So how come you can't buy a return ticket? I asked.

Grace, she said, please! Must you pester me? And then she went on her rant about how she was an adult and could make her own decisions, and she didn't need a fifteen-year-old telling her what to do, thank you very much.

She must have told Wiley before she told me, Jess, and Squid, 'cause Wiley was only in the room for a few seconds before he snatched a beer from the fridge and sat outside on the patio with his lawn chair facing the lilac bushes.

When I was really little it didn't seem weird that I didn't know anything about my relatives. It was just the way things were. Grandmothers were nothing but characters in story-books and movies. We never asked Mum about what Grandma was like or how it was growing up in England because she never told us anything in the first place. There was nothing to be curious about. It had never even crossed my mind to imagine what her life was like before Jess and I came along.

But when I was five some new neighbours moved in next door, and one of the kids, Darla, was my age. Darla's grand-mother lived with them in that house, and everyone, even unrelated people like me, called her Nana. Nana had her own little area on the top floor with a kitchen and everything. She was one of those grandmothers who really could've been a storybook character 'cause she had curly white hair like an angel and she was always smiling and chuckling at things we said, even if they weren't funny. She was round and soft and she'd smother both me and Darla with hugs as soon as we walked in the door, and it seemed like every time we visited, she happened to have a pan of ginger molasses cookies in the oven. She smelled like lavender and Ivory soap. That's when I started to wonder why I'd never met my grandma before, and why Mum had never taken us to visit her.

She's a very angry woman, Mum said when I asked about Grandma. And I'd rather not talk about her.

What's she so mad about? I asked. Maybe you can say sorry. I remember thinking this was a totally legitimate proposal. It seemed like all grandmothers had to be warm and jolly like Darla's.

It's nothing I did, Gracie, Mum said. It's hard to explain. Grown-up stuff.

I tried asking Mum again a bunch more times after that, but she just kept using the same excuses. Wouldn't say much about her sister either, said that she barely even knew Prim, and her dad had died of lung cancer when she was just a baby. But she did tell us a few things about Mere, the town in Wiltshire where she grew up. There was an old castle and a bacon factory, and lots and lots of farmland, just like here in the prairies except greener. She told us that when she first moved to Canada and went for breakfast in a restaurant, she could barely swallow the bacon 'cause it was so fatty — nothing like the lean cuts of back bacon she grew up with.

I couldn't believe that people who had enough money to go to restaurants actually *chose* to eat that, she said. Streaky bacon, we called it.

If we asked for more stories about Mere, Mum would just say it was a boring little town and we wouldn't like it anyway. Wiley made this cheeseball joke that they probably named it Mere because there was *mere*ly nothing there.

Probably, Mum said, not laughing.

But a few years later when we were doing the geography unit in Social, I learned that the word mere can also mean a lake or an arm of the sea. And even though I looked on a map of Wiltshire and saw that the town of Mere is nowhere near a lake or the sea, I still like to tell myself that's what the name means.

The day after Mum left, when I was taking Squid home on the bus after his concert, I told him that Mere was an underwater city where everyone was born with gills instead of lungs. Since he doesn't get any more answers from Mum than the rest of us, I figured it wouldn't hurt to make something up.

But Mummy doesn't have any gills, Squid said, curling his finger around his nose.

Well, I said, you just haven't seen them. They're these really small slits, and they're on the sides, sort of below her armpits. I scratched under my armpits like a gorilla to show him.

But how come I never saw them? Squid asked. Nuh-uh, he shook his head. You're just teasing.

Nope, it's true, I said. Think about it: Mum is always wearing shirts that cover up the spots under her armpits, right?

Squid narrowed his eyes.

Plus, I said, she doesn't need to use them when she's not in the water. So they're hard to see 'cause they just lie flat, like flaps of skin.

Squid was quiet. He crossed his arms, slid his fingers back and forth along the tops of his ribs.

Are we ever gonna get to go to Mere? he asked.

I dunno, I said, how long can you hold your breath?

Squid got all excited about that. Oh a long time, he said, nodding like a bobblehead. I'm the only kid in grade one who can blow up a balloon. The other kids say it's too hard.

You should probably keep practicing, I said. And you need to be a good swimmer too.

Like an amphibian? Squid asked. Amphibians are good swimmers.

Yep, you're right, I said. In fact, that's exactly what the people in Mere are. Amphibians.

Looking back now, I realize it was my fault that Squid got into trouble at school. When I got home the next day, the little red light on the answering machine was blinking. Wiley must not have heard the phone ring 'cause he was out in the garage. The message was from Mrs. Trainer, Squid's teacher.

Hello this message is for Belinda Spector, Sebastian's mother? This is Louise Trainer, your son's teacher. Yes I'm calling because Sebastian had some difficulties at school today. Please call me at your earliest convenience. Two-four-six, twenty-five-hundred, thank you.

Without even thinking, I erased the message. I didn't think it was any of Mrs. Trainer's business to know that Mum was away and couldn't return her call. And I got this feeling from the way she talked that she was probably just another prune-crotched ol' battleaxe (as Wiley says), and that whatever Squid did must've been her fault anyway. It's hard to understand why Squid does some of the things he does, but I guess I did some pretty weird things when I was younger too. For a while when I was four or five I insisted on drinking everything from a sponge because I thought it made things taste better. Didn't matter what it was — juice, water, chocolate milk — it had to be put into a bowl so I could soak it up with my yellow sponge. It was a real sponge too, not one of those cheap synthetic ones you can get at the dollar store. This sponge used to be a living thing. Makes me gag to think about putting my lips around it now, and I wonder why Mum even let me drink from something that was supposed to be for scrubbing our dirty bodies in the bathtub. Just goes to show you that those neuroscientists are probably right when they say your brain keeps growing until you get into your teens. You start looking back and wondering what the heck was going through your head when you did all those ridiculous things. And so because I knew that I did my share of freaky things as a kid, a tiny part of me wasn't all that surprised when Squid finally told me that he had taken the class newt out of its aquarium and accidentally killed it. Don't get me wrong, I was shocked, but not altogether surprised, if that makes any sense. Before I let myself lose it on him I tried to tell myself that 'accidentally' was the key word. Shit happens, right?

All right, I said to him. How did this happen? We were in his bedroom and I had made sure the door was closed even though Jess wasn't home yet. She'd stayed after school that day for bio tutoring, which was lucky 'cause I knew she would've freaked if she found out about this.

I was making a potion, Squid said quietly. The juice of a newt, remember? Suddenly everything made perfect sense. One of Squid's favourite books was about a friendly little witch who could stir up potions that would give kids superpowers. One of the kids in the story had wanted to be able to swim like a dolphin, so the witch prescribed the juice of a newt, which she said would give him the power to breathe underwater.

That was a *story*, Squid, I said. I was pressing my fists to my ears to stop myself from yelling. Just a goddamn story!

But I didn't think it would hurt! he said. Tears started to pool in his eyelids.

What did you do, squeeze the thing to death?

No! he wailed. I just scraped him a little. On his back. Squid made like he was scooping ice cream.

I could picture what had happened then. Squid holding the newt against the table and scraping its back with the plastic spoon from his lunch bag, the newt wriggling and Squid's fingers mashing down so it couldn't get away. Squid not knowing how hard was too hard 'cause he was only a kid and didn't think it made any difference.

I wondered if newts had blood, and what colour it was if they did.

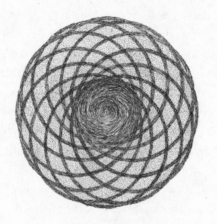

IX

IN ALL THE YEARS she'd lived in England, Belinda had only once seen Stonehenge. She'd been a sullen schoolgirl on a class field trip and she couldn't remember anything about the experience. She hadn't felt compelled to visit Woodhenge. History had not been a topic of interest in her mother's household. But when Belinda came across a diagram of Woodhenge in one of the crop circle books she was studying, she felt its importance resonate like an echo. The diagram mapped the site where archaeologists had uncovered the remnants of 168 post-holes arranged to form six concentric rings, and buried in the centre, a small child's skeleton. A dedicatory sacrifice, they presumed. The post-holes originally held wooden pillars, though the function of these was still a mystery. Some suspected the site had a religious purpose, and other theories touted moon and sun patterns to suggest it was a giant cosmological calendar that signaled the summer solstice when the dusk-light struck the pillars in a particular way. With Stonehenge just two miles away, a connection between the two monuments was almost undeniable. If you were to stand in the centre of Stonehenge with a map of all the archaeological sites in the area, you would be able to see Woodhenge in the distance, as well as dozens of surrounding burial mounds, simply by rotating on that fixed spot. You just needed to know where to look.

That Belinda had been raised in an English town only forty kilometres west of Salisbury was a coincidence solely of geography. She saw no significance in this fact. Twenty-three years before, she'd told her mother she would never return to Mere. It was a vow she would not allow herself to break. On the map of her memory, she'd drawn an invisible circle around Stourhead Gardens and Castle Hill, the town cemetery, the old bacon factory, the market square, and the perpetual clock tower — sealing the town behind a quarantine boundary, solid and unwavering. If she were to even think about how reachable the town really was, she might risk breaching that boundary.

On the phone the previous night, Wiley had begged her to come home. Belinda could hear the tightness in his voice. He'd obviously swung into one of his high-energy moods.

I've decided to reorganize the garage, he said. By myself. I'm going to turn it into a jam space. Maybe even build a stage.

Sounds great, Belinda said, knowing he would never follow through with the plans. So you're doing fine then?

Oh yeah, yeah, he said. I'm just fine. Wonderful, in fact.

Good, she said. I'm doing well, too. You might be interested to know that I'm going to Woodhenge tomorrow. It's going to be incredible.

Oh, Wiley said. That's nice.

Do you even know what Woodhenge is? Belinda asked.

Think so, Wiley said. Like Stonehenge, but wood, right?

You're impossible, Belinda said. Jessica says you haven't been helping out.

Jesus Christ, you're gonna nag me from across the Atlantic?

You're not giving me a choice, she said. I mean it — I need you to help the kids.

He sighed, and Belinda could tell he was rubbing his face. She could hear the phone in his hand, creaking. Please, he whined, just come home already.

What did he mean 'home'? she'd thought to herself, but decided it best left unsaid. Having always lived in the Canadian prairies, Wiley wouldn't understand how she could feel phantom pains from a removed landscape: a recalcitrant longing for rain-soaked air, pastures salted with woolly sheep, the knowledge that rocky beaches draped in solemn grey seas lay within an hour's drive.

And yet when she was finally there, riding the local Salisbury bus to Old Sarum where she and Pierre would take the footpaths to Woodhenge, the place seemed entirely foreign. Sitting across from her on the bus was an old woman in a flower-print skirt carrying a fraying basket of brown eggs. How quaint, Belinda thought. The woman's mouth was cracked and sunken like a deflated pudding. She seemed a quintessential accessory to the stone, brick, and timber façades reeling past the window behind her. Belinda had expected Wiltshire to have changed drastically since she was a child. It was enchanting to see that it hadn't, and yet the sight of the old woman made Belinda slightly sick to her stomach. With the bus bumping and lurching, Belinda felt the sensation of riding a merry-go-round, cantering on the slick back of a fibreglass horse while giant carnival tents revolved around her.

Pierre was an Englishman with a thick South-Country accent and uniformly crooked teeth, which Belinda hadn't expected. He wore a tweed flatcap and rough callouses on his red hands. For the entire bus ride, Belinda humoured him as he reminisced about growing up in a small Cornish village and his Mum's Stargazy Pie, the crispy sardine-heads stuck up through a golden crust. But when they'd stepped off the bus and found the footpath, she seized the opportunity to interject. She asked Pierre how long he'd been working with Dr. Longfellow.

Marshall? he said. I've known Marshall for — ohh . . . four years now? Ever since the crop circle appeared in my barley field.

A crop circle? Belinda repeated, nearly tripping on the long grass brushing her ankles. In your field? What was it like?

Pierre chuckled, pulled his cap down over his eyebrows and pushed it back up again. Well Ma'am, he said, it was like a circle is all I can say. It was just a plain circle, very large. Nothing like those extravagant pictures you see on the news reports.

But did you see it? she asked. Did you see it happen?

Ah, no, he chuckled again. I didn't think much of it until Marshall arrived on my doorstep and asked to take photographs. Pierre walked steadily, pulling up handfuls of grass along the path and picking off the seedlings ritualistically.

Tell me something, Belinda said gravely, and Pierre stopped walking and turned to face her expectantly. What's your opinion? she asked. Who do *you* think made the circle?

He smiled sheepishly, revealing a yellow eyetooth that stuck out like a fang. I haven't a clue, Ma'am, he said. I haven't put much thought into it, truth be told. I'd've mown it all down if Marshall hadn't come to my door. Didn't know a circle in a field could be worth something.

A nervous laugh trilled from Belinda's mouth. But — aren't you — a researcher? Dr. Longfellow's assistant?

He laughed again in response, with less sincerity. I suppose I'm something of an assistant, he said, grinning.

Belinda felt a finger of panic sliding up her spine. Pierre had begun walking ahead, and suddenly he was a stranger and

Belinda was sure his smile had an oily look to it, and they were alone. Alone together on a deserted country path.

Wh-Where are we going? she stammered, planting her feet in the dirt. What's going on?

Pierre stopped, turned, and removed his cap. His eyebrows furrowed. Belinda realized she looked like a petulant child with her fists pressed into her hips and her mouth set in a stern frown. She let her arms loosen and dangle.

I — I just mean . . . I'm confused, she said. I thought you were part of the research team.

The who? Pierre scratched his head. I'm sorry Ma'am, he said. I don't know anything about research. I was told you wanted to see Woodhenge. The lady should very much like to see Woodhenge, Marshall told me. And I know the way.

Belinda bit her thumbnail, searching his eyes for dishonesty. Was this really Dr. Longfellow's idea of an assistant?

Look there, Pierre said, and pointed to a grassy plateau up ahead, ruins like stony knuckles breaking its green surface. Old Sarum, he said, his finger tracing the ruins.

The sight of a famous landmark quickly dissolved Belinda's uncertainty. It didn't matter what Pierre was, she told herself. He was only showing her the way. The remains of Old Sarum's magnificent motte-and-bailey castle emerged from the green like a misty spectre. Pierre followed behind her, and stood at a distance as she wandered among the old walls hanging off the hillocks in conglomerate sheets. This was what she had come for, she thought. To be awed. Surrounded by enigmatic wonders and left to her own silent contemplation.

We'd best be off, he announced after watching her for some time, and she obeyed, hoping her compliance would constitute an apology for her outburst. After this first glimpse of the ancient history bound to the land around her, she felt invigorated. The sky was a swatch of boundless grey, and the air tasted as crisp as an apple. She asked Pierre good-naturedly how far the walk to Woodhenge was.

Not far, he said, only about six more miles.

Six *miles?* Belinda cried. But that will take us all day!

Pierre shrugged. Do you have another engagement? he asked.

The sun was setting by the time they caught the bus from the parking lot at Woodhenge back to Salisbury station. Belinda asked why they hadn't taken the bus all the way there and Pierre told her, with a hint of disdain, that he'd thought she would enjoy the walk. Belinda had trudged along silently for most of it, and Pierre had quickly resigned himself to her irritable attitude like a guilty husband. In the end, Woodhenge had been much smaller than she'd imagined. Crooked concrete posts, pocked and devoid of any ornament, marked the places of the original timber posts, long since decayed and crumbled away. Dozens of tourists loitered about the posts like bored construction workers.

Belinda searched for a feeling of reverence, but she could only think about Dr. Longfellow. Had he planned this all along? She thought about his letters, and how her mind could not, even with the greatest effort, reconcile the gracious, encouraging character of those compositions with the man she'd met the day before. She wondered if the letters, the invitation to come to England, the meeting, the field trip to Woodhenge, had all been attempts to placate her, in the same way that she would sometimes indulge Sebastian's pleas to help with the laundry, knowing he would quickly grow bored or frustrated and leave her to re-fold the messy, balled-up bundles he left behind. Caught up in her thoughts, she forgot to remind herself of the child's grave in the centre of the monument. She had intended to walk over it and contemplate the scene, imagine the bones beneath her feet, even though she knew they'd been long since extracted by archaeologists for analysis. How many hundreds of years had the sacrifice outlived the wood? Before she could think to wonder, she'd walked away, leaving the posts with their lengthening shadows like heavy black capes.

10 Hide and Seek

MOST PEOPLE DON'T KNOW that the Lost City of Atlantis is
actually a real place. It's a chain of hydrothermal vents in the
mid-Atlantic — basically a series of underwater volcanoes.
The vents look like giant chimneys with smoke pouring out,
which is partly what makes it look like a city. But the chimneys
are also between thirty and sixty metres high, so the chain
in its entirety looks something like the Walt Disney castle
covered in algae. And because of the hydrogen and methane
produced when the cold seawater reacts with the mineral-rich
magma, there are actually thousands of weird microorganisms
living on and around the vents, feeding off the chemicals and
basking in the warm water. Of course, those microorganisms
attract invertebrates like snails and shrimp who prey on them,
so it's really one big deep-sea smorgasbord where everyone's
invited. My kind of party. All you need to think about is
eating, and no one cares how cool you look or who you talk to.

It depresses me sometimes to think about how trivial life on
earth is. Wiley always says that high school is supposed to be
the best time of your life, which pretty much makes me wanna

slit my wrists and get it over with. Last year I had this friend named Nikki. She was one of those girls who would check her reflection in the vending machine whenever she passed by the cafeteria, thinking no one would notice. She was always talking about her boyfriend, *Doug said that movie blows* and *Doug hates when people say that* and *yesterday Doug and I did this* and on and on. Doug was the scrawniest kid I've ever seen, and he always wore these skinny black punk-rocker jeans that made his legs look like tube balloons. I couldn't help picturing a clown grabbing one of those legs and twisting it into a poodle or a butterfly, Ta-da! I really didn't want to think about what his legs looked like without pants, but Nikki did her best to force that on me.

He's got so much hair all over his legs, she said, and at the tops of his thighs it just stops. Then it gets all bushy again around his thing. It's so funny. It looks like he's wearing white shorts with a hole cut in the crotch.

Don't wanna know, I said, covering my ears. Luckily Rose was there too, and she'd just gotten dumped by her boyfriend a couple of days before. His name was Zack and he bleached and gelled his hair in a swoop to look like Zack Morris from *Saved by the Bell*. Dead serious. I only met him once when his basketball team was playing against our school's team, and Rose made me sit in the bleachers with her and watch. It was more stimulating to watch Zack's hair flopping out of its do as he jogged back and forth across the court and him smoothing it back into place every chance he got than to actually follow the game. Rose had spent three hours making an orange poster-paper banner that said ZACK ATTACK in huge cloud letters. She'd drawn the letters by hand on sheets of blue construction paper, and by the time she was ready to cut them out and glue them to the banner, bits of the paper were flaking off where she'd pressed hard with her pencil and then erased the lines over and over again, trying to make them look perfect. I helped her cut the letters out 'cause I felt sorry for her spending so much time working on it after school, but she'd made so many overlapping lines that it was hard to see which one to cut along. In the end it was a total waste 'cause nobody else in the bleachers had a banner, so hers just sat rolled up at her feet during the whole game. I saw her bend down a couple of times to touch it, but I could tell she was too embarrassed to just whip it open and wave it proudly over her head. Anyway, when Nikki was nattering on about Doug that day, Rose was feeling all cynical because Zack had dumped her with a note scribbled on a piece of looseleaf — *Looseleaf?* Rose had said, Can you even imagine a more jerky thing to do? — so she told Nikki to shut her hole, we didn't want to hear about Doug's bony white ass.

Nikki looked shocked at first but then she just shrugged. S'okay, she said, you're allowed to be a bitch after what happened to you.

I'm not friends with Nikki anymore, which is kind of a relief. She made me feel like I was turning into one of those typical girls who just wants to be popular, and wants people to think she's so badass — the kinds of girls that I hate. When she heard Mum was away she insisted we have a drunken sleepover at my house, even though I reminded her that Wiley would still be there.

So what, your stepdad sounds cool, she said. He won't care.

Actually, I said, he'll probably tell my Mum. She's got him on a leash, remember? I didn't feel like telling Nikki that I just didn't want drunk people in the house with Squid. She wouldn't have understood anyway.

Come on, she said, you deserve some fun after your mom left you all this crap to deal with.

I'd been complaining to Rose and Nikki about all the

housework and babysitting I'd had to do since Mum left, and I'd exaggerated some of it just 'cause I liked to hear them say *Oh no way* and *I would die if I was you*. Truth was I hadn't really done anything around the house, and neither had anyone else. On Saturday I went straight to Rose's house after we got back from lunch with Da, and when I got home that evening I nearly cried 'cause I saw how disgusting everything looked. You'd think for all of Jess's Mum-ness she'd have taken care of it, but cleaning was one thing Jess didn't have a clue about. I hadn't noticed how bad it was until I knew people were coming over. There was hair all over the bathroom floor and in the sink and a huge skid-mark in the toilet. The dining room was still a disaster zone from Jess's collage project that had been due three days before, *Chatelaine* magazines splayed open on the table with their gutted pages furling out, little bits of paper scattered like snow all around the feet of the table, scissors and glue and markers spread on the pulled-out chairs. We'd made a stack of pizza and chicken boxes and put them beside the back door 'cause they'd started making the kitchen smell like corn chips. Seemed like a good idea at the time. There were pots of dried-up mac 'n' cheese stacked on the kitchen counter along with a couple of days' worth of dirty plates and cutlery left there 'cause no one had wanted to empty the dishwasher. All the unswept crumbs on the floor made the linoleum crunch under my feet. But the worst part was that the kitchen table was literally covered in hundreds of little screws and nails and bolts, and it looked like someone had just dumped them out of an old box. There was grey dirt dusted all around them. Seeing it from the other end of the house it actually looked like the tablecloth was silver.

Wiley was nowhere and the house was silent.

I only had time to do a half-assed job of cleaning everything, but I was feeling pretty sorry for myself the whole way through. By the time I had finished washing the pots I'd gotten myself all riled up. I was so mad I was sweating. I remember thinking I could probably call up Child Services, get Mum and Wiley arrested for neglect. When Jess came home from the park with Squid I was on my knees scrubbing a sticky puddle of grape juice off the floor, and when Squid saw my face he raced straight up to his room. I screamed at Jess, told her the dining room looked like a goddamn pigsty.

Jesus Christ, you sound like Mummy! she yelled back.

I knew it was true but I punched her anyway. Smack in the boob. Of course she shrieked like a harpy which made me want to punch her again, except she ran off to her room crying and ranting about how much she hated me and wanted to kill me. I didn't blame her, 'cause there have been times when I've wanted to kill her too. Jess is the only person who has ever made me feel like I truly wanted them to die. And I really did when I told her my friends were coming over so she had to watch Squid and she said, Too bad, I'm going out to see a movie. I wailed on her until my vocal cords felt ready to snap, but she went storming out of the house anyway.

Nikki and Rose showed up two hours later and my hands still hadn't stopped trembling. My hair was plastered to my forehead with sweat. I'd just managed to get everything looking somewhat decent, all the junk stuffed into closets and a pan of McCain Superfries cooking in the oven.

Honey, you need a drink, Nikki said to me when I opened the door. She had her backpack slung over one shoulder and pulled around her front. She unzipped it and the long glass neck of a bottle with a red cap peeked out. I had this feeling that Squid was behind me so I stood in the doorway trying to block Nikki.

Jeez, are you gonna let us in? Nikki pushed her way past me.

Squid was standing at the bottom of the stairs when I turned around. He watched Nikki and Rose heel off their sneakers and toss their coats on the couch. I could tell by the little smile on his face that he wasn't going to leave us alone.

Can I have some French fries? he said quietly.

Yeah, I said, acting annoyed. I made extra so you could have some.

Whoa man, this is your little brother? Nikki said. He's cute.

Uh huh, I said. You guys hungry? I really wanted to change the subject, but Squid was totally sucking up the attention. His dark eyelashes were practically fluttering and his blue eyes were round as Bambi's. No one can pour on the syrup better than Squid.

He's got such blue eyes, Rose said. You guys don't look like brother and sister at all.

Yeah, well we are, I said.

That's 'cause I have a different dad, Squid said.

They *know* that already, I told him.

Oh my God, he is so cute, Nikki said. He's going to be totally hot when he grows up.

'Kay, can we just get the food and go down to the basement? I said.

Nikki sniffed the air like she just caught a whiff of something toxic. Oh, you're making fries? she said. Doug says McCain fries aren't even real potatoes.

So what are they then? Rose asked.

Like filler and stuff. Cardboard. Nikki has this habit of playing with her hair when she's bullshitting or lying: she lifts it up at the back and twirls it around her hand, then lets it fall.

I only made them for my brother, I said. I wanted to kick myself after I said it.

What's your brother's name again? Nikki said.

Squid! Squid cried out, taking Nikki's hand and shaking it up and down like Wiley had taught him to do when he introduced himself. I laughed the way Mum does when people give her compliments, all high and forced, and I took Squid by the shoulders to pull him away.

No no, I said. His real name's Sebastian. I patted him on the head, ruffled his hair a bit. We're trying to get him to stop calling himself that, I said. Squid pushed my hand away and started petting his head, gave me an exaggerated glare like Hey, you're wrecking my hair. I knew he was only faking it for attention. I could just see the hyperactive juices starting to filter into his veins.

Aw, come on Gray, leave him alone, Nikki said. He's cool.

Squid grinned when he heard that, shot up onto his tippy-toes. And now, he said, pointing a finger to the sky, we resume the investigation! He learned to say that after he heard it on an episode of *Inspector Gadget*. The first time he'd repeated it Jess and Wiley and I had laughed our heads off 'cause it sounded so funny coming out of a six-year-old. Naturally Rose and Nikki thought it was hilarious, and Squid skittered off into the living room with that big grin still on his face like he knew they'd be thinking *what a funny grown-up thing for a little boy to say* and wondering what he was doing now.

I huffed out a sigh, and rolled my eyes to signal that this was really not as cute as it seemed. I knew that Squid was hiding behind the curtains, thinking we'd go chasing after him. It was his favourite hiding spot ever since I used it to scare the bejeezus out of him during a blackout, but the curtains were sheer so it was probably the worst place to hide during the day.

Okay, I whispered to Rose and Nikki, now's our chance to escape to the basement. I scooped the fries onto a plate and left them on the counter for Squid while Rose and Nikki snuck into the basement. I locked the basement door behind us and felt a rock settle in my gut.

Nikki whipped out the bottle of vodka right away, shook her head when I asked her if she wanted some cups.

Doug says vodka's the best straight out of the bottle, she said. His dad's Russian. She held the bottle out to me and I took a swig, pretended it was totally normal for me to be drinking vodka, like I'd done it a million times before. I was afraid I might choke or spit it out but it actually wasn't that bad. It reminded me of the stuff Mum used to paint on the ends of my hair to make me stop biting it. It came out of this little brown bottle and it was supposed to be painted on fingernails to stop people from chewing them 'cause the stuff tasted so bad. Didn't work for me and my hair though. I just sucked off all the paint and went on biting.

Rose took a tiny little sip and her whole face scrunched up. Nikki and I laughed at her and then we heard the doorknob jiggling at the top of the stairs.

Oh shit! Nikki whispered. She and Rose started snickering into their hands.

The doorknob jiggled again, a little harder this time. Rose and Nikki let out a few giggles and I pressed my finger to my lips, gave them a stern look. Then came a few taps and a couple of knocks.

Hello? Squid's muffled voice said. Hello? Where are you? Grace, where are you?

I took another mouthful of vodka, smiled at Rose even though I felt like puking. The liquid felt kind of good burning down my throat, like super-strength cough syrup. A scene flashed in my head of me diving off the Centre Street bridge with my arms behind my back, the fish in the river watching my face smack the water.

We sat there quietly passing the bottle around for what seemed like an hour, listening to Squid rattle the doorknob, his little voice getting louder and louder, *Grace, Grace, I'm here*

Grace, not getting the point that I was doing it on purpose because why would I ever do something like that? I was on the verge of running up the stairs and bursting through the door with a million sorrys and a great big bear hug, but then the rattling stopped. The three of us looked at each other and Nikki raised the bottle in the air.

Cheers, she said, and took a big gulp.

I sat on the floor with my back against the wall and let my shoulders go loose. I felt a flood of tingles rise into my brain like 7 Up.

Aw crap, Rose said in a whiny voice, I have to pee again. When she got up her denim skirt was shifted to the side and hiked up around her waist, but she didn't seem to notice. She headed to the bathroom with her arms swinging too much, the way I'd imagine a sloth would walk if it could stand up on its hind legs.

Okay, Nikki said, hands on hips. Enough of the bore-fest already. That TV work?

I nodded and pointed to the remote, watched Nikki fiddle with it until the screen buzzed and flashed. The sound of TV channels flipping was relaxing, like a lullaby.

You know how in cartoons, they always show a conscience as two different characters, like an angel and devil? Well I think my conscience has three sides: the good side, the bad side, and the side that tells the other two to *Shut up, I'm trying to do something here.* And that side really likes the taste of vodka. With Squid gone, I started to think this felt pretty okay. This was fun, I thought. Me sitting slumped against a wall with the bottle pressed between my knees and Nikki dancing to Mariah Carey on MuchMusic, her hips swirling just like Mariah's. My head started swaying to the music and I didn't care that I hated how Mariah Carey always sang so high to impress people, but it ended up just sounding like screaming.

Rose got back and the music seemed to give her a second wind. She took Nikki's hands and they twirled each other around like it was the most fun they'd ever had. I just sat there and watched them 'cause that's what I felt like doing. I kept tipping vodka into my mouth like a robot stuck on repeat. Then 'Baby Got Back' came on and Nikki started showing Rose how to do this sexy move where you drop down and slink back up with your butt sticking out, like a stripper, and I felt really cool 'cause my face stayed serious even though somewhere deep down I was telling myself to be grossed-out. Sitting around my house getting drunk started to seem like something I deserved — everyone else got to do it, so why couldn't I? Anyway, I was holding my liquor way better than Rose. Her face was the colour of a tomato and her head was lolling like a rag doll's.

Nikki asked me to pass the bottle again when I was about to sip, and I accidentally knocked it against my teeth and some of the liquid dribbled on my chin. That was funny, oh boy was it funny. I started cackling like Beavis, and that made Rose and Nikki go right off. So we were giggling away like fruitcakes and pretty soon we forgot what we were giggling about. That was when we heard the bang.

It sounded like a boulder had hit the floor above us. The ceiling made a cracking noise, the same noise you hear in the first split-second of a thunderclap. At first I couldn't figure out what was happening. Then I noticed that Nikki and Rose had stopped laughing and were looking straight at me.

That's the garage, I said, pointing to the ceiling.

Next thing I knew I was at the top of the stairs, rattling the doorknob like crazy 'cause I'd forgotten I'd locked it. All I could think about was Squid pinned to the concrete floor under a toppled shelf, buried in paint cans and power tools. His body limp and mottled like a leaf of rotting lettuce. It was so clear in my mind that I was sure I was already seeing it. And when I finally got the door unlocked I had never hated myself more in my entire life.

When I burst through the door to the garage I must have looked like I just came out of *Night of the Living Dead*. My mouth was a gaping half-moon and my eyes were bulging and I stumbled a bit over my feet. I had to grab the railing to stop myself from spilling down the stairs. I stood there on the landing and it took a few seconds to focus my eyes. First thing I saw was Wiley kneeling in the middle of the floor in front of his big green travel trunk. He had a pair of pliers in his hand. A can of Coors was sitting on the floor by his feet.

Oh, hi, he said.

Squid's head popped up. He'd been kneeling next to Wiley. Hi Grace, he said. We're getting the treasure.

This is my old friend Bill, you remember Bill, right? Wiley said.

No, I said. I hadn't even noticed the man who was standing in the frame of the open garage door. He had a thin mustache and he was wearing a Bart Simpson t-shirt that was ratty around the neck. He waved, took a long drink of Coors. I was nearly positive I'd never seen Bill before in my life, but my head also felt like it was it was packed with Jell-O so I couldn't be sure.

He's the bass, Wiley said. *Was* the bass, I should say. Of Handbrake, remember?

Handbrake was the name of Wiley's band that broke up ten years ago, before Mum knew him. Wiley had a picture of the five of them posing with their instruments, and they all had the same long feathery hair that had been teased and poofed like Farrah Fawcett's.

I rock with Bossa Nova now, Bill said.

Things had started to sink in by this point — Squid wasn't

dead and nothing bad had happened. And for some reason that made me flippin' angry.

What the HELL are you doing? I yelled. My eyes were burning a hole into the trunk, the stupid green trunk that had sat at the foot of Mum and Wiley's bed draped in blankets and dirty clothes ever since I could remember. Wiley had said the locks were busted and he couldn't get it open, but he refused to give the thing away 'cause he said he couldn't remember what was in it. It could be important. He'd thrown out his back trying to lug it up the stairs when he moved in. He'd obviously recruited Bill as reinforcement this time, although Bill's flabby arms looked pretty useless.

Whoa-ho-ho! Wiley said. Chill! He'd never used the word 'chill' before. It sounded all stiff, like he was putting on an accent. He kind of laughed and I could tell he was embarrassed. Bill perked his eyebrows, chuckled as if to say, Dude, I'm glad I'm not you. He was way too old to be acting like that.

We're just trying to crack it open, Squid said. He slid his little fingers along the trunk's seam, pulled at one of the locked clasps. They tried to throw it but it's still locked up, he said.

Wiley picked at the other clasp with the pliers but they just jogged and snapped. Hm, Wiley said. Bill says he remembers there being some old LPs inside. Could be worth something.

So you tossed the trunk off the stairs? I shouted. I was practically frothing.

We tried everything, Wiley said. Anyway, whaddyou care? Don't you have friends over?

I'd forgotten about Nikki and Rose. I'd forgotten about being drunk. Wiley was giving me a queer look and I suddenly knew what he was thinking. I was out of there in a shot, and on my way back down to the basement I could hear Wiley and Bill laughing like two kids who'd just egged somebody's house.

I went down the stairs slowly, partly 'cause I felt like my top half was going to tip right over like one of those drinking bird toys, and partly 'cause I was trying to think of a way to get Nikki and Rose to go home.

They heard me coming and Rose yelled, What happened? I could tell by the worried sound of her voice that they'd heard the shouting through the ceiling. Rose came to the foot of the stairs and she had the bottle of vodka in her hand. It was already half empty.

I got in trouble, I said. My stepdad's home.

Oh shit, Nikki said.

You guys gotta leave, I said. He promised he wouldn't tell anyone if you guys left.

Nikki already had the cap in her hand and grabbed the bottle from Rose. She stuffed the vodka back into her backpack without saying anything.

Should we go out the patio door? Rose whispered on the way up the stairs.

Yeah, I said. Hurry, he's in the garage right now.

They waved goodbye at the screen door, Rose's eyes drooping like *You poor thing* and Nikki's going side to side like a metronome. I mouthed Bye and tried to look worried. Rose and Nikki crept through the backyard like a couple of stray cats.

Once they'd left I didn't feel all that woozy anymore but I got an Alka-Seltzer from Mum's medicine cabinet anyway. I didn't know what it was supposed to do but I'd seen people in movies dropping an Alka-Seltzer into a glass of water after they got drunk and did dumb things. The taste was like wet chalk.

In my room I had a whale calendar, and I sat there for a really long time staring at it and sipping my chalky drink. The picture for May was of a sperm whale underwater, and the way the sun was shining through the water made a tortoise-shell pattern in light blue lines all over the whale's body. My room was beside the garage and I could hear Wiley and Bill's muffled voices through the wall, but I couldn't understand what they were saying. They must have been whispering 'cause at one point I heard Squid's voice, *But I don't gotta go to school tomorrow!* Every so often the hiss-crack of beer cans being opened interrupted their whispers.

I figured out while I was sitting there that if I stared at the whale hard enough, I started to forget that the pattern wasn't really part of the whale's skin. It started to look like the whale was made of paper that had been scrunched up really tight and then smoothed back out again.

I thought about how sperm whales are the largest toothed mammals on the planet. One tooth can be as big as your forearm. They're pointy too, which I didn't expect. If you were looking at one and didn't know it was a tooth, you would probably mistake it for a bull's horn. But the weird thing is that no one really knows why sperm whales even have teeth. In fact, there are lots of perfectly healthy sperm whales that don't have any teeth. They don't need them for catching or eating their prey 'cause they just chase it down and swallow it whole. Some scientists think that maybe the teeth are just for showing off, proving to the other whales who's boss. Back when people used to hunt sperm whales, they kept the teeth as trophies and carved figurines out of them.

Wouldn't it be ridiculous, I thought, if there were little animals that collected human teeth and showed them off to their friends, *look how big?* It would never happen. I ran my tongue over my wisdom teeth at the back of my jaw. The dentist said I was lucky 'cause I only had three of them and they all grew in straight. That meant I didn't have to get them pulled and miss a week of school and walk around with chipmunk cheeks like other people my age. But I remember feeling disappointed, like I wasn't lucky at all. It was just another stupid thing that felt like missing out.

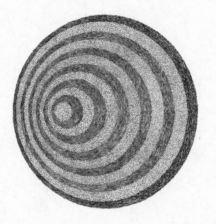

X

BELINDA HAD BEEN CALLING twice a day since she left, hoping
Jessica would pick up. She was the only one Belinda could only
rely on to carry on a conversation and update her on the true
state of things around the house. Wiley was too melodramatic,
Grace too withdrawn. They both made her worry.

Grace is being such a brat, Jessica told her the day before.
She skipped school on Thursday.

What? Belinda sighed, although she wasn't too concerned.
There were worse things girls Grace's age could be doing to rebel.

Yeah, Jessica continued, she just left before fifth period and
went to Squid's school. All his teachers were like, Who is *that*
person? She looked like a total creep.

She told you this?

Yeah, I think she thought it was funny or something.

What was she doing at Sebastian's school? Belinda asked.

He had that assembly, remember? Jessica spoke as if it
were a crime that Belinda forgot about the assembly. Anyway,
she said, I think it was just an excuse to get out of Math, to be
honest.

Well, I wouldn't worry too much about it, Belinda said. I'm sure the teachers will deal with it.

So you're not even gonna talk to her?

Not about missing school. I'll talk to her about how she's doing, though.

She's at Rose's house right now, Jessica said. And besides, you know she won't tell you that. She never says anything about her life.

All right then, Belinda said, how do *you* think she's doing? How are *you* doing?

Fine, I guess, Jessica said grudgingly. I've been doing practically everything around here. Wiley just holes himself up in the garage all day eating junk food. He was in there all morning. We had to take Squid along with us for dim sum.

Well, take a break tonight, Belinda said. Tell Grace she has to do her fair share of looking after Sebastian. And let me talk to Wiley.

I'm on my way out, Wiley said without a greeting. Got errands to run.

Why don't you take Sebastian with you, then? Belinda replied icily. You could spend some time with your son?

I already helped him clean the terrarium, he said. And Jess is taking him to the park anyway. She promised him. I've got important things to do. Alone. This house is driving me insane — you should see the mess.

I'm not coming home early.

Are you coming home at all?

Listen, she said, I don't want to get into this right now. I've got to get some sleep. I'll call you tomorrow. Please help the girls.

A hard click and Belinda knew Wiley had hung up. She was relieved rather than angry. She'd initially thought that frequent phone calls would make her more anxious, but they seemed instead to lessen the weight of her guilt. Life was going on without her. If Grace missing school for one afternoon was the biggest disaster they'd encountered thus far, they were coping just fine. The world she'd stepped into upon arriving in England was focused on issues far more consequential than the trifles of domestic life. It occurred to Belinda that the trip had already widened her scope for wisdom; she was gaining a panoramic perspective on the world.

All journeys of great discovery had their low points, and one of hers had occurred just hours before. After spending the day with Pierre and hordes of tourists at Stonehenge, she'd met with Dr. Longfellow for a late dinner and declared that she would buy a plane ticket back to Canada that evening if he didn't want her there. Dr. Longfellow hadn't seemed surprised. He calmly explained to her how he assumed she wanted to start off with a few low-key activities, to get her bearings. He apologised for the misunderstanding and Belinda felt her whole body exhale in gratitude.

I think I was over-excited, Belinda admitted. Perhaps I pushed it a bit too far. It almost feels like culture shock, being here again.

Of course, Dr. Longfellow said, I feel it every time I start working in the field after a long break. It's important not to expect too much of yourself right off. He cut his chicken meticulously, gently mashing each small piece before spearing it with his fork. Watching him eat put her at ease; if this was the way he ate, he probably approached his work in a careful and calculating way as well. Belinda decided during their meal that he had definitely been out of sorts for their first meeting. It hadn't been personal, she reassured herself. And after they had finished eating, Dr. Longfellow told her to be packed up and ready to leave Salisbury early the next morning. A new fractal formation had appeared at Windmill Hill in East Sussex.

I've heard it's a gigantic formation, Dr. Longfellow said, his eyes gleaming. And it happens to lie on the same northerly magnetic bearing as Stonehenge.

Belinda felt a shiver run through her. Was it possible that the formation had appeared at the very moment she was at Stonehenge? And if it had, did it mean something? Dr. Longfellow had evidently been contemplating the same possibility.

Perhaps we should be calling you our lucky charm, he said with a smile.

11 Mothers and Fathers

I USED TO HAVE a lot of bad dreams — ones about killers coming through my window in the dead of night to stab me to death. I could feel the knife slicing through my belly button, my intestines squirting. I would wake up in a cold sweat just like they do in movies, and the whole house would be dead silent. I'd always wake up just before the moment I was going to die, so the silence really did feel like death. For a while I'd lie there, listening to my drumming heartbeat and fanning my sweaty chest with my shirt. Eventually I'd calm myself down enough to go to Mum's room and tell her I'd had a nightmare, and she'd take me back to my room and read me a story to make me forget about it.

But one time, instead of reading to me from one of my books, Mum told me her own story. It was about a little girl who found an abandoned kitten in an old shed. She loved the kitten oh so dearly, and every night she'd give the kitten a saucer of milk to drink. Her parents were so poor that they could only afford to give the girl one glass of milk a day, but she preferred to give it to the kitten and go without. What she didn't know was that milk is actually bad for kittens when it's not from their mothers. So the kitten got really sick and died. The little girl wouldn't tell anybody about the kitten dying because she felt like it was her fault, she'd been a bad Mum. So she made a bed for the body using a tin tea box, and to make it more comfy and cozy she lined the box with goose feathers plucked from her pillow. She made it look like the kitten was curled up and sleeping.

Nobody ever found out about the kitten dying. The little girl kept the box under her bed until the kitten's belly started to cave in and its fur looked stiff and matted, and her Mum kept asking what on earth is that smell in here? Her Mum had forgotten that she had the kitten. No one else had remembered this friend she had loved so much. It had been too small a thing to notice.

I know, it's not the kind of story that you'd think would make a kid feel better after a nightmare. But for some reason, it made me feel good and safe. It made me feel like dying was just something that happened to everyone and everything. You can't control it, so why bother worrying?

Of course I begged and begged Mum for a kitten for weeks after, told her I would make sure it didn't tear up the carpet or pee in the house plants, I'd watch it every minute and clean its litter box every day. Absolutely not, was all she said. When I told her she needed to give me one good reason she said, I hate cats.

I gave Da the same spiel and he gave in without a fight when I told him Mum had said No, flat-out. Da named the cat Sally. She was all black with one white paw, and Jess and I helped him pick her out from the SPCA. It was just after we moved into the townhouse with Mum, and at that time Da was making sure he saw us every single weekend. It got really boring 'cause there was never anything to do at Da's house, and it wasn't like our home anymore so it felt weird just doing nothing. The place was freezing all the time, and Da hadn't bothered to buy any more furniture or decorations to replace the stuff that Mum had taken. Too expensive, he'd said. Does she know how much they charge for curtains these days?

You could still see the indents in the carpet where the armchairs had stood, and there was a perfect rectangle on the dining room wall that was a shade darker than the rest because Mum's Thomas Kinkade print had hung there for so long. I never wanted to take off my socks when I was there even though I used to go around barefoot all the time when I lived there. I feel bad about it now 'cause it was obvious that Da noticed. He'd stock his kitchen with things that Mum would never buy like liquorice allsorts and mangoes and canned spaghetti. But he never seemed to get that neither of us really liked any of those things anyway. Whenever we asked when he was going to drive us home, he'd duck into the kitchen and come out with a treat, *Look what I've got!* We pretended to be excited, rubbing our tummies and licking our lips. It didn't feel like there was any other option.

When we went to visit Da the weekend after we brought Sally home, it looked like he hadn't cleaned her litter box even once. She had started to poop on the concrete floor in the basement instead. Da said he guessed we were going to have to come over more often to look after our cat. He only kept her for a couple more weeks after that. He told us he had to give her away to a woman he knew at work because he couldn't even watch TV anymore — the cat had started to climb up on his lap and dig its claws into his thighs every time he sat on the couch. We saw it happen the first time and it was hilarious to watch, Da's feet up on the coffee table and Sally jumping up and walking across his legs like a bridge, Da's whole body frozen stiff 'cause he was too afraid to touch her or even shoo her away. Sally's claws digdigdigging into his jeans and Da yelling at us, Get it — aw! *Shit* — get the cat OFF!

After he gave Sally away, Mum called him up and told him he couldn't just get rid of our pets without asking us. Jess had come home crying and saying she never wanted to see Da again. Da told Mum he thought we wouldn't notice Sally was gone since we were barely ever there, and anyway, she was costing him too much money on top of his child support payments. Mum called him a selfish miser.

To smooth over the Sally fiasco, Da got into renting James Bond videos and enticing us over with movie nights. We watched the whole series from Sean Connery to Timothy Dalton, Da's favourite. We always got to watch them on the TV in Da's bedroom. For some reason it was more fun to lie in bed with Da while we watched movies and ate popcorn than to do it on the couch in the living room. He'd spread his arms out so we could use them as pillows, me on one side and Jess on the other, and by the time the movie was halfway through we'd both be asleep. But after we got through *Licence to Kill* and there weren't any more Bond movies, it wasn't fun anymore. Da tried to get us to lie in his bed with him on the nights we were sleeping over, but we told him we couldn't fall asleep, it was more comfy to sleep in our own rooms.

When we got back to Mum's, Jess would tell her everything that Da had said and done like she'd been working undercover.

And then, she'd said, he wanted us to sleep in his bed with him a*gain*. Does he think we're like, five?

He needs a girlfriend, Mum said, as if having a girlfriend would solve all Da's problems. As if having a boyfriend or a girlfriend ever made anybody feel less lonely.

He still does that thing you hate, Jess went on. The thing with his belt. Da had this ritual every day after work when he was changing out of his dress pants. He'd stand in front of the closet dangling his belt by the tail end, and he'd try to jerk the buckle so that it would jump up, loop around, and tie the belt into a knot. Sometimes he'd stand there forever, just jerking the belt over and over, *jing-jing, jing-jing*, watching the buckle flail in the air and then drop back down. It drove Mum totally batty to watch him concentrating so hard on looping a strip of leather into a knot while she waited to hear about his day at work. She asked him if he expected a goddamn fireworks display on the day he finally did it.

What's really funny is, I think Da and Wiley are pretty similar in a lot of ways. Seems like neither of them ever wanted Mum to be a wife. When Mum and Da were married, Mum would pay the bills at the bank, wash the laundry, schedule events on the fridge calendar, and make sure all of us were fed three times a day plus afternoon snack, tucked in at night and kissed sweet dreams. Of course, that's the only way that Mum would have it. It was different for a short time when Wiley first moved in, but before you could say *abracadabra* Mum was paying Wiley's bills, washing his laundry, scheduling his piano lessons, and feeding him his three meals, all four food groups. Switcheroo, just like that.

But I'll be the first to admit that Mum has always done way more than her fair share of the responsible adult stuff. When New Wiley showed up on the scene, I started helping out a lot more. There was one day I was vacuuming the whole house and I thought Mum would be so happy when she came home to see a clean floor. I even tried to scrub out some of the stains in the carpet that always made her sigh when the afternoon sun lit them up. When I heard the garage door opening I moved to a spot where I could be seen from the back door. I wanted Mum to walk in and see me scrubbing away. I wanted to see the big smile spread across her face. But when the door opened it was Wiley. He walked in with his shoes on.

Hey! I yelled. I'm cleaning the floor here?

He stopped and quickly heeled off his shoes, leaving them in a jumble in the middle of the hall. Then he brushed past me without saying a word. He looked like he was rushing to get something.

Where've you been? I called after him. Weren't you s'posed to have students coming today?

Nope, he called back as he raced up the stairs. Got some important business to attend to!

I knew right away that Mum wasn't going to be happy about whatever he was doing. And right on cue she walked in the back door.

Hi, she said. I thought I saw Wiley driving up . . . Then she smiled. You're cleaning? she said. Isn't that a nice surprise. She looked down at Wiley's shoes. I could tell she was trying to hold back a grimace.

Wiley came pounding down the stairs, tucking his wallet in his back pocket. He beamed when he saw Mum.

I did it! he said. I finally bit the bullet and did it!

Did what? Mum said, looking at him like he was a rattle-snake ready to attack.

Bought a new synth! Wiley said, throwing his fists up in the air as if he'd just conquered the world.

What, Mum said. Her voice was dark and deep. You bought what?

I was still kneeling on the floor, watching Mum's face go pink. I didn't dare move.

Now I know I already have one, Wiley explained, but the technology's come a long way in the last three years. If me and the guys are gonna get our band up off the ground, we need state-of the-art.

Are you joking? Mum said. You can't be serious. Don't those things cost thousands of dollars? Her voice quivered.

It's okay, Wiley said. Think of it as an investment. We'll get it all back once the band makes it big.

Mum asked me to leave the room then. She asked me to go out to the backyard and pick the dead heads off the petunias. I left the rag I was using and the carpet cleaner sitting on the floor where they were and went straight out the door.

Mum had spent a lot of time planting the garden that year, and I hadn't really noticed how lush it was and how much work it must have been until that day. It was the middle of the summer and all the flowers were in bloom, a quilt of pinks and purples and greens and yellows. There were a lot of shriveled petunia heads to pluck. I started picking at one end of the garden, gathering them in my palm, and every so often I'd catch a snippet of Mum and Wiley's fight. I heard Mum saying, What do you expect me to do? Wiley yelled back, Support me! Believe in me!

I didn't blame Mum for not believing in him. I wouldn't either. And that got me thinking about how much Mum had resting on her shoulders. When things went wrong in our family, it was always Mum who fixed them. I remember wondering, as I sat on the porch steps and arranged my dead head collection into a neat little pile, how long it would be before Mum got tired of being a mother to everyone.

XI

THE MARRIAGE COUNSELLOR HAD asked Belinda about patterns.
Why do you think you follow these patterns? she had asked,
sliding a pen out from the coil of her notebook. She was a
petite woman who wore her hair the exact same way every
time Belinda saw her: parted down the middle, combed and
smoothed immaculately with the stiff, upturned ends hovering
just above her shoulders. She insisted that Wiley and Belinda
call her Norma. Belinda found this odd; if she were a doctor,
she'd want her patients to call her 'Doctor.' Dr. Spector sounded
quite distinguished, she thought.

I'm sorry? Belinda said. What patterns?

Norma's eyebrows lifted for a brief moment. Well, she said,
you had mentioned before that you've experienced the same
feelings with different people in your life. Suffocation, feeling
burdened with responsibility . . .

Yes, Belinda agreed. She could see what Norma was driving
at, but she was determined not to give in.

Do you think it's a coincidence that you keep feeling this way
with different people? Your mother, Dazhong, Wiley?

I — I don't know, Belinda replied, with a firm YES resounding in her mind. Belinda had thought Norma was a good counsellor; in their joint session the week before, she'd coerced Wiley to admit his unhealthy dependency on Belinda. Leeching, Belinda called it, but Norma had deemed that term insensitive. Fair enough. But this sudden attempt to expose Belinda's faults now that she'd gained her trust seemed unfair. Predatory.

I don't see, Belinda said, how you can compare my mother to my husbands. And anyway, since when is this about me?

Norma slid her pen back into the notebook. Your marriage isn't about you? she asked plainly.

That was the last time Belinda visited Norma's office. She had no use for Norma's cunning speculations, her cultivated skill for taking Belinda's words and turning them against her. True, she had used the word suffocation to describe feelings she'd experienced with her mother, her husbands, and her children, but it was only because her vulnerability and apprehension about expressing her feelings to a stranger barred access to a more descriptive vocabulary. It was her mother's relentless decorum and her false, callous demeanour that Belinda had called suffocating, but afterwards she had thought that suffocating wasn't the right word. Stifling seemed more fitting. At any rate, she had resolved her issues with her mother long ago. Wiley was the one who needed diagnosing.

But she had nonetheless considered Norma's suggestion, reasoning that patterns ought to be something she'd be drawn to. In cereology, patterns were prized like diamonds. The more precise, complete, and calculated the pattern, the more valuable the crop circle. Anomalies and inconsistencies were indications of fraud. But in terms of social behaviour, it was the formulaic aspect of patterns that bothered her; the notion of being bound to a pre-fabricated design seemed dooming. She tried to imagine herself as a pattern, wide and sprawling, made up of thin, needled lines. Hers would be a guilloche pattern like the ones printed on cheques and bank-notes: a swirling mass of ribboned lines threading over and under each other in endless arcs and swoops. The pattern appeared smooth and uniform on first glance, but when examined closely, it revealed many layers of lines turning in unpredictable directions. It occurred to Belinda that it was natural to want to resist seeing herself as symmetrical and invariable. The flawless uniformity of crop circles was proof of their unearthliness. They were too perfect for humans to conjure. To prescribe a pattern for herself was, in a sense, dehumanizing.

But what would she feel when she stood inside a crop circle and became part of the pattern? During the drive to Sussex, she considered the possibilities. Probably awe. She hoped euphoria, clarity, a sense of harmony with the land, as the eyewitness accounts had led her to expect. Perhaps she would feel nothing, but this was unlikely. Belinda knew the mind had the power to translate faith into feeling. Just moments earlier she'd been transfixed by a dime of light whizzing across the interior of the van, until she realized it was only the reflection of her watch face. She'd wanted it to be a sign.

Dr. Longfellow had rented a van with enough space for eight people, although the team was only five, including Belinda. She had the middle bench to herself. Two men named Rich and Sampson sat in the back, Dr. Longfellow in the passenger seat, and Monika Treadstone at the wheel. Monika had the long black hair that Belinda had imagined, except streaked with silver filaments and pulled back into a tight bun. She wore a dark blue sweatshirt that said EPCOT in white letters. She was a fairly large woman — larger than Belinda, and giant compared to Dr. Longfellow's slight frame — though she wasn't fat. She had scowled at the sight of Belinda's paisley skirt.

Rich and Sampson were both American, one from Detroit and the other from somewhere in Florida, but Belinda couldn't remember which man was from where. They told Belinda they'd visited hundreds of crop circles over the last six years. She had taken out her books at the beginning of the trip and laid them on the seat beside her, and the men had shown little interest. Belinda could feel her limbs vibrating with pent-up energy, as though her seat belt were the only thing keeping her from bursting out of the vehicle and coasting across the vacant fields like vast green roller-skating rinks.

Sampson and Rich talked amongst themselves, flipping through the curled pages of their tattered notebooks and pointing figures out to each other. In the front of the van, Dr. Longfellow read the paper, the broad grey sheets enclosing him in his own paper room, and Monika focused on the road ahead, her small brown eyes darting to the rear-view mirror every now and then to check the back window, but never the passengers. Belinda considered how like a family road trip it was — the bored and dutiful parents taking their three children on a day trip, and the children boxed into the vehicle's back seat, anticipation seeping out the cracks around the windows. Belinda had never sat in the back seat on a road trip; her mother had never driven her beyond the town limits, and every road trip she'd taken with her own children followed a strict itinerary which she had designed herself. She'd always sat in the front passenger seat, playing the responsible role of navigator, snack-distributor, and spill-mitigator. And there had always been a clear direction to take towards a definitive end, no surprises. To be chauffeured about England without knowing exactly where she was felt luxurious and self-serving, like taking a midday bubble bath with unsparing dollops of expensive oils and salts.

And yet, seeing herself in this situation made her feel vital.

She was on a scientific expedition, she told herself. She was a member of a research team, a group of brilliant scientists searching for the centre of an imperative mystery. It was up to her in the next few days to become a valuable and respectable member of the team. Belinda listened to Rich and Sampson's conversation, nodding along and allowing their terminology to fall about her like snow as they spoke of Milk Hill, magnetism levels as high as 4.36, and centrifugal deposits.

In the soil? Belinda cut in, and the two men stared at her and smiled.

He's a soil man, Rich replied, pitching his head at Sampson, the one with the handlebar moustache.

Sampson grinned. Soil is the secret, he said proudly, and Belinda could tell this was something of a mantra that the team joked about. It takes a keen eye, he continued. You have to know what you're looking for. We've been finding these little balls, see. Little metal balls scattered on the surface of the soil.

What are they? Belinda asked, her eyes growing wide.

Iron, mostly, Sampson said. But they're these little balls, see, and that's the important bit. Sampson cupped his palm and pinched at the air inside with a thumb and forefinger to illustrate the size of the balls. That means, he said, that they were once *molten*. So we find these once-molten balls of iron inside the crop circle, and what do you think that means?

They must have melted! Belinda shouted, nearly springing out of her seat. Rich began to chuckle and she blushed, touching two fingers to her open mouth. I mean, she said, it sounds like something must have melted them, some kind of force. Something hot enough to melt metal in the soil. That would be my guess.

I like her already, Sampson said to Rich. His smug grin displayed large square teeth like Chiclets.

You said something about centrifugal dispersion, Belinda said. Does that mean the balls are dispersed in some sort of pattern?

Uh oh! Rich cried, clapping a hand to his knee. Marshall, he called up to the front of the van, Sampson's doing missionary work back here! He's got his first follower!

Dr. Longfellow glanced back and shook his head like a disapproving father, then re-settled himself into his reading.

As a matter of fact, Sampson said loudly to drown Rich's chuckling, I would argue that the concentration of the balls increases as you get closer to the formation's perimeter. Like an explosion, from the centre out. Sampson's hands mimed an expanding mushroom cloud.

Is he talking about his balls again? Monika called out. She eyed the three passengers in her rear-view mirror, a sly smile stretching across her face.

What else? Rich replied.

Let her make up her own mind, Sam, Monika said, still smiling.

Oh no, Belinda said, I think it's fascinating. She was quite certain that Monika was joking, but the team's constant teasing of Sampson seemed cruel. Monika said nothing in reply, and her smile stayed frozen in place as she turned her eyes back to the road.

I'm a mathematics nut myself, Rich piped up. Never did too good in grade school but now I got calculations coming out the wazoo. He passed his notebook to Belinda, the pages spread open. The paper was chicken-scratched with numbers and small sketches of circular formations dissected like pies.

Show her your other one, Sampson said, elbowing Rich in the side.

Sure, Rich said, I don't mind sharing. He reached into the backpack tucked under the seat in from of him and pulled out another, smaller notebook which he tossed on top of Belinda's books. She flipped through dozens of pencil drawings of spiral galaxies, so loose and large that they fell off the pages like the clumsy scribblings of a small child.

Beautiful, Belinda said. Did you do these?

They come to me when I'm inside, Rich replied.

Belinda had begun telling them about her children then, which she hadn't wanted to do. She didn't want to come off as a disenchanted mother, trying to escape the sad reality that her children were her world. Belinda's sense of adventure was informed and legitimate, not escapist. But she had mentioned Sebastian's interest in crop circles, how he loved to draw circles over and over again and never seemed to bore himself, and then it had seemed unavoidable to talk about Jessica and Grace as well. She resisted the urge to pull photographs out of her purse, but Sampson and Rich still seemed to receive her talk of her children as motherly yearning.

Ah yes, it's hard being away from the little rascals, isn't it? Rich said. Glad I don't have any to worry about.

I've got a daughter, Sampson said. Nine years old. She's always expecting presents when I come home after a couple of months of fieldwork. And then there's the wife — oh, boy. You could come home with the Holy Grail and it wouldn't be enough! Sampson palmed his forehead in mock exasperation.

You can consider that a warning, Rich said, and Sampson chuckled in agreement. For a brief instant, Belinda contemplated telling Rich and Sampson that she wasn't sure she *would* be going home. The words almost slipped out of her mouth before she decided she didn't know them well enough yet. She could imagine the judgmental grimaces that might distort their jovial expressions. For all their experience as researchers, it was clear that they considered crop circles a part-time occupation. Going home at the end of the season was never in doubt.

Belinda had barely spoken to Monika past initial intro-
ductions, but she felt certain that Monika did not have
children. Her commanding presence put Belinda in mind of
a school principal. Belinda always saw principals as people
with too much good sense to burden the world with children
of their own; instead, they made it their duty to manage
those of others. But it was mainly the way Monika was able
to joke with the men in that coarse, nonchalant way that
gestured her freedom from the grave and wary responsibility
of motherhood.

Monika and Dr. Longfellow had virtually ignored each
other for the entire trip, and Belinda wondered if they'd once
been lovers and were forced for the sake of their joint research
to continue working together despite awkward personal
tensions. She had a difficult time imagining Dr. Longfellow's
spindly arms around Monika's wide and solid girth, but the
thought of their ungainly pairing gave her comfort. Belinda
was glad that Monika had turned out to be much different —
less attractive and graceful — than she had expected. Rather
than a shiny charm for Dr. Longfellow to wear, Monika was
human and imperfect, with untamable grey hairs and a large,
kidney-shaped mole next to her left eye. She wore souvenir
sweatshirts and scowled at other women. She was more interesting when Belinda did not have to envy her.

12 Foreigners

ROSE HAS THIS PEN PAL named Jesus. He lives in Paraguay. She's been writing to him since grade five, when everyone in her class got assigned to a pen pal as a language arts project. I think the only reason she still writes to him is 'cause she gets to say: I correspond with Jesus.

Isn't that sort of sacrilegious? I asked her. Like, wouldn't Catholic people find that offensive?

Whatever, she said. It's just a joke.

But I know it wouldn't be funny to Rose's parents, considering Rose isn't even allowed to say God when she's not praying. Whenever I say Oh my God Rose corrects me, *Don't you mean oh my gosh?* I don't think she actually cares; it's more like a habit. I accidentally said Oh my God once at the dinner table with her family, and I saw Rose's eyes look straight at her dad like he was a jack-in-the-box ready to pop. Nobody said anything, but Rose's mom looked down at her plate and her eyes went wide for a second. I could tell she was thinking that I was going to end up in hell. Rose's mom is the only person I know who says Oh for Pete's sake whenever something surprising happens. She even yelled it out one time when she opened the fridge and an open can of tomato juice fell out and spilled all over the floor, and then she laughed and shook her head while she stared at the puddle making its way across the tiles. Mum would've screamed Shit, shit, shit, ripped off about ten sheets of paper towel and thrown them on the floor like her whole day was ruined.

The funny thing is, Rose's parents actually know all about her pen pal. They see the letters come in the mail. Her mom pronounces Jesus's name Hay-zoos. You got another letter from Hay-zoos, she told Rose one day when I was over at their house. I must have looked confused 'cause then her mom turned to me and said, That's how the Latinos pronounce it. Rose's dad peeked over her shoulder to look at the stamp from Paraguay and said Ooo, that's a keeper. Rose just rolled her eyes and pressed the envelope to her chest. She won't open the letters until she's alone in her room, and sometimes she won't even tell me what they say. It's private, thank you very much, she says.

I'm pretty sure that Rose's parents don't know she sends Jesus pictures of herself with every letter. She once bought a disposable camera and made me take a whole roll of them. Some full-body shots in different poses, with her wearing a spaghetti-strap tank-top that shows the tops of her boobs. She also got me to do a bunch of shots zoomed right in on her face with black eyeliner and mascara and pink lipstick all over it. One time, she held the camera out in front of her and made a kissy face. She showed me the letter she got back after she sent it and Jesus had gone on for a whole paragraph about how hot she was, and how he wished he could caress her smooth skin and look into her beautiful eyes and all kinds of sleazebag crap like that.

Barf, I said when I read it. I laughed through the whole thing and Rose said I was just jealous, which was probably the dumbest thing I'd ever heard. Rose is the one who gets jealous about everything. When I won the Social award in grade nine, she avoided me for a week. I didn't even care about the award, it was just a stupid plaque with my name on a rectangular piece that had been glued on. They put my Chinese middle name on it without even asking, so it wasn't like I was going to display it for everyone to see. I told her she could have it and peel off the name part if that would make her happy and she said it wouldn't. Go figure.

The other thing Rose gets mad about is copying. She always thinks I'm copying her when I'm just minding my own business. One time, she got mad 'cause I chose the same gummy candies as her at the 7-Eleven. She'd taken three marshmallow frogs, six sour soothers and ten jumbo coke bottles, and I took the same. It just seemed like good proportions.

What are you doing? she asked. She watched me twirl the plastic baggie and tie it in a knot. She was looking at me like I had a puppy in a chokehold.

Buying gummies, I said.

I thought you liked Swedish berries, she said. She stood there scowling at me until I untied my baggie and threw a few Swedish berries inside. I only did it because I knew that if I didn't, she'd say she felt like going home when we left the store. Sometimes Rose can be such a spoiled brat.

So when I told her I had my own my pen pal, I wasn't really surprised that she got all defensive.

What's *your* pen pal's name? Rose asked.

Prim, I said.

Prim? What kind of a name is that?

It's an English name. She's from England.

You can't have a pen pal from England, Rose said. They're supposed to be from a third-world country.

I thought they just had to be a stranger you write letters to, I said.

No, Rose said. That's not a pen pal. That's just a stranger you write letters to. And anyway, you're not supposed to just send random people letters.

Well I guess she's technically not a stranger, I said, biting my hair. We're sort of related.

You're related? You're writing to someone in your family? Rose sighed and blew her bangs out of her eyes like *whatever are we going to do with you.* Hel-lo, she said, the point of a pen pal is to get to know someone new?

I've never seen her before in my life, I said. She doesn't even send me pictures of herself.

So what? Rose said. Her face was getting red. It still doesn't count. You're not even doing it for school.

Neither are you, I said.

Well, not any*more*, Rose said, but Jesus and I aren't strangers anymore either. We're close. Then Rose started telling me all about how people in Paraguay can drop out of high school before they graduate and no one cares because most people don't have much education anyway. Jesus told her he was going to get a job and save up to come to Canada. He would live at her house for a while until he got a job, and then they could move out together. She was talking so fast I didn't even get a chance to explain that I started writing my letters before I even knew she had a pen pal, and by the time she finished yakking it didn't seem important anymore.

The first few times, it felt creepy to send letters to someone I didn't know. I'd accidentally found the address in Mum's Rolodex when I was looking for her work number, so it wasn't like I was sneaking around like a stalker to find her. I even asked Mum if that was her sister's address and she said No, Prim wasn't living there anymore. I could tell she was lying. The first letter was kind of like a test, and then Prim wrote back asking all kinds of questions about how old I was and if

I had any brothers and sisters, so of course I had to write back. But I didn't really want to. I didn't know what to say. *I am 14 years old. I have one sister (16) and one brother (5).* It sounded so dumb, like something a grade two-er would write. And how was I supposed to ask her the things I wanted to know? *I was just wondering what you're like, and why your mother disowned you.* Yeah, right. It seems weird to me that people like Rose can just convince themselves that someone they've never met who lives on the other side of the equator or across an entire ocean can be their friend — even boyfriend. I mean, it's not like you can really know anything about that person. Jesus could be a total perv, for all Rose knows. And Paraguay might as well be on a different planet. Rose can't even pick it out on a map.

Sometimes I wonder if people are meant to stay where they belong. I've heard people talk about feeling culture shock when they go to a different country. It makes me think of this story I read a while ago about a bunch of foreign jellyfish — mauve stingers, in fact — freaking out and attacking a salmon farm in Ireland. Mauve stingers are pretty small jellyfish, but they travel in groups of a billion or more, tightly packed together like one huge pulsating jelly-monster. Most people don't know that a large group of jellyfish is called a bloom, which I think is perfect 'cause you can just imagine billions of them floating together in the water like the petals of a huge red flower, their tentacles waving in the ocean wind. So anyway, this bloom of mauve stingers was native to the Mediterranean, and no one really understood why it had travelled all the way up around the freezing-cold coasts of Ireland. But jellyfish aren't actually strong enough to swim against the tides, so when this bloom drifted into the salmon farm it seemed like the jellyfish were disoriented and confused. They drifted right over top of the salmon cages and just started stinging like crazy. The fish were stuck in their cages and all those jellyfish smushed together made a poisonous blanket over them so that the farmers couldn't do anything about it. The bloom was more than ten miles wide and thirty-five feet deep and it turned the sea into a red beating heart. The farmers just stood there watching while the fish got stung, and when the tide carried the bloom away there were 120,000 dead fish floating on the surface of the water. The jellyfish hadn't eaten a single one of those fat and juicy farm fish. You can tell that story to anyone who thinks animals only kill when they want food. Those jelly-fish ended up somewhere they didn't belong, and their first instinct was obviously not to be friendly with the locals. It was basically their way of showing culture shock. Really, we're not all that different. The only difference is we have more brains to stop ourselves from freaking out and doing bad things, even though our bodies may be telling us to.

I've never been outside North America, but Wiley says travelling is overrated. Maybe that's 'cause he's never been to a different continent either. Da keeps saying that he's going to take me and Jess to Malaysia someday whether we like it or not, and Jess always says NOT and then wrinkles her nose up like she can't imagine anything more revolting. She'd rather go to England, and even though I wouldn't be able to learn how to scuba dive in England, I think I'd rather go there too. Wiley says all they have there is bad weather and worse food, but I still think it would be kinda neat to see where Mum came from. I always imagine Auntie Prim as an older version of Mum and my cousin Sebastian as an older version of Squid, so I bet it would feel like stepping into the future or even some parallel universe. It makes me wonder if there's another version of me out there somewhere.

I can still remember the time when I was little and I sud-denly realized I was me, and there wasn't anyone else quite like me in the world. I was eating a Popsicle and staring up at a woolly mammoth. See, when you take the train to the zoo you get off in this long concrete tunnel that leads up to the entrance. The middle of the tunnel rises up into a skylight, with a life-size mammoth sculpture standing beneath it. The tunnel was my favourite part of the zoo, 'cause it was dark and clammy like a sewer, with only the dim rays filtering down from the skylight and a few yellow safelights along the walls. Your voice would echo all around you, even when you were just talking softly. The animal carvings on the walls made it feel like a prehistoric cave. Your footsteps would echo too, and Jess and I would always skip ahead of Mum and come running back just to hear the drumming music our feet could make. In the middle of the tunnel there's a big circle with the mammoth plonked in the centre, and a few dinosaurs and sabre-toothed tigers around the sides. You can stand right under the mammoth and the shadow of just one tusk covers your whole body, and when you're a kid you can really imagine it's a live animal towering over you. My pink Popsicle was melting and dripping on my fingers and I imagined the mammoth's mouth dripping saliva like a dog. The mouth was a bit open and painted dark grey inside.

For some reason, looking up at that mouth that was the perfect shape for my puny little head made me think about how amazing it was that I was born as me, as if I could have been any one of the millions of other people in the world, but it was some stroke of pure chance that made me *me*. It was like I imagined that people were made up of different pieces that got put together randomly, as if God or whoever was responsible had one of those machines they use for Bingo where all the balls fly around inside and a certain few get sucked up into the tube, one by one, until you have a set of lucky numbers.

Of course, Mum would say there's no such thing as luck. It's all part of the cosmic design, she says. But it seems like if she really believed that, she never would have gone to England.

If she believed that everything happens for a reason, there wouldn't be anything to run away from.

Jess told me that she didn't think Mum would have gone on her trip if she knew that Wiley was going to start acting even weirder than usual. I'd made the mistake of telling her about Wiley and the trunk the night before.

Mum wouldn't have left us with a crazy person, Jess said. She would never leave us in danger. I hadn't even said anything about danger but it was obvious that Jess was scared. Her fingernails were bitten down so far that there were dark red curves tracing the edges.

Whoa, drama queen, I said. I just thought it was weird, that's all. I don't think it's exactly normal for someone to stay up in the garage all night trying to crack open a useless old trunk.

Ya think? Jess said. It's *crazy*, that's what it is.

Relax, I said. It's not like he's gonna come after you in the night and stab you with a screwdriver.

How do you know? Jess said. You don't know that. She crossed her arms and looked me straight in the eye, the way Mum does when she's made up her mind.

Oh God, I said. I laughed at her and rolled my eyes as if what she'd said was completely ridiculous, but it was actually the only thing I could think to do to make her stop talking about it. As dramatic as it sounded, it was kinda true. The Wiley we were living with wasn't the guy who played 'Eye of the Tiger' on our piano just to hear us giggle and taught us how to tie-dye our own t-shirts. New Wiley was the kind of guy who didn't care if we ate pizza three times a day or got drunk in the house. New Wiley could spend eight hours straight in the garage drinking beer with his buddy while Squid was wailing 'cause he'd had a nightmare. He was supposed to be our stepdad, but we didn't know him at all.

XII

BELINDA NEEDED A STRATEGY for leaving. She never got anything done without a plan. If she went to the grocery store
without a list, she would go home with bagfuls of frivolous
items like jars of pickled vine leaves, raisin bread, and peanut
butter swirled with strawberry jam — foods that made her
feel hungry. She'd decided long ago that she couldn't trust her
instincts. Her instincts had kept her in her mother's house for
seventeen years. The plan got her out.

The plan to leave her mother began when Belinda refused
to grind the crabapples one autumn. It was one of her mother's
nonsensical obsessions to collect every crabapple that the
tree in their front yard put forth. It was unthinkable to let
them grow and fall to the ground, or to allow the occasional
small animal to enjoy the fruit. Every edible morsel had to
be plucked and hoarded, any worms or scars or bruises cut
out of the flesh. Vestiges of wartime mentality: to waste food
was treasonous. And so her mother would insist on grinding
the crabapples to a pulpy sauce, which could be preserved
in Mason jars and stored in the cellar. Since her mother had

arthritic wrists, it was Belinda's job to mill the apples by hand in a contraption that looked like a saucepan with a sweeping blade set on the inside and a crank handle sticking out the top. Belinda was forced to crank the handle around and around as her mother added newly manicured and peeled apples to the mix, watching the dirty yellow sauce swirling at the bottom of the grinder. The same task had once been assigned to Prim, who, as her mother insisted, did a lazy job of it.

You don't want to turn out like her, do you? her mother reminded Belinda at every opportunity. Look at her. Poor, alone, stuck with an invalid child. Likely alcohol poisoning, so I said. She drank like a fish, couldn't help herself.

She spoke about Prim as if Belinda knew her, had some magical means to know what Prim was like then, and what her life was like now. But all she knew was that whatever her mother said about Prim was not the truth. Her mother had turned her back on her own daughter, rejected her for no good reason. Sometimes it even seemed as though she was jealous of Prim's freedom.

Before you know it, her mother would continue, she'll be old and useless. No life of her own to speak of.

Belinda knew these were only stories, constructed by her mother to keep her in fear. Still, it worked. As much as she was convinced her mother was lying, she had no way of knowing if there was some small element of truth in her words. And rather than allow herself to admit that, she continued to grind the apples, shutting out her mother's mantra with her own visions of Prim.

You'll thank me, her mother had said, when you're eating a nice hot bowl of crabapple sauce on a cold winter's day. She said this every single year, and not once did they open a jar. The jars collected in a corner of the cellar, the crowded stacks of glass like the towers of a miniature city glowing vague and flaxen in the perpetual darkness.

Refusing her grinding duties was Belinda's way of taking a stand. Asserting her independence was the first stage of the plan. The next stage was to do something serious and unexpected. She smashed all the jars to pieces. She didn't do these things for her mother's sake, but rather for her own. Her mother didn't find about the smashed jars until the following autumn, after Belinda had left, when the sauce had caked and dried in crusty puddles and the shards of glass had become features of the cellar's landscape, furred with dust and dirt. Belinda thought of her plan as confidence-building. She smashed the jars to prove her capability for irresponsible destructiveness. She was proving wrong her own self-doubt.

After the jar-smashing, she'd found a job at the convenience store at the other end of town. This hadn't seemed possible while the jars were still intact, harbouring all of their preserved evidence that year after year would always bring more apples. The job — the money — fulfilled the practical part of her plan. Practicalities signalled the final stage.

With Dazhong she'd had to up the ante. When the time came to leave him she was no longer a meek teenager. She'd proven her independence by starting piano lessons — something that Dazhong didn't value and couldn't possibly share with her even if he'd wanted. Although she'd specifically chosen a male piano teacher, the attraction to Wiley was not planned. But it made her rash act of defiance a natural progression. Next, getting a job at a clothing store in the mall was easy; she carried the aplomb of an adulteress, flaunting poise and certainty like shiny gold bangles. They liked that in retail. She'd received three job offers, and Talbots offered her the highest wage. Selling clothes had seemed glamourous until it became clear that the clothes at Talbots were only considered stylish among women over the age of sixty. Things had a way of changing — or perhaps what really changed were Belinda's perceptions of things.

But with Wiley it had been different. *He* had changed, too. When he wasn't feverishly professing his love and admiration for everyone around him, he was spending entire days holed up in dingy bars contemplating the worthlessness of life. In personality, he'd become a caricature of himself, with certain traits grossly exaggerated and others diminished to feeble proportions. His disposition was either exuberant or despondent, nothing in between, and his moods seemed to last for weeks on end.

He'd been in the thick of one of his erratic, charged-up moods when Belinda made the mistake of telling him, before she made a plan, that she intended to leave. It had happened weeks before she even conceived of taking the trip to England, but she was still being punished for it. Wiley hadn't been sleeping for more than a few hours each night and his eyes had acquired the unsettling glaze that often accompanied this persona, as though he were seeing the world in some mesmerizing new dimension. And in his intensified way of jumping to overblown conclusions, he'd convinced himself that Belinda had used him as a way out of her marriage to Dazhong.

You manipulated me, he'd sneered. You wanted a way out. You even had a child you didn't want for the sake of justifying it. It's despicable, you're going to hell, you're going straight to hell. He'd screamed the words over and over until Belinda almost began to believe them.

She called it a slip-up, and it was. She was frustrated; she'd taken the wrong approach. And she'd given Wiley leverage when she asked him not to tell the children what she had said.

You're looking for absolution, he accused. I will not absolve you. You are a *bad* person. She'd been particularly stung by the weight of these insults. His accusations made her out to be thoroughly, innately *bad*. Evil.

Later that evening, after they'd been forced to smooth things over for the kids' sake, she realized that Wiley was probably right about her desire for absolution. It had been too providential for Grace to ask about purgatory at the dinner table the very same day. And Belinda had felt the need to defend herself, even when the conversation really had nothing to do with her.

Purgatory is a place of torture, Wiley told Grace. You get tortured there, for the bad things you've done. He aimed his manic stare directly at Belinda.

It's more of a state of being than a place, Belinda had said. Grace looked confused about that response. She'd been going through a spiritual phase, and Belinda knew it had to do with fitting in. She had a friend who was Catholic. The friend, Rose, looked like the kind of girl teenaged boys would find attractive. She had thin, long limbs, fair skin, and designer clothes. She wore push-up bras under low-cut tops. She played on the volleyball team and chewed bubble gum obsessively. Grace's envy of her was as palpable as an overripe cheese. Her inquiries about religion were merely attempts to unpack Rose's character in that enamoured way of jealous adolescent girls. She could not have known that Wiley was simmering on her words, and reveling in their invocation.

So . . . Grace said, it's something you just make up in your head?

You might say that, Belinda said. Catholics believe that some people have to be purified before they can go to heaven. The ones who did some bad things like everyone does, but are still good people. She could see Wiley out of the corner of her eye, mashing his baked potato with his fork as though it were a thrashing, living thing that needed to be squashed before eaten.

So they just float around in their dead bodies, like ghosts? Grace asked. Waiting until they can get into heaven?

I don't know, Belinda replied, truthfully. She could see how waiting for an absolution that might never come could be torturous.

13 Mean Streak

PEOPLE THINK I LOOK innocent 'cause I've got Da's round cheeks and Mum's big eyes. When I was little Mum cut my hair short and I looked like one of those monkey toys that crashes a pair of cymbals when you wind it up. In fact, I can still make the best monkey face you've ever seen in your life. All I gotta do is pull out my ears and puff my cheeks and voilà: it's like chimps on parade.

But I can be a real bitch when I feel like it. Up until a few years ago, I cheated at board games all the time. When we still lived with Da we had this neighbour named Chelsea who would come over to play games, and she wasn't exactly the brightest crayon in the box. Or at least I was pretty sure I was smarter than her even though she was a year older than me. We played Scrabble and I just made up words like BICZA and told her they were real, and I acted like such a smarty-pants snob that she believed me. The funny thing was that she didn't care about losing. She just kept giggling and spelling out lame words like IT and GO and saying things like I'm so bad at this game! and I'm so dumb! Yeah, you are, I would say back, acting annoyed at her for losing all the time. She went to my school and nobody really liked her, so I told people that she peed her pants all the time. It wasn't exactly a lie; she did pee her pants once when she was at my house. She'd been wearing purple leggings and there was a big eggplant splotch on her butt, but she didn't even do anything about it. She just pretended it wasn't there. The reason I know I have a mean streak is that even when I think about it now, I don't feel sorry for Chelsea. She just grosses me out.

The other mean thing I do is make fun of Jess's mole. She has this big mole on her left cheek beside her nose. It sticks out like a blob of chocolate pudding and it grows two little tiny hairs on it. I know she's really self-conscious about it 'cause she's always trying to hide it with her hand when she talks to people she doesn't know, and when she gets pictures taken she tries to turn her head to the side. A couple of years ago she asked Mum if she could get it removed, and Mum told her she'd need plastic surgery and it would probably cost hundreds of dollars. After that she started plucking out the little hairs with Mum's tweezers. It's pretty pathetic, actually. But sometimes I get in these moods where absolutely everything Jess says is obnoxious, and as she's talking to me I'm staring at the mole thinking about how ugly it is and how much I hate that mole, and meanwhile Jess has stopped talking and she's looking at me and waiting for me to say something. Sorry? I say. Your mole was staring at me.

If she cries it makes me even more pissed, 'cause then I have to deal with Mum's *do you enjoy making people miserable?* lecture. And I just have to sit there and let her lay into me 'cause I can't very well say, Yes, I actually do sort of enjoy it.

But as mean as that is, I still think the meanest thing I ever did in my life was spank Squid. Spank is the word that Mum uses, but if spanking is a little whap on the bum like the ones

Mum and Jess both gave him, then what I did was something else altogether.

He was two years old, terrible twos as they say. I used to call it tornado twos in Squid's case. Even when we put up his baby gate in the door to the kitchen so he couldn't run too far, one of us would be trailing behind him pretty much everywhere he went with a wad of paper towels and a garbage bag. I was only eleven but I felt old. When I followed him around I dragged my feet like they weighed a hundred pounds, and when I scrubbed the jam or spilled juice or soft-boiled egg off the floor I grunted and groaned like an old maid. And that was just on a regular day. That particular day he'd eaten a huge bowl of macaroni-and-cheese that had little pieces of hot dog mixed into it, and he had the orange sauce all around his mouth like someone had tried to paint a sun on his face. He saw me coming with the dishcloth and scooted off into the living room, and he ran around and around in circles trying to sing "U Can't Touch This" by MC Hammer. He was obsessed with that song at the time. Since he was only two he couldn't quite say it right. Cantukis! Cantukis! he kept yelling. I was so tired of running after him that I was just shuffling around, swatting at him like a sloth and trying to get his arm. Of course, as soon as I caught him he puked his lunch out on the carpet, pure KD orange smoothie with rubbery red floaties.

It was a Saturday, and Mum and Jess had gone out shopping for the whole day. That was back when Wiley still taught piano lessons, and since Saturday was always his busiest day he wasn't around either. I like to tell myself I was set up. It was common knowledge that anyone who was stuck in the house watching tornado Squid for more than a few hours at a time would be ready to have a conniption by the end of it. Truth is, no one else would have handled it the way I did. I know it's just an excuse.

So anyway, I looked at the puke and this big gasp came out of my mouth. Squid thought that was pretty funny. But I kept my cool, for the most part. I picked him right up, carried him to the bathroom and started filling the tub. While the water was running full-blast I yanked off his clothes so hard that I ripped one of the buttons off his overalls. You might think it was pretty harsh of me not to be worried when he just puked up his lunch, but he was still giggling away and his arms were flapping so much I could barely get his shirt off. See, Squid has always had this problem where he doesn't get it when people are mad. It's like he doesn't know the difference between kinda ticked off and ready to explode; you could be foaming at the mouth and he'd still think it was some kind of game. Besides, there I was getting him ready for a bath and he always loved baths. It was like I was rewarding him.

As soon as the tub was full I shut it off and gave him a look. A warning look. It was the look I always gave him before putting him in the bath, and both of us knew it meant *don't even think about splashing.* For a second we stared at each other and everything seemed eerily silent and intense. A drop of water dripped from the tap with an echoey *bloop,* as if it were the exclamation mark on the end of my warning.

And so I plonked him into the tub. He sat quietly while I added some soap to the water and swished it around. I thought he had calmed down by then, so I knelt down and cupped some water over his shoulders. But he'd only been waiting for the bubbles. I saw that huge cheeky smile of his and it looked even huger than usual with the orange sauce all around it.

And then he started splashing. Arms thrashing and legs kicking, water flying out of the tub and landing *splatsplatsplat* all over me and the floor. Our tub had sliding glass doors and I flung them shut. There were pools of water on the floor, soaking into my socks and the bath mat. A clenching feeling lodged itself in my belly, pulling tight like my insides were turning to rock. My jeans were sopped and my hair was dripping. And still Squid kept splashing away. Usually he would stop splashing when I closed the doors 'cause it wasn't fun for him anymore when I wasn't watching him. But that day he kept on going. He was squealing and laughing and I was screaming STOP! STOP NOW! STOP IT! at the top of my lungs. If anyone else were listening they would have thought I was being murdered the way I was screaming. But Squid's laughter was piercing, like a devilish little song that was mocking me, humiliating me. He was splashing so hard that foam and water were coming over the glass door like rain. I may have been on the outside, but I felt trapped. I was trapped in a bathysphere, far below the surface, the water rushing in through punctures, fissures in the glass. I started sobbing but it didn't make a difference. The water kept pummeling the glass doors and trickling back down into the tub. STOP IT! PLEASE! I screamed, and Squid only laughed and splashed more. I stood there holding out my hands and crying while more water came splattering down and little rivers spilled out the cracks at the bottom of the door, and all of a sudden I wished I would die. I imagined the room filling up with soapy water, my head going under and the water filling my nose and throat. Thick, lukewarm hands of water ramming fists down into my lungs. Squid's thrashing became the sound of my own arms fighting and the water pulling me down, sucking all the air out of my body. And then I saw myself floating on an ocean, so small you could mistake me for a dead fish. My skin was the grey of a dirty tin can.

At that point I wasn't even mad at Squid anymore. I was mad that he was so much stronger than me. He was two years old and I felt completely helpless.

Next thing I knew I reached in and pulled him out of the tub by his wrist. His skin was wet so he slipped a bit and one of his legs hit the edge of the tub on the way out. It made a big thunk but Squid didn't even cry. I dragged him into his bedroom and threw him on his bed, and he lay there, naked and skinny and shivering, looking at me like I was a meteor about to land right on top of him. And when I flipped him over and my hand came down on his wet bum, it sounded like a big fat encyclopedia being clapped shut. I felt him hold his breath. And then I hit him again. And again. Somehow, it didn't feel like I was hitting my brother. He was just a thing I hated, like Jess's mole. When I was done I left him lying on the bed and slammed the door. By the time I got to my room I was shaking so bad I couldn't stand. I had to sit on the edge of my bed and put my head between my knees, and my legs were bouncing up and down uncontrollably like marionettes. Squid was bawling but I didn't even hear him. All I could think about was the day in the supermarket with Mum, his evil little grin, when I was a stranger and he was not my brother. It seemed like eons had passed since then.

That was about the time that Mum and Jess got home. I heard Mum's feet racing up the stairs and Jess's going up after her, two steps at a time. What happened? Mum kept yelling. Where's Grace? Instead of feeling worried I felt relieved. Now that Mum was home I knew Squid would be safe.

But in the end it turned out that the worst part of the whole thing was the way Mum acted. She didn't ask me if I enjoyed making people miserable. She didn't yell at me. She didn't even look at me. Instead, she came into my room and told me in a very quiet voice that I wasn't allowed to look after Squid by myself anymore.

I nodded and my eyes filled up with tears. Mum turned around like she was going to leave, but then she came towards me and tried to slap me on the face. I cringed and she ended up slapping my forehead, where my hair was sticking to the sweat.

If you ever hit my child again, she said, pointing a finger at my nose. But she didn't finish. Instead, she said, That's called abuse, Grace. You are an abusive person. There was spit flying out of her mouth and it landed on my face.

The bruise on Squid's leg where he hit the tub was green and black the next day. I didn't even try to look at his bum, but Jess told me you could see the marks of my fingers. I don't know if Mum told everyone to keep it a secret, but nobody ever talked about it again or asked me about what happened. I didn't even have to say sorry to Squid. I guess it would have been stupid to say sorry. Sorry is what people say when they hurt someone's feelings or use a swear word. It doesn't really mean anything.

It's funny: ever since then I've felt like if anything really awful ever happened to Squid, it would be my fault. When Mum first told us she was going on a trip to England without us, I felt like I'd eaten a sackful of gravel. I didn't know it then, but looking back I think it was 'cause deep down I knew something bad was going to happen.

On Monday morning, almost a week after Mum had left, I woke up late for school. I'd jolted awake, the way you do when your body suddenly realizes you were supposed to be up a long time ago. My alarm clock was blinking 12:00. The sun was already pouring through the cracks in my blinds and I jumped out of bed and had my toothbrush in my mouth before I could even open my eyes.

Squi? I called out, my mouth full of toothpaste. Squi, ge uh, Squi! I bent down and spit in the sink, and when I came back up Jess was standing in the hallway looking at me. She had the bottom of her pajama shirt all balled up in her fists.

Suddenly I realized that Wiley's big green travel trunk — the one that had been sitting in the hall outside my room since he'd tried to break it open — had disappeared.

Wiley's gone, Jess said. And he took Squid with him.

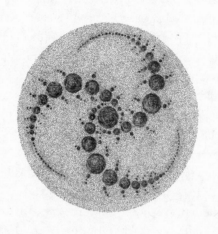

XIII

WHEN BELINDA WAS PREGNANT with Sebastian, Wiley had a pet potato. The potato had been the last one in the bag, and it had been sitting in a dark corner of the pantry for weeks because someone had shoved a new bag in front of it — one of Belinda's pet peeves. Wiley had found it one day rummaging around for snack food. The lone potato had flourished in its dark hiding place. A sheaf of long, bone-coloured arms sprouted from one end, gnarled like twigs. Wiley placed it on a saucer in a pool of tepid water and gave it a spot above the fireplace, alongside the African violet and a framed wedding photo.

By the time Belinda arrived home from work that day, Wiley had gotten Grace fascinated by the potato as well. Grace presented the saucer to her mother like a birthday cake.

We named it Squid, Grace had said. Doesn't it look like one?

Mmmhmm, Belinda agreed. She felt herself recoiling as though it were indeed a slimy, writhing sea creature. The sprouts did look like tentacles, the way they furled from the end of the potato, their curled ends reaching out as if poised to cinch unsuspecting prey. The knobs along them were bulbous and vaguely purple, reminiscent of a squid's suction cups. Just looking at the potato, monstrous with its maladroit limbs, sent shivers up the back of her neck.

Belinda had protested at first. That thing is hideous, she told them. It's going to rot. But Wiley begged and whined to keep it just a little longer, to see how long the sprouts would grow. Of course Grace had joined in, jumping up and down and pulling on Belinda's sleeves. She was eight years old at the time, and Wiley's biggest fan. Belinda found it difficult to reject anything that supported their bonding. And so the potato lived. The arms grew and grew, longer, whiter, stiffer. They dangled off the mantel, small green leaves blossoming from their knobs. The growth of Belinda's rounding belly was barely noticeable in comparison. And even though Wiley continued to ignore the other house plants, he fussed over his potato, kept it watered and noted its progress, moved it around to shadowed regions of the house if it didn't seem happy enough. Belinda reckoned it was his way of nesting. While she painted the baby's nursery and folded tiny sleepers into drawers, Wiley practiced his nurturing instinct on the potato. She joked about it, first in a lighthearted way, but later with a tinge of jealousy.

How's *your* baby doing? she'd ask him when she caught him peering at the mantel. He'd joke along, attend to the potato and stroke its sprouts, cooing *You happy there, little Squid?* For some reason, this drove her wild. As the potato grew, she found it more and more grotesque. The sight of Wiley poking the skin or fingering the stiff sprouts repulsed her. It was as though he were touching something vile and diseased, like the innards of a dead animal. She told herself it was hormones.

But when she went on maternity leave she'd had to spend full days alone with the potato, and the first three had been too much. On the fourth day she snatched it from the wet saucer and the grip of her hand squashed the supple flesh. She'd had to snap off the sprouts to fit them in the garbage. The sound was crisp, like snap peas cracking between teeth. The thought of the severed sprouts, bunched and bent into a warped loop inside the garbage bin, made Belinda shudder.

This was the first thought that came to Belinda's mind as she stood on the shallow incline at the edge of the field and gazed over the long, curving chain of circles laid in the wheat before her. A coiling arm, each circle like a razor-edged suction cup. A tentacle. Its length stretched hundreds of feet into the horizon, beyond the furthest point they could see.

Lord almighty, Rich said.

Gorgeous, just gorgeous, Sampson whispered. She's a beaut.

You're telling me, Rich replied, grinning open-mouthed like a puppet. It's a Julia, eh Marshall? Another Julia set!

It appears that way, doesn't it? Dr. Longfellow said, placing his hands on his hips. Monika stood next to him, taking pictures with a camera that sported a long, expensive-looking lens.

On first glace, he continued, it looks quite authentic. He smiled to himself and sniffed the air as though it were fresh and not muggy.

Don't get ahead of yourself, Marshall, Monika said. She lowered her camera and fixed a condescending stare on Dr. Longfellow. We haven't yet stepped ínto the bloody thing.

Hold on, there's two of 'em! Sampson said, pointing to the south. The others looked over in unison like a flock of curious seagulls. To Belinda's right, she could see the curve of another arm leading off to the south. It was an unusually clear day, and the wind pulsed across the field in bold strokes as if liberated by the cloudless sky. With the wind blowing waves over the grass surrounding the circles, Belinda could swear the arms were moving.

Three, Monika said, directing her lens to the east.

Three Julia sets! Rich cried, reeling. Belinda could hear his breathing, shallow and clipped. His eyes were wide and gleaming as he flipped to a fresh page of his journal and jotted notes.

She was familiar with the original Julia set. It was a formation that had appeared the previous summer. The aerial photo showed a snail-shell spiral drawn with a beaded string of circles, larger around the centre and progressively smaller towards the tail end. The large circles were flanked on either side by mirrored sets of smaller circles. According to reports, the formation had appeared in broad daylight, less than a mile away from Stonehenge, but no one had actually witnessed it happening. The farmer had visited the untouched field that morning, and a mere forty-five minutes later, a small plane had flown over and the crop circle was there. Cereologists had named it the Julia set for its resemblance to a fractal of the same name, discovered by a French physicist named Gaston Julia. Belinda had found his biography at the library, and learned that he had lost his nose in the Second World War. She couldn't remember anything about the fractal; it had all been mathematical jargon. She could only remember the portrait of Gaston Julia, wearing a leather strap over his unsightly missing nose.

Now, looking at the new formation from the ground, she saw the spirals as huge, snaking tentacles, detached from their mammoth body and floating at the surface of a golden sea.

Shall we take a walk? Sampson asked her, gently touching her elbow. She had been very quiet, and he probably thought she felt overwhelmed. Perhaps she did; she wasn't sure.

There's another group of people here, Sampson said. We should get going before they trample everything. Rich and Monika had begun following Dr. Longfellow towards the first circle, which appeared to be large enough for just one person to stand inside at a time. Belinda followed behind Sampson. She was the last to step foot inside the end of the tentacle.

She stood still for several moments, listening to the wind eddy in her ears. Although the wheat was only knee-height, she felt enclosed.

I am standing in a crop circle, she told herself, but didn't quite believe it. She had assumed there would be a purpose, something to do when she finally came to this point, though she couldn't think what. Dr. Longfellow had recommended she bring with her a box of plastic Ziploc bags, a measuring tape, a notebook and pencil, and a set of binoculars, and these she had put in a backpack that she shrugged off and set on the flattened stalks. She bent down and examined the swirl of wheat at the centre of the circle. The stalks appeared woven together like a bird's nest. She'd seen countless pictures in books and magazines of wheat swirls that looked identical to the one she was staring at. It was like looking at a famous painting — a Van Gogh or a Monet. A screen of surreality fogged the space between her eyes and the image. It didn't seem real.

The next circle in the chain was separated from the first by a thin veil of standing wheat, only about three or four stalks in width. Belinda stepped over them carefully. Rays of sun dappled through them as through curtains of lace. They looked too delicate to touch.

Belinda wanted to suggest to the others that they remove their shoes, but no one else seemed concerned. To her, the space was like a cathedral — foreign and holy, the depth of its meaning out of reach. The way the team advanced up the arm, traipsing with eager feet and rapturous faces, seemed disrespectful, even foolish.

Pretty amazing, isn't it? Rich called out. He'd begun loping towards her, beaming and out of breath.

Yes, it's very — neat, she said, springing to her feet. I'm amazed, seeing this in person.

You're lucky this is your first, Rich said. My first was a dud — one of the fakes. I tell ya, it was the only time I ever questioned why I was doing this. Once you see a beauty like this, you're hooked. A true-blue croppie.

Is that so? Belinda said. I guess it's hard without something to compare it to. I mean, I can't picture — I wish I could see it from above.

Yep, Rich said. You can never take it all in until you see the aerial. But Marshall and Mon do that part. Gets pricey to send people up in helicopters, right?

Oh — of course, Belinda said.

She takes great pictures though, Rich said. Several circles ahead, too far away to have heard their conversation over the wind, Monika turned her head toward them. She stood feet apart and knees rigid like a statue, and her camera hung from the strap around her neck, heavy against her chest. She stared at them, her face stern.

Rich had of course been referring to Monika's skill with the camera, but Belinda found herself imagining what she would look like on the other end of the lens. Still staring at them, Monika adjusted the fanny pack belted to her waist and her bosom puffed like a peacock displaying its feathers. Her camera pointed at the skyline. Belinda thought of the photos of Queen Victoria in middle age, her square face sagging and manly, her chest a corseted barricade. Not in the least bit beautiful, and yet her presence as demanding as a mountain. The circle in which Monika was standing seemed so small and inconsequential. Her boots could easily trample it in the blink of an eye.

With a shift of her broad thighs, Monika dissolved the picture and began moving back towards Rich and Belinda.

Burning ears, Rich said, shrugging.

Did he give you his fractal lecture yet? Monika said as she approached.

I was warming up to it, Rich said.

Poor dear, Monika said. You can tune out if you like.

Actually, I'm interested to hear it, Belinda said. I looked into it before, but all the information I found was very — mathematical. She was about to say 'confusing,' but decided against it with Monika there.

Ha! Rich said, pointing a finger at Monika. So there! She *does* want to hear it.

Monika fluttered her eyelids and turned to Belinda. Have fun, she said, and she strode ahead.

All right, so, Rich began. They call this crop circle design a Julia set, but that's technically inaccurate. It's true that Julia sets are types of fractals with swirling patterns, but fractals are a lot more complex than regular shapes. We math-nuts call them self-similar shapes.

Belinda nodded, walking slowly alongside Rich as she listened. She watched Sampson up ahead, traversing the circles like a child playing hopscotch. He was collecting handfuls of earth here and there, sieving the soil through his fingers and into plastic bags. Monika walked past him and towards Dr. Longfellow, who was bent down examining the grain.

I've got a great analogy to explain self-similarity in layman's terms, Rich said. Everything in the natural world is self-similar. For example, think of a rocky mountain.

Belinda thought of the first mountain she ever saw up close and in person, back in Canada with Dazhong. They'd been driving the highway to Banff, marooned among prairie seas not unlike the one in which she was now walking. The road was cresting the peak of a hill when the mountain suddenly rose out of the horizon, an ancient, craggy spectre looming over their tiny car.

So if you picture the texture of a rocky mountain, Rich continued, you can see from a distance how rocky it is, right?

Yes, Belinda said.

Now think of being right at the foot of the mountain, and looking at a small part of its surface. The texture looks the same as it does from far away, right? Except on a smaller scale.

Yes, I suppose it does, Belinda said.

So if you think about it, every part of that mountain, no matter how small, is similar in texture. You can keep zooming in on smaller and smaller areas, and you'll get a similar texture every time. It's infinitely detailed, no matter how closely you look at it. See what I mean?

I think so, Belinda said. But that seems so . . . imprecise. I thought there was some sort of formula involved. An equation.

You're right, Rich said, in a sense there is. But every fractal includes a multitude of different equations. Trillions, in some cases. Every shape, every thing is made up of a whole bunch of tiny points, right? You can think of each of those points as a formula.

But then — isn't it just sort of random? Can't something just be random and beautiful, without a formula?

Everything has a formula, Rich said. We're *made* of formulas. Your body, every little cell of it, is a formula.

Belinda shook her head. It still doesn't make sense to me, she said, laughing. It's a different way of thinking, isn't it?

Sure is, Rich said. Unfortunately, you'll have to learn a lot more about mathematics before you can really understand it any further. He patted her shoulder.

It occurred to Belinda that anyone who was watching her and Rich would think they were flirting with each other. She wasn't exactly attracted to Rich, but she began to wonder if she could be. He was intelligent and kind, after all, and better-looking than Sampson or Dr. Longfellow. And they shared similar interests. She became aware of the way her voice had been softening through their conversation.

By this time they'd reached one of the larger circles, and Belinda stopped to take in the sight. The area was large enough to contain a house, and yet the swept grains followed the same swirling pattern as the smaller circles leading up to it.

I understand now why you might compare it to a fractal, Belinda told Rich. Even if it's not quite accurate.

Look over there, Rich said, and Belinda peered ahead. Beyond a shallow slope lay the centre of the formation. She could see a group of strangers gathered there. Dr. Longfellow and Monika were walking toward them, waving.

Who are they? Belinda asked.

Probably tourists, Rich said. I betcha one of the local farmers whipped up a tour to earn some extra cash. Might even be the guy who owns this field.

Terrible, Belinda said. Look at them stomping all over everything.

Rich shrugged. Part of the fun, he said.

But Belinda couldn't help but feel territorial. It was her first crop circle, and she wanted it to be hers. In her mind she had planted a big red flag in the centre of the formation, claiming it as her own. She felt sweat gathering on her chest as she and Rich increased their pace toward the centre. The strangers had begun speaking with Dr. Longfellow, Monika, and Sampson. Sampson displayed his bags of soil samples, holding them up like trophies for the others to admire. But one of the strangers stood off to the side, watching Belinda and Rich approach. She wore a large white sun hat that almost covered her eyes.

Belinda followed Rich along the winding path of the arm as it curved toward the central circle. The woman in the white hat followed them with her gaze, rotating her head slowly. As Belinda circled around her, she started to wonder if there wasn't something familiar about her. It seemed as though the woman was staring straight at her.

And then Belinda's feet stopped short. She nearly fell over against the momentum of her body. The woman wasn't real. Rich was continuing on ahead, unfazed by the woman's gaze. Belinda was having a vision. And the vision was an image of herself, staring into a mirror. The woman was her. Under the wide brim of the white hat, Belinda's eyes stared back at her. Her mouth was slightly open.

Belinda didn't dare move. She held her breath, staring at herself, waiting for a sign. This was the moment, she knew, when everything would become clear. She would know what to do. She would understand her purpose.

The woman's hand pressed to her mouth. She lifted the white hat off her head, and Belinda could see that she was smiling.

Belinda! the woman yelled across the field. Belindaaaa! She waved the hat in the air and the wind gusted, almost blowing it away.

Everyone turned to look at her. At that moment, Belinda felt as though she were watching a slide show, and the picture had suddenly changed. The face she was staring at was not her own. It was a forgotten memory come to life. There in the centre of the circle stood her sister. It was Prim.

14 The Abyss

AT A CERTAIN POINT, darkness can't get any darker. It happens
at a depth of about four kilometres, where the water becomes
the blackest black there ever was and no tendrils of sunlight can
penetrate even one inch deeper. It's hard to imagine 'cause most
regular people never experience it. In a dark room, your eyes
will always adjust until you can see the vague outlines of things
around you. I know how hard it is to create complete darkness
'cause I've tried it myself. I locked myself in the bathroom and
jammed towels under the door and taped cardboard over the
white slivers shining through the cracks. I sat on the toilet seat
and didn't move, just looked around me and imagined I was part
of the black, a sinking plumb-line in the ocean. And for a few
moments I could actually imagine the whole world and everything in it flat as a piece of paper, and myself just an invisible
speck on that paper. Not even a speck, but a nothing. Or maybe
not even nothing. Maybe I *was* that piece of paper and so was
everything else that had ever existed, no matter how big or
small.

But after a few minutes I started to see a faint grey line, and pretty quick I knew that the line was the edge of the faucet. And then there was a counter top. The lip of a sink. Two toothbrushes. If I was a kid maybe I would've seen things different. The slick back of an arrowtooth eel, the window of a submarine.

In the abyssal zone of the ocean, black is black. No light, period, so your eyes would never be able to adjust. In fact, your eyes would implode into your skull long before you even got to those depths. Your head would come out the size of a crabapple and your bones would be crushed like crackers. You might think that sounds kinda gross, but oceanographers think it's pretty funny. When they're dropping an ROV or a package to take samples, they get their kicks by attaching a Styrofoam cup or ball to the plumb to see how much it will have shrunk by the time it gets back to the surface. A full-size cup turns into a shriveled thimble at four kilometres. Sometimes they do it with heads too. Styrofoam heads like the ones you see in the Ladies department at The Bay, only without the ugly hats and feathers sticking out the sides. The deeper they drop, the smaller they shrink. I bet if you saw one of those heads coming out of the ocean you wouldn't be able to help but imagine how small your own would be if it was you attached to the plumb. Maybe it's a good way for the oceanographers to make themselves feel better about not being able to explore the deep ocean first-hand.

I used to tell people I was going to be a deep-sea diver some day, but I've always known it would never happen. It was a good thing to tell people 'cause it gave me a reason to talk about the ocean all the time, plus I could brag about how deep-sea divers earn tons of money to make up for how dangerous their work is. Even Da thought it was cool when I told him that hyperbaric welders have the highest salaries of any job.

But seriously, I could never actually be a deep-sea welder, and not just 'cause I'm a total klutz and I'd probably torch my arm off. Truth is, I'm a bad swimmer. I seize right up as soon as my body hits the cold water. I've never even attempted swimming in the ocean, but there was this one time we went to Sylvan Lake in the summer, back when Squid was five. It was the first time he'd ever been to a beach and we thought he'd never get tired of throwing sand up in the air and letting it fall into his hair like rain. Everyone else wanted to sunbathe so I helped him build a sandcastle and took him up to the water's edge and we let the water swirl around our ankles. Mum told him he was too little to go swimming. That was just asking for it, as far as I was concerned. He kept looking out at the older kids who were swimming way out by the buoys, floating heads splashing around with water noodles and footballs and yelling and laughing and cackling like pirates.

So then I got the idea to take Squid walking along the docks to see the boats. It seemed like a good way to keep him busy so he wouldn't go running out into the lake the second I turned my head. He liked the algae growing on the wooden pillars. Bright green and shaggy like fur. We found an empty dock and lay on our bellies looking over the edge, letting the sun bake the backs of our legs. Squid said the pillars going down into the water looked like monster legs.

Lookit Squid, I told him, and pointed at the surface of the water. It's a giant squid!

Where? he said. His face got all serious and he peered into the water, right through his reflection.

There, I said, right there!

His eyes scanned the ripples. He had his hands bunched up under his chin and his lip was practically quivering.

It's right there, I said, right next to the queen goblin mermaid! I made a gobliny face, stuck my tongue out and rolled my eyes back. When I looked over at Squid he'd figured it out and he was flapping his hands by his ears.

It's a squid, he yelled.

It's the biggest squid I've ever seen, I said, watching our reflections. But mostly I was looking at me. Something about me looked different, and it wasn't the goblin faces I was making. It might have been the way the sunlight was beaming behind our heads, but my face looked gigantic compared to Squid's. I looked huge and dark and awkward, as if I was staring into one of those fun-house mirrors that makes all your features look stretched and widened. Next to little Squid and his tiny wiggling fingers, his blond hair lit up gold in the sun and his pink lips spread into a smile, I felt like a big ugly buffalo.

You know how when you're little, your parents sometimes get sidetracked while they're listening to your annoying chatter so they sort of shut off part of their brains and start saying things without even thinking? You could ask something like Did a dingo eat your baby? and your mom or dad would answer Yes dear or Mmhm and you'd know that they weren't paying attention. Well, a similar thing happened to me that day with Squid. I can't even remember what he said to me or if he said anything at all, but all of a sudden the image of me as a big ugly buffalo burst into a frothy splash, and there was Squid, his arms thrashing in the water.

Of course I jumped in after him even though I knew I wasn't a good swimmer. And when the lake went over my head I became a sack of stones and the water wrapped around me like a boa constrictor, tighter and tighter. The few seconds I was underwater felt like ages. I remember opening my eyes and the brown water stinging, bubbles whizzing around like frantic flies. I could have sworn I was sinking. I thought I was inches away from the muddy bottom of the lake until one of my arms broke the surface of the water and then I was paddling. The first thing I saw when my head came up was Squid, kneeling on the edge of the dock and watching me. He looked like an obedient dog kneeling there with his wet hair dripping over his eyes. At the time I thought I was hallucinating, but when I finally climbed back on the dock I realized I'd jumped in for nothing. He'd saved himself.

Neither of us said a word about what happened when we got back to the beach. I hadn't even said anything to Squid about keeping it a secret. After I got out of the water I lay flat on the dock for a long time, breathing in and out loud as a rhino and saying nothing. Squid sat down beside me and waited. I didn't ask him why he jumped in because I knew he didn't know. The way he was sitting all curled up and looking at his knees made me feel like there wasn't any point in yelling at him or telling him he was bad. Instead I just lay on my back letting water trickle off my skin, and after I rubbed the water out of my eyes I pressed my fingers hard over my eyelids and let myself stare at the magenta sunspot floating in the black like a winking satellite.

I like to tell myself that I knew what it was to be a mother then. It's a cheesy thought but it also makes me feel less anxious about little things in life like the way my hair looks or getting a good mark in Science. To a mother, there's nothing more nerve-wracking than realizing that your kid is an entirely separate person. You don't even know it, but for the longest time you think of that kid as a part of you, like an extra arm or leg. But really, there's a space between you and him that you'll never be able to reach through. A no-man's-land. And that means that no matter what you do, your kid's life is out of your control.

∞

It was like I was back in that lake when Jess told me Wiley and Squid were gone. I ran up to Squid's room to check if he was there because I didn't know what else to do. I looked under the pillows and threw off the covers and rifled through his shelf piled with stuffed animals. Jess was standing in the doorway, watching me and whimpering softly. I wanted to slap her.

What should we do? she said. She had a big cowlick in her hair and she was smoothing it down with one hand. What about school? He's supposed to be at school.

Yeah, I said. So are we. I don't think that's our biggest concern right now.

Jess left and I could hear her in Mum and Wiley's room, opening drawers and clacking hangers.

Some clothes are gone, she called out, but we both knew that didn't mean anything 'cause there was no way to tell whether the empty hangers were for Wiley's clothes or Mum's. I joined Jess in their room and sat on the edge of the unmade bed. Jess was staring into the closet and chewing her nails like crazy.

Maybe they went for a walk, she said.

With the trunk? I said. For a split second I started thinking about the green trunk and how it was the perfect size for Squid's little body but then I made myself erase that thought. And anyway, I said, the car is gone.

Maybe they went to Wiley's friend's house. What was his name? Bill something?

All I got was Bill, I said. He seemed like a creep.

Jess was already rummaging through Wiley's dresser drawer. We both got our hands in the drawer and there were a ton of prescription bottles and a box of condoms that we just pretended to ignore. My stomach started to feel queasy.

Here, Jess said, pulling out a small black address book. She flipped the pages but every one was blank. She looked at me like she'd just been tricked.

We have to call Mummy, she said.

How do we call Mum? I said. She told us yesterday that she's moving hotels. We don't even know what city she's in right now.

We'll try calling the old hotel, Jess said. Maybe they know where she went.

I just shrugged and let her run downstairs to the phone. It was a dumb idea but at least it was something. I tried to remember if I'd heard what Wiley and Bill were whispering about the other night in the garage. I'd been feeling so sorry for myself that I hadn't bothered to pay attention. All I could remember was Squid saying that he didn't have to go to school the next day, and when I thought about that it started to sound like something Squid would say to get invited along. But that had happened on Saturday night, and Wiley had been home for the whole day on Sunday. He and Squid watched infomercials all morning while I did my homework at the kitchen table. Wiley even helped Squid and Jess clean out Princess Leticia's terrarium. I saw him at the kitchen sink, scrubbing the algae off the plastic water dish, and I remember thinking he seemed eerily happy. He was using the dishcloth we're supposed to use for the countertops and grinning away to himself like it was the most fun he'd ever had.

I felt pin-prickles race up my neck.

Jess appeared in the doorway, huffing from running back up the stairs. They don't know where Mum went, she said.

Surprise surprise, I said.

But she'll call, right? I mean, she's got to call at some point. She'll call and give us her new hotel number.

So what, we just wait around twiddling our thumbs?

I don't know, Jess whispered. Her eyes filled up with tears. I don't know what else to do, she said.

Usually I'm not much of a sap, but as soon as I saw Jess crying I felt tears running down my cheeks too, a feeling like horseradish burning in my nose. I suddenly started thinking about how crazy and twisted this whole thing was; it would never happen to anyone else I knew. If Nikki woke up one day and her dad and her brother weren't there, she wouldn't bat an eye about it. She wouldn't have any reason to worry about her dad and brother being off somewhere alone together. She would probably think to herself, Huh, that's kinda weird, and just assume everything would make sense later. But then I realized that something like that would never even happen at Nikki's house in the first place, because her mom would be making breakfast in the kitchen when Nikki woke up, and she'd explain everything before Nikki had a chance to notice. Thinking about that made me feel like my life was really messed up. My brother was alone with my stepdad and I'd never felt more scared in my entire life. And next thing I knew I had my arms around Jess and I could feel her tears soaking into the shoulder of my shirt.

I hate Mummy, Jess said into my shoulder. Her voice vibrated through my skin. On any other day, I wouldn't have thought much of what she said. Everyone says they hate their parents at least once in their lives. The difference was that Jess wasn't talking about hating Mum because she was too strict or nagged us all the time. I think what she really hated was the fact that we needed Mum, and she didn't need us.

We spent the rest of the day watching TV and the clock. We watched three episodes of *Friends* in a row and didn't laugh once. Jess kept picking up the phone to make sure we had a dial tone and putting it back down. We'd decided that there was no sense panicking when they'd only been gone for a few hours. I told Jess I was sure that they'd show up for dinner and that seemed to make her feel a little better even though there was no reason for us to believe that at all.

When it got dark enough that we had to turn the lamps on, Jess switched off the TV and said, I'm going to leave here when I graduate.

What? I said. How?

I'll get a job, she said. And Sebastian will come live with me. She was staring at me like a robot, her eyes blank and no expression. You can come too if you want, she said, and she started fingering a stain on the couch.

You can't move out, Jess, I said. You have to go to university. The thought of Jess living somewhere on her own was so ridiculous I couldn't even imagine it. She'd be calling Mum every five minutes.

Then I'll move in with Daddy, I don't care, Jess said. I'll tell him he has to let me bring Sebastian. I'll pay rent or something.

You're not making any sense, I said.

This doesn't make any sense, she said. What kind of a mother leaves her kids with a crazy person?

At that moment, the phone rang. Jess stared at me for a second as though she didn't believe what she was hearing. I jumped up and ran to the kitchen, chanting in my head Let it be Squid, let it be Squid, let it be Squid.

Hello? I said.

Hi honey, Mum said. You okay? You sound out of breath.

Oh — hi, I said. I'm just. I was running to pick up.

Well I'm sorry I'm calling so late, she said. We went straight to the field. I only just arrived at the hotel.

S'okay, I said. It doesn't matter. I held my breath between sentences, trying to disguise the shaking in my voice.

You weren't worried? she said.

Nope.

Oh. All right. So how are things there?

Fine, I said without even thinking. We're just doing nothing. Jess was standing in front of me with her hands spread out.

She mouthed Who is it? I put a finger to my lips and shook my head.

Okay, Mum said. Well everything is good here too. I saw my first crop circle today. We walked around inside it and everything. It just appeared yesterday. Over a thousand feet in diameter, can you believe that?

Wow, I said in a flat voice. Neat.

Very neat, she said. But I can't talk long. I'm just going to give you my new hotel number, okay? In case of emergency. Have you got a pen?

Shoot away, I said. There was a pen lying on top of the microwave in front of me but I didn't pick it up.

It's area code zero-one-three-two-three —

Uh huh, I said. I waved my hand at Jess to act like everything was normal. I wasn't sure if she could hear Mum's voice coming through so I ducked my chin down close to my chest. My head felt full of steam.

Eight thirty-nine, five-one-two. Did you get that?

Yep, I said.

And it's the Gladwyn Hotel.

Got it.

Good. So, nothing else is new? School is going well?

Peachy, I said. My voice almost quivered.

Okay, well I should go, Mum said. It's late here — I'm going to bed in a couple of minutes. Give Jessica and Sebastian hugs for me.

'Kay, I will, I said.

Love you.

Yep, you too. Bye.

I hung up the phone and rolled my eyes at Jess. It was just Rose, I said. Asking about homework stuff again. I started walking back to the living room so I wouldn't have to look Jess in the eye. The pits of my stomach twisted themselves into one big knot.

Oh, Jess said, following me. She plunked back down on the couch. How much longer do you think we should wait?

It's five o'clock now, I said. Maybe a couple more hours.

I didn't want to wait around any longer but it seemed like there wasn't anything else we could do. Jess nodded. I'm pretty sure she was thinking the same thing. And I knew that if I told her it was Mum on the phone, she would want to tell her everything, ask her what we should do, bawl like a baby and beg Mum to come home right away. Before I picked up the phone, I'd thought that was what I wanted, too. But as soon as I heard Mum's voice on the other end, it didn't seem fair. Mum was the one who left. I felt like she shouldn't be allowed to get involved in our problems. She didn't deserve to worry herself sick about Squid or feel like she could never forgive herself if something happened to him. At that moment in our lives there was nothing more important to me and Jess than Squid, and all Mum could think about were a bunch of useless circles — meaningless pictures stamped into grain fields in the middle of nowhere. As far as I was concerned, she didn't have a right to know.

Grace? Jess said. We were looking at each other in the blank screen of the TV. Jess was twirling her hair around one finger.

Yeah? I said.

What happens if Mummy never comes back?

I think I smiled then, by accident. It wasn't that I thought it was funny. It just made me feel really strange to hear Jess actually say it out loud. It was the kind of feeling you get when you hear something you know you weren't supposed to hear, like a raunchy sex joke. As if hearing it makes it possible, even real or true.

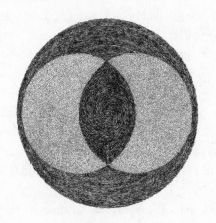

XIV

IT HAD BEEN NEARLY two years since Belinda saw the spacecraft. On that evening, she'd had a fight with Wiley and couldn't sleep. Wiley had announced that Handbrake, his old band, was getting back together.

It was amazing, Wiley had said when he got home from the bar. It was like — spiritual. We thought we were just getting together for beers for old times' sake, and then finally we all broke down. Turns out we'd been thinking the same thing. I was the first one to say it. I said, Guys, we really were a hell of a band, and I wish we would have tried to make it.

But you did try, Belinda said. Almost eight years ago. Didn't you go to an agent and get turned down?

Yeah, Wiley said. But we only went to the one agent and then we gave up. We could've kept trying. We could've gone without an agent for a while and built up our name ourselves.

Does that work? Belinda said.

Whaddyou mean does that work? If you're good, you make it work. That's the point. We didn't try hard enough, and now we're all regretting it.

Belinda let the silence hang for a moment. Wiley's eyes, bright as glass, waited for her approval. She wanted to smother them out, extinguish them with her fists.

You can't be serious, she said. You have a child.

Wiley's face contorted, a rude shock twisting his lips. So what? he said. This can't be a grown-up job? You think I should teach kids to play piano for the rest of my fucking life?

Belinda had gone berserk. She called him immature and irresponsible, a deadbeat. Wiley had called her a dictator. The fight had fed itself from there. It lasted too long, packed with the same tired complaints repeated over and over. Jessica, Grace, and Sebastian had barred themselves in the basement living room with the television blaring.

Everything always has to be your way, Wiley kept saying. Nobody else matters. It's all about YOU.

Hours after the fight had ended, after they'd grown tired of screaming and offered their empty apologies, his accusation still clamped on her thoughts. Wiley had fallen asleep just as quickly as any other night, and Belinda hadn't even been able to keep her eyes shut without strain. She couldn't make sense of Wiley's argument; it had no basis. How could she be selfish? She who had no life of her own, whose every decision and every action was made for him and her children? She was back in her old cycle — the marriage she thought she abandoned years ago. She'd left Dazhong because he didn't allow her to be her own person. Somehow, she'd continued to drift since then, chasing after the pieces of herself, strewn and floating in different directions.

As she lay in bed staring at the ceiling, a craving for a cigarette interrupted her thoughts. She hadn't smoked once in the nineteen years since she'd quit cold turkey, and this was the first craving she'd felt since Jessica was born. Without restraint, she slipped out of bed and down to the garage, and found the packet Wiley had hidden years ago in an old plastic cooler. The smoke soothed her lungs like a warm wind. She found herself opening the garage door to let the night shine in. It was fairly balmy because it was summer, but Belinda's skin prickled under the fresh air. Outside it was silent.

When Belinda was a small child, her mother told her stories of the witching hour to keep her from leaving her bed at night. It happens in the middle of the night, her mother said, when everyone is asleep. If you're not asleep, the creatures of the night will come for you. The witches and the demons and the ghosts. You'll know they're on their way when everything is dark and deadly silent. That's how you know they've got you.

That night, as Belinda stood on the driveway and listened, she couldn't make out the faintest sound or movement. Up and down the street, the trees and houses and cars and telephone wires were part of a photograph, silent and suspended in time. The crackle of her cigarette as she drew in seemed as loud as a bonfire.

And then, she felt the atmosphere brighten ever so slightly, as if a match had been struck somewhere behind the dark curtain of the sky. She looked up and the sky was blotted with inky blue clouds, a few dull stars like grains of sand sprinkled between them.

The spacecraft appeared in a blink. Three round lights pierced the dark, each one glowing white as a moon. Together they made the three points of an empty triangle.

It must be an airplane, Belinda told herself. Some sort of high-tech military craft. But then the lights began to move, or rather, glide, fixed in their triangular orientation. They glided in a diagonal motion, a quick slash across the sky like a checkmark. Belinda had never seen an airplane or any other machine move with such grace. The craft changed direction in a sharp but seamless motion and glided west, more slowly this time. There was something organic, even delicate about the spacecraft's movements; it seemed to dangle from an invisible hand, letting the wind carry it like an enormous kite. Belinda held her breath, willing her memory to record what she was seeing. The lights hovered only a few seconds longer before they went out, as quickly as they had appeared, snuffed by the shadows weaving through the sky.

Belinda didn't move. She fixed her view on that spot in the sky, her eyes flicking across the vague outlines of clouds, searching. Minutes passed. The cigarette tucked between her fingers smouldered into an ashen claw. The lights never reappeared.

When Belinda got back inside the house, her hands felt numb and she realized she had been cold. The time on the microwave said 3:58 AM. She had been standing on the driveway for almost an hour, wearing only her pajamas and slippers. But she felt as though she'd just emerged from a mountain lake, fresh and clean, the air against her skin like tiny bites of electricity. She had witnessed something extraordinary. The lights had been real — there was no doubt in her mind. And no matter how she tried to make sense of what she saw, she couldn't escape what she knew to be true. It was a UFO. A flying object like she had never seen. It was unexplainable.

The RCMP seemed the best place to call. She'd heard of people reporting UFO sightings, but she'd never taken such stories seriously before. The police would probably be less sympathetic, too busy with more pressing matters.

I'm calling to report a UFO, Belinda said into the phone. And I'm not crazy.

Can I get your name? the woman on the other end asked. She sounded unsurprised, even bored.

Belinda Spector, she said. It happened about an hour ago. Just over my house, these lights —

Can you please describe what you saw, Ma'am? The woman sounded as if she were reading from a script.

When Belinda finished her story, the woman said, All right, Ma'am, we'll look into it. Thank you for letting us know. She hung up.

Belinda considered calling back, but she didn't know what she would say. She wanted the woman to believe her. Anything she could think to say — *You have to believe me!* or *I'm telling the truth!* — sounded hackneyed.

She realized then that this would be something she would always keep for herself. She was the only one who would ever really believe what happened. And rather than feeling discouraged, she felt a small thrill. The vision — the knowledge that such a beautiful moment could exist — was hers. It was a gift that no one else could share.

Days later, she'd tried to make a sketch of the spacecraft, as a record. But after she'd drawn three dots, she hadn't known what else to do. She connected the dots with lines, knowing they were only part of her imagination. And then she'd given up. It was impossible to recreate what she had seen. But she kept the drawing anyway, tucked it in her journal. Eventually it came to represent more of a place marker, like a red dot on a map. She saw the sighting as the beginning of her journey, the start-point of her path. Since that day, she thought she had been drawing a course for herself, a jagged line that navigated through paranormal mysteries to someday reach a definitive end. But she'd never been able to picture that end, because she'd never known what she was looking for to begin with. She'd assumed that once she found the answer, the question would become clear.

Instead, the path had led her to the centre of the Triple Julia Set crop circle. She had been following an arc, so wide and sweeping that she hadn't noticed herself turning back toward its beginning. She had ended up where she started — far beyond crop formations or spacecraft. Against her will, she'd travelled in one huge circle, all the way back to her childhood. Back to Prim, and back to the Snow White fairy-tale she'd forced herself to believe.

When Prim had called out to her, the world seemed to turn inside out. The field around her softened, the ground bent away like toffee. Before Belinda knew it she was leading Prim off by the elbow, gaining distance from the group, *Come this way,* her voice hushed. She'd shooed away Rich with his look of concern. All of this without thought. It felt necessary, but she didn't know why. Now they stood on the edge of the innermost circle, Prim shelving her fingers under her eyelids, tears dripping off her knuckles. She looked old for her age, coral lipstick smudged on one side and filling the wrinkles around her mouth. Her hair, unruly and streaked with white, blew across her face. Her cheeks flared pink with heat.

You look exactly how I imagined you, Prim told her. Her smile clawed into Belinda's memory. She remembered a dream she'd once had of Prim in a long white sundress, the hem dragging on the ground and swept with grass stains. Her hair in a dandelion crown. As a child Belinda had imagined this as a scene from Prim's wedding. For years she believed it had really happened, that she had channeled her way into Prim's life through her dreams. But this Prim, the one standing in front of her, would never have worn a white dress like that. She was not that kind of woman — too severe, and in no way ethereal.

Belinda coughed. She had no words.

All this time, Prim said. Aren't you going to say anything?

Belinda let her eyes wander across the field. She focused on the furthest line of the horizon, where the wheat became a blonde fringe brushing against the grey sky. Her throat felt closed-off, filled with cement. She was thinking about how she had come to this place, her mind reeling through every event that had led up to this moment. She thought about her coincidences, how she treasured them. Stacked them up into golden towers and shut them away. She thought about the child's grave at Woodhenge, marking the centre like a bull's-eye.

Belinda? Prim said. What is it? Say something. Please.

Belinda looked at her sister, at the fleck of orange embedded like a searing ember in the green of her left iris.

A pocket of air left Belinda's lips, and her voice was free. She took a step backward.

You can't be here, she said. You have to leave.

15 Niches

MY LAST LETTER SAID that Mum was going on a quest to find herself. I think Auntie Prim took that to mean Mum was on a quest to find *her*. I suppose it did sound like a pretty convenient coincidence that Mum happened to be traveling to England and even staying in the same county where Prim lived. She addressed her reply to both me and Mum, but luckily I always made sure to get to the mailbox before Mum got home from work. Auntie Prim's letter asked for our phone number and the name of the hotel Mum was going to be staying at, and at the end she wrote that she hoped she could visit Canada someday. She'd never asked about meeting us in any of the previous letters. It was like she had been waiting for me to give her the green light.

I never wrote back. I guess part of me started to feel guilty about going behind Mum's back. It had been fun at first. It was like a game. I hadn't been thinking of Prim as a real live person, let alone a person who shared some of the same genes as me. She was like a character out of a storybook. I could imagine her my own way, and that made her something I could

believe in but also not take seriously. I imagined her with
Mum's hair and eyes but without the wilted look on her face.
She was always laughing and never tired, stressed, or angry.
She was an architect, or a lawyer. She wore cool clothes.
She was proud of her son, and she'd been there for every
major event in his life. On his graduation day, they went
skydiving together. She didn't have a husband because she
didn't need one.

When it came down to it, writing to Prim was like writing
to Santa Claus. Anyone who's ever written a letter to Santa
knows that you get a letter back, written in Santa's curly
handwriting. Of course, there's no doubt in your mind that
the letter is real. But still, somewhere deep down, you don't
actually believe that Santa is real. His letter is like evidence
of some kind of magic.

It was the same way with Prim. Her letters seemed more
real than she did. So when I thought about actually meeting
her in person, I started to realize how disappointing it
would be. No matter what, she couldn't possibly be the way
I imagined her. And neither could my cousin Sebastian. As
nonsensical as it sounds, I saw Prim and Mum as the same
person. For me, Prim was Mum in a different life, maybe the
way Mum would be if she'd never left England, never met Da,
never had us. Prim was a way to imagine how the whole world
could be completely different.

And at the same time, I wondered if Prim would be disappointed in me. Would she be expecting me to be a blonde-haired,
green-eyed, mini-incarnation of Mum? I wasn't even sure if she
knew anything about Da. I could just picture her coming out
of the gate at the airport, seeing Mum and then seeing me, the
look on her face. That look I've seen a thousand times before
with the searching eyes and the slightly open mouth that makes
me want to say Yes, we *are* together.

Truth is, I don't think Mum and Prim are really meant to see each other again. The more I think about it, the less believable it seems that they could exist in the same place at the same time. Any words they could think to say to each other would sound so stiff and awkward. *How have you been, for the last thirty-odd years?* Just because they're sisters doesn't necessarily mean they have anything to talk about. Jess and I have a hard enough time talking to each other even though we see each other every day. It makes me realize how easily people can become strangers. The only good thing that came out of Squid and Wiley taking off was that Jess and I really had no choice but to talk. It was the only thing that kept us from losing our heads.

It had been past midnight when Wiley and Squid walked in the door. I'd spent the entire evening alone with Jess, talking about things we remembered from when we were kids as if we were about to take our last breaths, the whole time trying to pretend that Squid and Wiley hadn't been gone for more than sixteen hours. We talked about how Mum used to make us cover our eyes for the hoochy bits in movies, but we could hear all the kissing and breathing and knew what was happening anyway. Jess remembered that we used to cover our eyes with our headbands so our hands wouldn't have to do the work, and we'd tell Mum we were being Geordi from *Star Trek* but she didn't think it was funny. We talked about how on rainy days, we used to put on our matching rubber boots and walk down the street to the sewer grate because Jess told me that there were fairies living in the pipes and they only came out when it rained. We'd kneel over the grate with Jess holding an invisible fairy in her cupped palms, and I'd listen quietly for the soft hum of a fairy-song. And we talked about how Mum used to buy us a tub of white icing and a package of plain cupcakes every Halloween, and how mixing up the icing with food-colouring to make orange and green and black potions was always way more fun than decorating the cupcakes like Jack-o'-lanterns.

By midnight we had fallen asleep in the living room. I was woken up by a sound — a moaning sound. It was stretched and deep, like the sad underwater cry of a whale. I sprang up and saw Squid standing in front of the couch, and the next second Jess was on him, her arms wrapping him up like a bundle of laundry she didn't want to drop. She was moaning and sobbing in thick gulps, and even though I couldn't see Squid's face I knew by the way he was standing completely stiff that he had no idea what was going on.

Hi girls! Wiley called from the back door. He sang it out as if it was just a regular day, as if he were coming home from a long day at work all ready for a home-cooked supper. I heard the door swing shut behind him.

I had spent the whole day imagining myself at that moment, screaming and swearing at Wiley and tearing a strip right off him. What the hell did you think you were doing? I imagined myself saying. Do you have any fucking idea how scared we were? But when the moment finally came, those things sounded so lame and cliché. They sounded fake, like lines straight out of a movie script. Instead, I stood at the end of the hallway that led to the back door and stared at Wiley while he pulled off one rubber boot and then the other, not looking up. Each boot scattered a little shower of sand on the floor when he yanked it off.

Your mother call? he asked. Then he looked up and saw my face.

I wish you were dead, I said. I didn't yell it. I looked him straight in the eye and said it the way you would state a fact, like Cows eat grass. I don't know what possessed me to say that. It seemed like the meanest thing I could manage to say.

Hey, Wiley said. He frowned. He must have heard Jess's sobbing then because he said, Whoawhoawhoa, what's going on?

Are you serious? I said. I could feel sweat prickling my forehead.

Wiley blinked.

You left, I said. You didn't tell us where you were.

He looked at me like *Is that all?* Sorry, he said. I forgot. I thought you'd be at school all day anyway.

You couldn't have left a goddamn note? I yelled. But my voice sounded limp, as if the words had no air behind them. I felt drained. Listening to myself made me feel like a melodramatic teenage brat. And all of a sudden I couldn't figure out why I was so upset. I couldn't figure out how to put it into words.

We went to Sylvan Lake, Squid said. He and Jess had come up behind me, and Jess was smearing her wet cheeks.

We didn't know where you were, I said again. And the trunk was gone and we thought maybe you ran away or something.

It was a school day, Jess joined in. You were gone when we woke up. It looked like you were trying to sneak off.

Oh, Wiley said. Well, sorry. It was kind of a spur-of-the-moment type thing. Bill's parents have a place up by the lake and he got a last-minute gig at the Legion.

Jess and I stood silent.

Really, I'm sorry, Wiley said. I shoulda called.

We brought you some rock candy, Squid said.

That set Jess off. Rock candy? she screamed at Wiley. So giving us candy is supposed to make everything okay? She looked to me for some support, but I didn't say anything. I'd already given up.

No, Wiley said, that's not — Jesus! I didn't think there was a law against surprising my son with a day at the beach.

There's a law against kidnapping, Jess said. We were about to call the cops.

Wiley's face turned into a wince. He looked at Jess like she'd just stabbed him in the gut. Then he looked at me. I lowered my eyes to my feet.

What do you think I am? he said. His voice was quiet and sharp.

Jess stared him down hard. But behind her eyes I could see the faintest flicker, and I knew she was feeling the same way as me. Like a fraud.

Wiley sighed. And right then it was like an invisible hook came down and took hold of his disguise, the one made of all the little changes that had built up since Squid was born, and lifted it clear off his body. All that moodiness and irresponsibility and impulsiveness peeled off like a robe and floated away. For just a few minutes he was Old Wiley again, good Old Wiley, and he was older and wiser and knew more about life than we possibly could.

I'm his father, Wiley said. He didn't need to tell us that we weren't Squid's mothers.

It took me a long time to make sense of everything that happened in those couple of days. I barely slept that night 'cause I felt so frustrated, crying on and off and not knowing why. I felt angry. I was so mad that I had to keep stuffing my pillow in my mouth and biting down hard. I was mad that Squid had come back and I was just supposed to be relieved and happy, and everything was supposed to settle back to normal. I was mad that I had looked like the one who was wrong, and Wiley didn't have to admit to anything. I had felt so useless. But like most bad feelings people have, even the feelings that seem too awful to ever survive, they eventually blew over and became something in the past. A memory.

It seems like every time you revisit a memory it means something else, especially when you've been able to forget it

for a while. It's like the things you experience in the mean-
time make the memory change. Just the other day we were
talking about ecological feedback systems in Bio, and Mr.
Ramsay brought up the subject of niches. We'd learned about
niches before in Junior High, but I'd forgotten all about them.
That turned out to be kind of a good thing though, 'cause I'd
had it all wrong before. When we first learned about them in
grade seven Science, I kept thinking that a niche was a place,
like the African savannah or the Great Barrier Reef. I blame
Mrs. Lambert for that. She was the one who told our class
that the word niche comes from the French word 'nicher,'
which means to nest. So naturally I thought nesting had to
do with the place an animal calls home. But then we learned
about them again in grade nine and it seemed like niches
actually had to do with the roles that organisms play in their
environments, like how certain types of marine fungi exist so
that certain types of fish can eat them, and those fish make
it possible for other types of fish to exist, and on and on and
on. I thought it was about how every ecosystem depends
on a whole bunch of little components that stay in perfect
symbiosis with each other, and how every component of that
environment plays a crucial part in the great big circle of life.
Take away a chunk of forest or wipe out a certain species of
caterpillar and the whole cycle goes completely out of whack.

But it's actually a lot more complicated than that. The way
I understand it now, niches are more about the ways that
organisms make a place for themselves. It's about how they
adapt themselves to fit into their worlds. If a certain species
of phytoplankton goes extinct, another slightly different
species might take the opportunity to increase its population
tenfold so it can step in and fill the position. Or maybe not. I
talked to Mr. Ramsay about it after class, and he told me that
some biologists believe there are thousands upon thousands

of vacant niches, left by organisms that have died out over the years. But other biologists think that niches are defined by the organisms that live in a given ecosystem, so the idea of a vacant niche is impossible. Once a species gets wiped out, the niche is gone too.

Really, I think it's just a matter of how you want to look at it. If it were true that vacant niches existed everywhere, then it'd mean that very few ecosystems, if any at all, would ever manage to reach a state of complete balance. There would always be a gap somewhere in the circle. If vacant niches didn't exist, then any gaps that appeared would just get closed up, and the circle would get a tiny bit smaller.

Now that I've thought about it, I think I'm okay with believing either scenario. It makes me feel better to know that no matter what, all organisms have to keep learning new ways to make up for what's missing. Eventually, they must get really good at pretending to be something they're not.

XV

THERE HAD ONLY BEEN one other instant when Belinda had
questioned her motives for going to England. It had happened
as she was counting the money — the bills she'd saved from
eighteen years' worth of birthday cards sent by her mother.
It was just enough to pay her airfare. She considered the irony
of rejecting her mother's money all these years, only to finally
spend it on a flight back to Wiltshire. Suddenly she wondered
why she had kept the money at all. She could have sent it back,
or donated it to charity. But then she remembered that she
hadn't wanted to begin an exchange with her mother; she didn't
want to suggest her consent to maintaining their connection.
And giving the money to charity felt wrong. Belinda felt it
wasn't right for anyone to benefit from her mother's attempts
to buy love.

Even as Belinda tried to rationalize it away, part of her wondered if there was more significance to her decisions. For the
briefest second, she wondered if on some level she had known
all along she would use the money to return to England one day.
She dismissed the idea almost as quickly as she'd conjured it.

But she faced the same scenario again with Prim in the crop circle. Up until that moment, she'd believed that a series of coincidental events had led her on this journey. She'd opened herself to them, let them sweep her along. But meeting Prim forced her to wonder if she'd had more control than she realized. When she told Prim she couldn't be there, what she'd meant was that she couldn't bring herself to believe that Prim could be standing in front of her, a real live body marked with lines of age and imperfections. She didn't want to see the ghastly white streaks in Prim's hair, the drooping, wrinkled skin under her chin. This was not the way Belinda wanted to imagine her. And this was not the way her crop circle experience was supposed to turn out. It felt like a violation. It was as if Prim's presence in the crop circle called into question Belinda's purpose for being there. Had Belinda willed this into being? Had she subconsciously directed her pilgrimage of self-discovery back to the place of her birth? Had she chosen Wiltshire, deep down envisioning the possibility of a reunion? She was not willing to consider these thoughts. She wanted them gone.

And Prim left. It wasn't the reaction Belinda was expecting. She turned around and walked away without saying a word, as though she had been anticipating Belinda's rejection. She retrieved her small handbag lying in the field and took it with her, back down the curving arm of the formation and out of sight. Belinda, fists clenched at her sides, had watched her trudge away, holding her white hat by the brim as the wind lifted it like the lid of a kettle. Belinda's body felt rigid, as if all her muscles had swelled and stiffened, leaving her a statue.

Dr. Longfellow was first to leave the group and approach her. Did you know that woman? he asked.

No, Belinda blurted. I don't know anything about her.

He offered her a bottle of water and she took it, dazedly. As she drank, her hands, her mouth, the cold water running down her throat, felt separate from her. Dr. Longfellow peered in the direction in which Prim had gone. I'm sorry, he said. Everyone goes through something like this.

Excuse me? Belinda said. A bead of water trickled from the corner of her lips and ran down her chin.

Well, it was bound to happen, he said. Unfortunately, our line of work often attracts — unstable people. I hope she didn't upset you too much?

No, Belinda said, no. She looked at Dr. Longfellow for a moment, shaking her head mechanically. No, she repeated.

I was speaking with the owner of the farm, he said, pointing over to a man standing among the strangers. Apparently that woman showed up this morning asking if she could join the tour. He said there was something off about her from the start.

Off? Belinda said. She felt the bead of water hanging from her chin, poised to drop.

Well, Mr. Beaton told me it didn't seem like she was here for the crop circle.

I — I see, Belinda said.

She was with someone, too, he said. Her son, presumably. Very strange fellow, so says Mr. Beaton.

A man? Belinda said, wiping her chin. Where? Where is he? She scanned over the strangers in the distance, all of whom looked middle-aged.

Didn't come, Dr. Longfellow said. He was with her this morning, but she was alone when she returned for the tour.

Belinda gave the water bottle back to Dr. Longfellow. Her hand touched his and she held it there, her fingers pressing into his knuckles.

It was her son, my — she said, her breath swallowing her words. Dr. Longfellow looked at her queerly.

Don't be alarmed, he said. We'll find out how she got your name. I'm sure she's harmless.

I think — Belinda began, then nodded. I have to go, she said, and began to run.

When she reached the edge of the field, her pulse thumping in her ears, Prim was nowhere to be seen. Belinda followed the path out to the road. A line of vacant cars sat parked on the sloping shoulder. No one in either direction. She was about to turn around when she saw a shape moving through a grassy field beside a farmhouse, a few hundred yards down the road. Belinda ran as if the wind were chasing her, sandals slapping on asphalt. She had no idea what she was doing. She was following a blind hope, a sudden urge to understand what she was feeling, the hulking chasm in her gut — as if she'd been deceived. Cheated by her own fantasies.

Nothing had changed on the street leading up to her mother's house. She could picture it now, and herself running along it. Stick fences, slumping with age, standing at lazy angles to the square houses. The cobblestone streets collecting rivers of water in their cracks, covered with hairy patches of moss like a checkerboard. The pristine old bicycle propped against the front steps of the house on the corner, tangled in wild grasses. The patchy bit of stucco on the front of their house that her mother had tried in vain to repair, and rose stems climbing towards it on a rickety trellis. And her mother, alone, barely alive, sitting inside hunched over the embroidery on her knees. Up until now, her aloneness had seemed selfish. But there was something too familiar about that way Prim had turned her eyes, the way her mouth had begun to pucker at the edges. Prim was not married, not happy. Belinda knew without having to ask.

Prim saw her coming. She met Belinda on the drive leading

up to the house, but her smile had faded. She held her hands in a tight heart against her chest.

Belinda, winded from the run, clutched her knees and let the sweat river down her face. She took a moment to catch her breath. Prim watched her, expectantly. Belinda wasn't sure what she wanted to say.

Where's Sebastian? she finally said.

At home, Prim said. He can't be around strangers for too long.

Belinda felt her eyebrows twitch.

He's autistic, Prim explained, a sudden sharpness to her voice. Belinda recognized it as bitterness.

Oh, Belinda said. She resisted her impulse to apologize. Sebastian was well over thirty years old by now, Belinda figured.

Prim looked down at her feet, nudged a small stone with her toe. Belinda stared at the gravel on which they stood, breathing heavily, searching for words. She examined the gravel's rocky texture, imagined zooming in on a patch of ground and seeing the same texture repeated. Zoom further, same texture. The same pattern, again and again, into infinity. A formula — fixed, unyielding.

I named my son Sebastian, Belinda said, more to herself than to Prim.

I know, Prim said.

Why? Why did I do that? Her mind was spinning, the words flinging out like splashes of mud.

Prim stared at her blankly. I'm not sure what you're asking, she said.

I haven't seen you in thirty-six years, Belinda said. I want to know why I'm so — afraid of you. I've always been afraid of knowing you, knowing anything about you.

Prim bit her lip. I don't know, she said, squeezing her eyes shut against her tears. I don't know. She wiped her palm over her eyes. Perhaps . . . perhaps you didn't want to turn out like me.

Belinda turned her gaze to the fields, stretching out in long waves behind the house. She focused on the thin lines of wheat stalks, trembling together in the wind. The crop circle was just visible in the distance, a shadowy inkblot, like a spill on the landscape.

And when she looked back at Prim, she saw nothing but a woman. She was just an ordinary woman, like anyone else. Nothing special, as her mother had always said. All these years Prim had remained stagnant — a woman, a mother, reduced.

But I did, Belinda said. I turned out just like you.

16 Camouflage

I USED TO BELIEVE that people couldn't change. Now I realize that if other people are anything like me, they hold on to certain memories like pieces of themselves, and take them along wherever they go. We're made of the things that happen to us, so that no matter how much things change around us, we will always be who we are. I try to think about that when I get stressed about change. I try to remember that I'll always be me, no matter what is going on around me.

But even so, sometimes it really gets to me when I find out that a place I remember so clearly has changed. When Rose got back from Disney World last summer, the first question I asked her was if she liked the *Twenty Thousand Leagues Under the Sea* ride.

Huh? she said.

Twenty Thousand Leagues Under the Sea, I said, slowly. You know — the submarines?

She blinked. I don't know what that is, she said.

It's only the best ride in the whole park, I said. You've seriously never heard of *Twenty Thousand Leagues Under the Sea*? Jules Verne? Captain Nemo?

How long ago was it that you went to Disney World again? she said. Weren't you like, twelve?

Yeah, I said. Four years isn't that long, ya know.

Well I didn't see anything like Under the Sea or whatever, Rose said. They must've taken it out.

How could they take it out? I said. There's this ginormous pool for all the submarines. It's huge.

How should I know? Rose said. Maybe it was busted. Or maybe no one knows what that is anymore so they shut it down. Who cares, anyway.

After that I just kept my mouth shut 'cause it was obvious that Rose was in one of her moods where everything I say is lame. And anyway, part of me really didn't want to know that the submarine ride was gone forever. I wanted to remember it in my own way, and I wanted that memory to stay true forever.

When I went to Disney World with Da, the submarine ride was the best part of the whole trip. We'd only had the one day to do all the rides 'cause Da's conference was in Miami and it was his only day off. Up until then I'd been hanging around the hotel swimming pool by myself during the day, bored as all hell. The pool had waterfalls and a floating bar in the middle. But when you're twelve there's only so much wading and suntanning and pineapple juice-drinking and magazine-reading you can do before you start wishing you had someone you could splash or play Marco Polo with. Jess hadn't wanted to come 'cause she'd already signed up for Horseback-riding camp with her best friend for that week. I'd told her she was nuts to turn down a trip to Florida, but she said it probably wouldn't be fun with Da anyway. Turns out she was kinda right.

I don't remember much about Miami. I remember going down to the beach outside the hotel and seeing a lady doing cornrows in girls' hair for money. Da had given me ten bucks

and that got me two cornrows, one on either side of my head.
Da was pissed when he found out how much I'd paid. How
could you be so stupid? he'd said. I thought he was being super
mean at the time, but looking back I have to admit it was
pretty stupid. And the trip wasn't all bad. Once Da was done
with working and we drove to Disney World in Orlando, he let
me drag him around wherever I wanted. It was a pretty fun
day, all things considered. Da really wanted to go on It's a Small
World so we did, but when it was over I made sure he knew how
dumb it was, how freaky all those little robot children looked,
and he had to agree. When we came out of Space Mountain a
bird landed on Da's head and I laughed hysterically watching
him swat at his hair and run around in circles, *Get it off, Jesus
Christ!* But when we left the park that evening we both agreed,
hands-down, that *Twenty Thousand Leagues Under the Sea* was
the best part of the day.

We knew it was going to be good 'cause the lineup was the
longest of any ride. When we finally boarded we got seats
next to one of the little round windows at the back of the
sub, where it was darkest. It was a nice break from the hot
sun of the day and all the screaming and flashing lights and
stomach-wrenching drops. Everyone was quiet in the sub,
little kids included. We watched the blue water bubble and
rush past, listened to Captain Nemo's voice telling us scientific
facts about the creatures peering at us with shiny glass eyes.

And when we came up on the giant squid near the end,
even Da gasped. It was really the only sea creature along the
whole ride that you could almost believe, so it made the fake-
looking fibreglass fish and the mermaids with cartoon faces
and stick-straight arms forgivable. In the dark, murky water,
the squid was bloated and pink like a muscle. Its tentacles
coiled tight around the belly of another submarine. A single
glowing eye, big as a Frisbee, glared in our direction.

Full repellent charge! Captain Nemo ordered. Lightning flashes flickered in the water and our sub zoomed ahead. The eye, bright and unblinking, followed us like a waning moon.

A couple of weeks after we got back from Florida, Da surprised me with a book called SEA MONSTERS: GIANT SQUID. It had a black-and-white drawing of a squid attacking a submarine on the cover.

Just like the one we saw, remember? he said, grinning.

It was a nice thing for Da to do, but I remember thinking it was kinda dumb at first. It looked like a kid's book, and at that time I was trying to get into sophisticated adult books like *Animal Farm* and *Great Expectations*. The book sat uncracked on my bookshelf for months until one day, just out of curiosity, I decided to flip through. It turned out that the book actually had some cool facts inside. For instance, that all squid have camouflage capabilities. And not camouflage like the way some moths have wings textured like bark so they look like part of the tree. Squid have chromatophores in their skin that can actually shift and morph the pigment in the cells to change colour. If they want to, squid can blend right into their surroundings no matter what they are — coral, rock, or even sand — and they can do it so well that they practically turn invisible. One minute you see a squid and the next there's only a tangled bunch of seaweed. They have the power to change into whatever they want to be. That means that wherever a squid goes, it'll never be somewhere it can't fit in.

That's when I decided I wanted to be a marine biologist. I read that book cover to cover. Then I took out a whole bunch of other sea-life books from the public library. I dug up the boxes of Wiley's old *National Geographics* in the basement and went through every single one looking for underwater photographs in coral reefs and deep-sea trenches.

I dreamt of squid. I kept having the same dream where I was swimming in the hotel pool in Miami and I felt something brush up against my legs, but when I looked down into the water there was nothing there. I tried to swim away but something was holding me by the ankle. Somehow I knew it was a giant squid, in camouflage with the clear blue water. Invisible. I kept kicking my legs but the squid held on, and then it began to swell up like a sponge, larger and larger, until the whole pool filled up with slimy squid flesh. I was trying to climb out but I kept slipping and sliding on the squid and falling on my face and getting squid juice in my mouth. The swelling flesh rose up around me like a thundercloud — and then I'd wake up.

I made the mistake of telling Jess about the dream and of course she looked it up in her dream dictionary, even though I've told her over and over that I don't believe in that psychoanalysis crap.

Let's see, she said, finding the page and running her finger down the list. Here it is — Squid. If you see a squid in your dream, you may be feeling unconsciously threatened.

'Kay, I said. Big whoop.

Wait, Jess said, there's more. Your judgment might also be clouded.

This stuff's so bogus, I said. It's like horoscopes. Everything they say is so wishy-washy that it'd be easy for anyone to convince themselves, Oh yeah, that's totally me.

Jess just ignored me. Alternatively, she said, a squid can also symbolize greed. You may be thinking about yourself while disregarding the needs of others. Oh wait — there's also something here about eating squid . . .

I wasn't eating it, I said.

Didn't you say you got some in your mouth? It says here that —

Ugh, just forget it, I said. I don't believe in this stuff anyway.

Eating squid indicates that you are feeling self-conscious, and you worry about how others perceive you.

Oh my God, I said. Can we stop now?

Fine, Jess said. She tossed the book on her bed. She had a little smile on her face, as if she'd just learned some dirty secret about me. That look always makes me steam like a hot sausage. I threw a hissy-fit and stormed out of her room, which probably made her think she was even more right. It's not like I cared, anyway. I mean, who *isn't* self-conscious? Certainly not Jess, Miss I-talk-to-myself-in-the-mirror.

I had the squid dream a few more times after that. I wouldn't call it a nightmare because by then I'd decided that squid were pretty much the coolest creatures on earth. And probably the neatest thing about them is that no matter how hard scientists and oceanographers try, they still don't know much about them. There was one oceanographer who tried attaching cameras to the backs of sperm whales on the slim chance that they might come into contact with a squid. Surprise surprise, it didn't work. And as much as I like learning new things about deep-sea creatures, I'm glad the squid is still so mysterious. It makes the things we do know seem like treasures.

My absolute favourite thing to tell people about squid is that they have not one, but THREE hearts. Nobody believes me at first when I tell them that. They think I'm making it up. I admit, it does seem kind of excessive. Why would a squid need three separate hearts when most other sea creatures get by just fine with one? Well, the reason is that squid need to circulate lots of blood in order to breathe at such low depths. They have one main heart that takes care of most of the body, and two smaller hearts, like mirrors of each other, that feed the gills on either side. Now, most people ask me why they don't just have one big heart that pumps more efficiently instead. I don't really know the answer to that. I've never been able to find it. But sometimes, just 'cause it's more fun than saying I don't know, I'll say, Because three is my lucky number. That's what I said to Rose, but she just clucked her tongue the way her mom does when her dad makes a corny pun.

Right, she said. 'Cause that makes a whole lotta sense. I guess that's also supposed to explain why you're wearing three rings?

I shrugged. They're my Mum's, I said. I can't decide which one I like best.

Well, she said, you could at least wear them on different fingers.

Yeah, I said, maybe. But I didn't want to. I'd been wearing them for long enough that there was a slight indent in my finger, as if the rings were starting to fuse with my skin. When I took them off it looked like some of my finger was missing. The skin that the rings usually covered was smooth and shiny, like the scar left by a bad burn.

AUTHOR'S NOTE

Many books and articles were instrumental in helping me to understand the culture and controversies surrounding crop circles. Particularly useful were: *Crop Circles: Exploring the Designs and Mysteries* by Werner Anderhub and Hans-Peter Roth; "Anatomical anomalies in crop formation plants," published in *Physiologia Plantarium* (92) by W.C. Levengood; *Secrets in the Fields: The Science and Mysticism of Crop Circles* by Freddy Silva; and *Crop Circles: The Greatest Mystery of Modern Times* by Lucy Pringle. The crop circle illustrations in this book were inspired by the drawings of Leora Franco, featured in Pringle's book.

ACKNOWLEDGMENTS

I wrote this novel during my time at the University of New Brunswick, where I had the unfailing support of my fellow graduate students, professors, and administrators in the English department. I cannot thank them enough for all that I learned and experienced in those two short years. I am indebted to John Ball, who helped shape this book from the very first chapter, and believed in the strength of my story even when I did not. I was honoured to receive the insightful critical perspectives of Mark Jarman, Jennifer Andrews, and Heather Sears. Many thanks to Fred Stenson for his comments on early chapters, and to Eden Robinson for marathon-reading my first draft and sharing her wizardry for structure. I greatly appreciate the assistance provided by the Social Sciences and Humanities Research Council of Canada.

Thank you to everyone at NeWest, and especially Doug Barbour for knowing exactly which questions to ask.

I would not have become a writer if not for Linda Bialek, Suzette Mayr, Nicole Markotić, and Aritha van Herk. You were far more than teachers to me, and you continue to inspire me in everything I do.

To my partner, Andrew: I could not have done this without you. And finally, to my family, in all your various incarnations: thank you for being the place where I belong.

CALGARY-BORN CORINNA CHONG is a writer, editor, and graphic designer based out of Kelowna, B.C. Her writing has appeared in *Grain, NōD, Echolocation,* and *The Malahat Review.* She currently teaches English Literature at Okanagan College and edits *Ryga: A Journal of Provocations.*